The
LAST
LETTER
from
PARIS

BOOKS BY KATE EASTHAM

An Angel's Work
When the World Stood Still
The Sea Nurses

THE NURSING SERIES
Miss Nightingale's Nurses
The Liverpool Nightingales
Daughters of Liverpool
Coming Home to Liverpool

The
LAST
LETTER
from
PARIS

KATE EASTHAM

bookouture

Published by Bookouture in 2023

An imprint of Storyfire Ltd.
Carmelite House
50 Victoria Embankment
London EC4Y 0DZ

www.bookouture.com

ISBN: 978-1-80314-935-6
eBook ISBN: 978-1-80314-934-9

PROLOGUE

MONTAUK, LONG ISLAND, JULY 1933

Come away, O human child!
To the waters and the wild
With a faery, hand in hand,
For the world's more full of
Weeping than you can understand.

W.B. Yeats

A foundling. It sounds romantic, something from a fairy tale or perhaps just plain accidental, stumbled upon by chance. I was left in the long grass on the shores of Southampton Water in the summer of 1917, a year before the end of the war. *A foundling during wartime*, all very dramatic. As soon as I was old enough to be aware, my adoptive mother, not wanting a secret to act like grit in a wound that would be hard to heal anyway, told the story of my *finding*. Easy for her, she was the one who witnessed it as she stood leaning on the rail of a small pier. She was tantalisingly close to the woman with dark red hair – exactly like mine – who left me next to the gently lapping salt waters.

I've never found out why I was abandoned, left to wonder if my birth mother was desperate, terrified, or merely too poor to take care of me, especially since I needed an urgent surgical repair of the harelip that I'd had the fortune to be born with. My special mark, as my adoptive mother, Evie, calls it, tracing it gently with her fingertip. It's a fine silver line but it pulls my top lip slightly out of shape. Now, in my teenage years, I see the scar as a huge, deforming mark which I cover with my fingers every time I stand in front of a mirror – which is often. Gone are the days when the other kids in class would ask about it then grab my hand and pull me into a game of hide and seek. Now some of my peers narrow their eyes, look closer, make derogatory noises or offer sympathy. 'You won't get a boyfriend with a scar like that,' Justine Murray said the other week. I had to bite back a response of, 'Neither will you, with your ugly mug.' Stuff like that doesn't usually get you anywhere except left out in the cold. Not that I'd ever let anyone truly intimidate me, I'd always stand my ground. If you've been dumped by your own mother, it pays to hold on to every scrap of self-belief that you have.

It was sixteen years ago today that Evie saw me being deposited by the woman with dark red hair. And without knowing my actual birthday, we always celebrate this as my day to remember. I've had cake and candles, even a sip of wine, and my best friend Martha bought me a leather-bound journal and a set of pencils. And this year, Evie gave me something very special – the necklace that my birth mother had hidden in my clothing when she left me. It has a silver chain and an enamelled pendant with a distinctive spiral pattern... I've worn it all day, I'll never take it off. When Evie fastened it around my neck, she said, 'The woman who gave birth to you meant for you to have this, Cora, it shows that she loved you very much.' Then we both cried, her more than me.

After we'd hugged and dried our eyes, Evie retold the story of my finding. Starting with her working as a nurse at Netley hospital, leaning on the rail of the small pier jutting out into Southampton Water. She'd been taking a break after completing a busy shift nursing wounded soldiers brought back from the trenches. The smell of the salt water, the gentle lap of the waves, she described how it gave her solace, reminded her of her roots in the fishing village of Anstruther on the east coast of Scotland.

Then she paused for effect and spoke of a rustling sound behind her, a woman's voice muttering jumbled words in French. The light was beginning to fade, she couldn't see properly so she walked back along the pier. 'Hello,' she'd called softly and the woman had screamed and then she'd stooped down to what looked like a blanket bundle on the ground and started to sob. When Evie called out to her, she'd immediately turned and run away. Evie's instinct had been to chase after her, try to help. But when the bundle had started to writhe and she'd heard the first piercing cry and a tiny arm had shot out of the blanket, she'd bent down and pulled *me* out of the long grass.

I love the next part, when she describes how loudly and angrily I protested. It gives me a presence I wouldn't necessarily have if I'd been gently accepting of being abandoned by my birth mother. It's hard to describe how it feels to have been left, like a package, and then for your mother to actively run in the opposite direction. It's taboo, surely, severing a bond that should be so strong it can never be broken, not even in the direst of circumstances.

I try to put it out of my mind; I was so lucky to be found by Evie, I know she is a very special person. She's not only tough but she's bright and funny and she still has the closest friends ever back in Scotland – other women who she worked with during the herring season, and, of course, my Aunt Iris who lives in Paris, a fellow nurse who she met during the war. But sometimes, the more I try to rid myself of thoughts of my birth mother, the more her leaving me behind infuriates me.

. . .

She haunts me... I feel her whispering presence during my waking hours, and in dreams, her ghost moves through me, flavours almost everything I do. It tears me apart, sensing her presence yet never knowing anything beyond her red hair, her French accent and the spiral-patterned necklace she left with me. I used to cry into my pillow when the thoughts came but now I grit my teeth, steel myself, knowing I have to find a way of living through this. It makes me impatient to be older, so I'll know whether how I'm feeling right now is a passing phase. And if it isn't, well I'll... I don't know what I'll do. I only know that I'll have to be tough, even tougher than I am now.

My given name is Cora Mayhew – Evie called me after her Scottish grandmother and then she married my adoptive father so that's the Mayhew. I'm proud of the name, it means that instantly, the moment I was pulled from the edge of the water, somebody else wanted me. Wanted me so strongly that she got my cleft lip fixed straight away and then made complex arrangements for my care and paid too, so that she could continue her work of nursing the wounded soldiers. When I was little, I felt able to pass as Evie's child. But now with my body changing, I'm growing tall and skinny with no hint of my adoptive mother's short stature or her curves, and it feels like I'm leaving her behind. Increasingly, people tell me I don't look anything like my mother or my father... and I don't always want to go into the detail of being adopted, so it feels awkward, something hanging around my neck. As a child I prayed that I'd grow to look like Evie or Adam but with my distinctive red hair and pale skin, I stick out like a sore thumb.... I've even considered dying my hair brown to stop people asking all the time. Then I start to wonder... do I look like my birth mother or my real father? Do I even look like anyone at all, or am I an oddity?

It seems strange that Evie never had any children with

Adam. I sometimes wonder if that's my fault. Did me being here, like a cuckoo in the nest, block any others from being born? I know it's a ridiculous thought and I know my mother and father love me as if I'm their own flesh and blood. My adoptive parents are the best people ever, they are the ones who have raised me, I owe everything to them.

But here I am, an only child, an adopted child which means *I am* and *I am not* Cora Mayhew. Somewhere out there I have another name, maybe it's still spoken, still whispered on my mother's lips. Is she strong-willed like me, is she striving to forget me as powerfully as I'm imagining her? There are so many questions and never any answers and it makes my head hurt. That's why, one day when I'm older, I will go to France and I will do everything in my power to find the woman who abandoned me... to find myself.

CHAPTER 1

PARIS, JUNE 1940

Iris stood tightly gripping the wrought-iron balustrade of her apartment balcony with both hands. She made herself breathe deeply, fighting to control the dread that clawed in her chest. For days she'd seen the flashes of explosions in the night sky, heard the drone of German planes and the thud of war move ever closer. Now, with the loud rumble of military vehicles and the rhythmic tread of jackboots echoing across the city, she knew for sure that the time of waiting, of keeping spirits up and hoping for the best, was over. As she'd stood here last night, in this same spot, even as she'd heard the twelve deep chimes from Notre Dame and been aware of the direness of their situation, she'd still hoped the German invasion would be averted. For days people had barely gone out, shops had been boarded up, nightclubs and cocktail bars closed. At night the city had fallen silent, and now, knowing the German army were here, it felt as if Paris had lost her spirit.

Having lived through one war, it seemed inconceivable to Iris that she'd hardly been prepared for Hitler's army taking Paris. And only now, when the reality hit her, did she feel almost as afraid as she had under enemy fire, clinging to the rail of the hospital ship *Britannic* as they waited to receive casualties from Gallipoli. Even though she'd heard about the British and French wounded soldiers being brought to the American hospital in Paris, it still hadn't sunk in. Now, as she felt the hard metal of the balcony dig into her palm, she watched as the tricolour flag on the Eiffel Tower began to lower. Iris drew in a heavy breath that became a sob, and reaching a hand to her cheek, she was surprised to find it wet with tears.

Shifting her gaze back to the powerful lines of the Eiffel Tower, she recalled its link to the Statue of Liberty, designed by the same architect, a symbol of hope with her arm raised in greeting to all those who approached New York by ship. The thought took her back to her days as a nurse stewardess for the White Star Line; she felt again the prickle of goosebumps on her arms and that ache in her chest each time they'd entered New York harbour. The Eiffel Tower had represented all that and more since she'd made her home in Paris. Even now, on this first day of Nazi occupation, it gave her courage.

The announcements on the radiogram had been clear: Paris had declared itself an open city, there would be no resistance to the invasion. No *official* resistance, she thought, seeing the tower now in sharp focus, a testament to the power of collective human enterprise and ingenuity. She'd heard from a neighbour on the floor below that if the Germans did come, the cables to the tower's elevator would be cut through to hinder the inevitable raising of the German flag. She gave a wry smile – if Miss Amelia Duchamp, the elderly American woman who had gifted her this beautiful apartment on the Avenue Rapp, had still been alive, she'd have revelled in stories like these. But she was long gone now and, remembering her distress when the last war had been declared, Iris was glad that her benefactor wouldn't be forced to endure yet another. One that, with the relentless rise to power of Adolf Hitler, now meant that Paris had been taken.

Still holding onto the balcony rail, Iris watched as a swastika flag was slowly, inevitably, raised on the tower. As the bright red, white and black piece of cloth reached its fullest extent, it flapped, then unfurled, and a feeling of dread clutched at her heart. She felt jarred awake as if from sleepwalking, aware that those carefree days she'd enjoyed in her adopted city were now well and truly over.

A stab of anxiety. Where was her young companion, Cora? She'd been gone long enough to buy fresh bread from the only boulangerie left open on the street. It seemed so foolish now to have carried on as normal even after they'd seen a German soldier on a motorbike speeding down the avenue. Cora was an American citizen and a fiercely independent young woman, she should be safe. But what would Iris's closest friend, Evie, think if she knew that Iris had paid so little attention to the safety of her precious adopted daughter that she'd let her wander the streets unaccompanied? All the heated telephone calls from Montauk with Evie begging for Iris to make Cora leave Paris flooded back to her. But how could she force a headstrong young woman to return to America when she had integrated so well into life in one of the most beautiful cities in the world?

Turning abruptly from the view, Iris strode through the French windows into the apartment. Taking a deep breath, she stood for a few moments to collect her thoughts. Visions of her beautiful young charge being accosted by drunken German soldiers ran through her mind. The worries that had come and gone over the last few weeks regarding her own safety felt like nothing now. It seemed almost irrelevant that she'd ever been concerned about her own status – still a British citizen, though she'd lived in Paris since the end of the last war, married to a man who was half German, half French. The time had flown by in her beloved city and even when war had been declared, there'd been no thought of her leaving Paris or going to stay with Evie in America. She'd clung to her home, the place where she'd loved and lost her darling husband, Lucien. She couldn't imagine leaving him here alone in the graveyard, and not being able to take the weekly fresh-cut flowers to his grave.

A bubble of grim laughter rose through her chest – her hair was peppered with silver, but there were enough strands of blonde to be eye-catching. So many times, when first married to Lucien Becker, she'd been mistaken for a German wife, but the illusion hadn't lasted long – as soon as she'd been required to speak, in the days before she'd honed her language skills, her stunted German responses had been an instant giveaway. Lucien had died three years ago from a sudden heart attack. She still mourned his loss but her contact with Cora helped her immensely. That and the ongoing support she had from Francine, an old friend from her days of working as a nurse stewardess on the transatlantic liners, living in Southampton during her onshore time. A French citizen, Francine had been the wife of a close friend and fellow crew member, Sam King, who had died tragically when the *Lusitania* had sunk. All those losses from the last war were still so raw, her mind reeled at having to deal with the new ones that were coming.

But there was no time to dwell, she needed to find Cora.

Iris strode towards the hallway, grabbing her grey linen jacket off the hallstand. Hastily pulling open the tall wooden door of her apartment, she emerged onto the white marble landing. Her side-button boots clipped in a firm rhythm on the pristine tiles as she walked to the top of the sweeping staircase. Hearing echoes from the floors below she snatched a breath, bracing herself when she detected the opening and closing of doors, a man's voice shouting, and the cry of a distressed child. Flashing images of Cora's pale face came to her, making her gasp for air as she ran down the stairs with one hand on the shiny brass balustrade. A scream from the floor below caused her to stop dead, and in the pocket of silence that followed, all she could hear was the sound of her own heart pounding in her ears. Her downstairs neighbour, pleading rapidly in French, silenced by a sharp command. Then quiet, making Iris more aware of the breath rasping in her chest as she continued down, one step at a time.

'Halt!' a uniformed man shouted as she rounded the next curve of the staircase. 'Papers! Show me your papers!'

Iris gasped, eyeing the gap between the thickset German soldier and the curve of the immaculate, white-painted stairwell. Maybe in her younger years, when she'd kept fit by running up and down the stairs on the ocean liners, she'd have stood a chance of dodging by, but not now.

The soldier was red in the face, out of breath from the exertion of the climb, but his dark eyes burned into her. 'What is your name?' he asked in broken French.

She replied smoothly, praying her assured tone and fluency would amply disguise her true provenance as a British citizen.

'Iris,' he rolled the sound of her name over his tongue with a slight hiss on the final consonant. Iris drew in a steady breath, her heart beating so violently in her chest that she was sure he would be able to hear it. Clearly, he was puzzled by her name. She spoke again, trialling her German this time – her voice wavered, but she'd kept up her language skills to stay close to Lucien, a way of recalling the happy hours they'd spent together, the sound of his laughter as all those years ago she'd struggled to get her tongue around the heavy vowels.

The soldier began to frown. Iris hoped that his puzzlement would work in her favour. He was nodding now, maybe her grasp of the German language was better than she thought. In the next second, when she was sure he was about to wave her past, a neighbour from a lower floor whom Iris hadn't spoken to for years after some petty disagreement over the redecoration of the entrance hall, appeared around the curve of the stairs, closely followed by a tall, well-built younger officer. The woman must have been around the same age as Iris, almost fifty, but her face was furrowed permanently into a scowl and her dark grey hair was plastered to her head.

'That's her,' the woman spat, pointing an accusing finger at Iris. 'She's the one who lives in the grand apartment, she's your enemy, she's *British*.'

'No, no, there's a misunderstanding,' Iris shouted in German, 'this woman hardly knows me.' But the red-faced soldier's mouth was set in a line now and he was grabbing her by the arm.

'Come with me,' he urged, raising his voice, his fingers digging into the soft flesh. When she held back, he started to drag her and she had no choice but to comply, simply to avoid falling down the marble stairs. As she passed her neighbour, the woman sneered at her and in that moment, just when she should have been weakened, Iris felt a surge of resistance blossom in her chest. She would fight this, she would not give up, not when Cora was out there on the streets, all alone.

CHAPTER 2

MONTAUK, LONG ISLAND, JUNE 1940

Evie scrambled down the stony path towards the beach, seeking the customary ease she always found in the sound of the waves breaking on the shore. Although the day was uncomfortably hot, being close to the sea where she'd lived and worked brought comfort. That first year in New York when she'd been a theatre nurse at the Bellevue hospital, working with her husband Adam – then a young surgeon – she'd had the waterfront close by and the salt smell, the cry of the gulls had provided some solace for her as she'd got used to living away from her hometown of Anstruther on the east coast of Scotland. But once they'd both had their fill of the frantically busy New York hospital and Adam had gained enough experience to work at a senior level, they'd moved to Coney Island hospital and rented a house next to the shore.

It had worked well for little Cora, being by the sea with easy access to the beach and the funfair. Every day had been full of life and colour, exciting. But after Evie had endured her third miscarriage, she'd been unable to bear the shrieks of happy families on a day out at the funfair and she'd started to withdraw from the world. Adam had been his usual understanding self, but he'd started drinking heavily when he wasn't on call. When another pregnancy came, she'd seen him suck in a breath, offer a smile that didn't reach his eyes. After a few short weeks, when the bleeding came, it almost felt like a merciful release from the agonising anxiety of wondering not if but *when* all hope would be shredded once again.

That was the point when Evie knew that she had to seek further help from a specialist, a friend of Adam's back in the city. The examination under anaesthetic went to plan, Evie was so hopeful that the bright young surgeon would be able to fix her problem, but the news was stark. Her first pregnancy and traumatic delivery of a stillborn baby boy, conceived when she worked as a fisher girl, had caused irreparable damage to the neck of her womb. Adam's friend had told her that she'd probably also had an infection which had damaged the lining of her uterus. It seemed that little Martin, who she had left buried in the graveyard at Anstruther, would be the only baby she would ever be able to carry to full term.

Evie wept for days, walked the shore, waded in the sea, but when she became aware of how sad and withdrawn little Cora was becoming, she adopted a guise of happiness which in time became more substantive and eventually led to a coming to terms with the stark fact that she would never have any more children. Cora at seven years old, with her shock of dark red curls and green eyes, was a wild, beautiful child, brimming with curiosity and excitement. It was a struggle for Evie to leave her dark, lonely place but eventually she was able to bury her losses, embrace her only child and take care never to get pregnant again.

She needed to move from Coney Island though, find somewhere quieter, more reminiscent of the wildness of her upbringing on the east coast of Scotland. At first, Adam resisted, saying he wanted time to develop his practice. But then came a storm that brought all her other losses flooding back – her father lost at sea when she was a child, her first love cruelly taken by the sea just before she found out she was pregnant with his child. With Cora safely tucked up in bed, Evie had lost control. She'd run out into the night, drawn towards the lashing waves, the wind stripping her hair back from her face. Adam had found her on the beach, raging at the ocean and weeping uncontrollably. He'd understood then how important it was for his wife to find a home where she could settle.

Within weeks, he'd secured an interview for a position as a family doctor in Montauk. Evie was keen, feeling in her bones that this was the right move for her. When she'd arrived, leading the way with Cora holding her hand and Adam following, she'd seen the house with a stripped wood door and heard the Atlantic rollers breaking on the beach, and fallen instantly in love. They'd rented at first but when the elderly owner could no longer keep up with repairs on the rickety, weather-beaten building, they'd bought it. Knowing that she had a house of her own – somewhere that felt like home even though it was far away from Anstruther and her brother and his family and the friends she'd made while working the herring season – Evie had felt like a contented bird in a feathery nest. And the house overlooking the beach had been a wonderful place for Cora to grow up.

They were idyllic years with Cora sharing Evie's love of the sea. They'd breathed the air together, enjoyed every moment. Time had passed quickly, too quickly, taken up with Cora's schooling, Evie's training to be a midwife and Adam's diligent practice as a family doctor. The house had gradually expanded around them, with the addition of a spacious porch with a swing seat where the teenage Cora could gaze out to sea and where Evie could sit once her daughter had gone off to college. Now, with Cora a grown woman living in Paris, Evie felt as if it had all happened in the blink of an eye. Those simple carefree days had been over far too soon and all she had left was constant nagging anxiety. Cora had travelled to France to try and find her 'real family', as she described the woman who'd abandoned her as a baby in the grounds of Netley hospital.

Evie had been devastated when her bright-eyed beautiful daughter had stood in the kitchen one day last year and announced her intention to travel to France to look for her mother. *Her mother.* Wasn't that what Evie had always been? It had almost made her double over with pain when the words were spoken, even though she'd understood why Cora would want to know more about the woman who had left her behind, and the reasons she'd done it. Even though Evie understood all of it, the visceral pain it caused her was hard to bear.

Seeing the tears spring to Cora's eyes when she'd realised that she'd upset Evie, Evie had tried to rally round, but the feelings she had ran deep and she'd sensed Cora taking a step back, starting for the first time ever to choose her words carefully. She didn't want to lose the closeness she had with her daughter, she didn't want Cora to be apologising, trying to comfort her. It had made her feel frustrated but also upset for her daughter. Of course she understood Cora's need to find her birth mother; she'd come from a close family, she knew the security it gave to know exactly who your kin were. She wanted to help Cora with her search, but the rawness of her past losses and the prospect of losing her daughter, the centre of her world, left her too choked up to even talk about it. She'd never told Cora about her miscarriages, she hadn't wanted to put even more pressure on her as an only child; and then with the upset over her wanting to go to France, the sorrow of those losses had become even more difficult to bear.

Evie had been distressed by Cora's wariness, the unspoken tension between them, neither one wanting to hurt the other. It had been a relief in the end when Cora had spoken again, tentatively at first, about travelling to Paris to stay with Iris. This time she'd presented the issue of looking for her birth mother as an aside. It had frustrated Evie, all she wanted was to have that openness they once had, but now they were dancing around each other. Evie had nodded along, saying yes it would be lovely for her to spend time with her aunt Iris... As if Evie hadn't ever noticed the way Cora, often subconsciously, reached for the spiral-patterned necklace that hung permanently around her neck. How she clasped it in her hand or pressed her palm lovingly against it. She knew she'd done the right thing by giving her the necklace on her sixteenth birthday, but back then, she hadn't realised how much Cora would treasure it. It made her feel jealous of the unknown French woman she'd caught only a fleeting glimpse of, but who now seemed to be pulling her daughter away from her.

And things were even more of a mess now because in the few months since Cora had travelled to France, Germany had declared war. Evie had been stricken with fear for her daughter's safety. She'd seen first-hand – working beside Iris on a hospital ship and at Netley military hospital – the devastation, pain and suffering the last war had brought. She'd pleaded with Cora to come back to America, but her daughter had repeated over and over that as an American she would be safe. Often Evie would scream with anguish after putting the phone down, frustrated at her inability to make her daughter see the danger she was in. It seemed inevitable that America would join the war against Germany, and then what? Even her quietly spoken husband had shouted when he'd tried pleading with Cora. Evie heaved a sigh; just the thought of it made her weary to the core. Yes, she'd been headstrong at that age, she'd gone off and followed the herring, season after season, pushed herself physically, thought that she was invincible... and then she'd fallen for a fisherman, something she'd vowed she'd never do, not after what had happened to her father.

It infuriated her that she couldn't make her stubborn daughter see reason. While part of her understood that Cora needed to make her own way in life, painful as that might be, it seemed cruel that all the pain Evie had endured couldn't be used in sparing her daughter the need to go through something similar.

She'd hoped she could count on Iris, who'd always been so level-headed, to step in and guide Cora. When they'd been nurses in the last war, Iris had been her senior, in rank as well as age, and Evie had always looked to her for advice and trusted her. But since Lucien had died, leaving Iris a widow, it was as if the roles had been reversed and Evie was the one trying to steady things and give sensible advice, while Iris was off in a daydream. Instead of offering guidance, she seemed to have fallen under Cora's spell, allowing her free rein and encouraging her to stay in Paris. Evie had been at screaming pitch when her suggestion that Iris should make her annual trip to America and bring Cora with her, thus removing them both from danger, had been rejected out of hand. Perhaps, never having had children of her own, Iris was incapable of understanding how she felt.

Evie tried to make allowances. She knew Iris was still mourning Lucien and couldn't bear to leave the place where they'd been so happy. But he'd been gone three years; surely it was time for Iris to move on? Perhaps Evie's anxiety over Cora was making her harsh in her judgement, but it seemed so long since she'd had any contact beyond a stilted telephone call that she felt she no longer knew Iris.

When they first met, on the hospital ship *Britannic*, she'd regarded Nurse Iris Purefoy as buttoned up, driven by dedication to duty and professionalism. The horrors of war had broken through that carapace; Evie had got to know the authentic Iris, seen her passion, her courage. Without the support and strength they'd drawn from each other, they couldn't have endured the horrors they'd lived through. The two of them had blossomed and basked in the glow of their friendship. But now, all she had was this stranger, a shadow of her old friend. All Evie could do was hope and pray that somewhere behind those blue-green eyes and the finely lined but still serene face which she knew so well, Iris had enough fire left to sort Cora out and deliver her home to safety. Even if she couldn't bring herself to leave Paris, she could at least send Cora back to her.

Now, as Evie kicked off her sandals and walked the shore, feeling the shells beneath her bare feet, the waves breaking against her legs, the memories of Cora as a small girl were so strong it was as if she were right here beside her. She could practically hear her laughter as she splashed through the water, the squeals of delight when she turned back to see Evie chasing her, the tangle of red curls streaming out behind her as she ran free. It brought tears to her eyes, thinking of her now, far beyond her reach in Paris. Adam had been quiet this morning as he'd flicked through the newspaper before heading to the doctor's surgery. She'd heard him heave a sigh as he neatly folded the bad news of war in on itself and placed the paper squarely on the table. He'd walked away with his shoulders slumped.

It seemed like madness now to have agreed to let Cora travel to Paris unaccompanied, but a year ago it had seemed unthinkable that Europe would again find itself in the grip of war. Listening to this morning's radio broadcast with its grim report of German troops poised to enter Paris, she'd cursed herself for giving in to her daughter.

Evie felt a whispering shift in the air around her. She stopped in her tracks and looked out to sea. A heaviness crept over her, and in that moment, she knew something was badly wrong with Cora. She'd had sudden flashes of anxiety before that had been easily soothed by making a telephone call to Iris's apartment, but this felt different. Before she knew it, she was sprinting across the sand, her every step haunted by images of weeping fisherwomen and the white face of her first love, seaweed clinging to his hair, his lifeless body sagging as he was hauled from the water. Her heart was beating painfully as if it would burst at any minute.

She flew in through the door, her chest tight and heaving, desperately trying to catch her breath as her shaking finger dialled. Her voice was hoarse and rasping as she gave the operator Iris's number, and then she waited, her heart pounding, as the ringtone sounded. She pictured the black telephone set on the oak table in the hallway of Iris's plush apartment. It was ringing and ringing... surely it should be answered by now. She prayed for Iris or Cora to answer, knowing that, if no one picked up, she would be swamped by anxiety. Still she clutched the handset, tightly gripping a pebble she'd found on the beach in her other hand, needing to feel the hard edge of it dig into her palm. She knew that Iris had been constantly in the apartment over the last two weeks; it made her frantic now that the telephone wasn't being picked up. The lonely, mournful sound of the unanswered ringtone reduced her to tears.

Then her agony was over, the phone was picked up.

'Hello, hello... Iris, Cora,' she shouted into the mouthpiece.

She could hear breathing, why didn't they speak? She called their names again.

Then a gruff man's voice, unmistakably German, spoke in a staccato sequence impossible to understand. Evie felt the impact like a punch. She fell to her knees on the hard terracotta tiles, letting the receiver fall from her hand. The man's voice still calling, demanding a response, making her heart contract with fear.

CHAPTER 3

PARIS, JUNE 1940

Cora tucked the warm baguette wrapped in brown paper beneath her left arm and kept her head down as she passed through a maze of side streets. This part of the city had seemed deserted when she'd set out from Iris's apartment but now startled citizens dodged past her laden with bags. One plump middle-aged woman bizarrely carrying an ornate lamp with a frilly pink shade. She knew that Iris would be starting to worry because she'd taken so long to buy the bread, but their local boulangerie was all boarded up, so she'd had to walk further afield. She increased her pace, starting to run now as she began to feel that something wasn't quite right. Grateful for the time she'd taken since she arrived in Paris last year to learn the secret maze of side streets and alleyways, she dodged her way back to the Avenue Rapp.

Breathless, resting for a few moments at the top of the avenue, she saw it deserted apart from a stray poodle dragging its red leather leash, and two gendarmes walking away from her. As Cora judged the distance to the door of the apartment building, she paused for a moment, glancing up to the Eiffel Tower.

She felt shocked, like a punch to her chest, as her eye caught the red and white swastika flag flying there.

Reality hit her – could she be confident that she would be safe here? Only last week she'd listened to talk between her work colleagues at the American library, those who'd chosen not to join the exodus out of the city. Maybe it'd been bravado, but they'd repeated the claims that as citizens of a country that was not yet at war with Germany, Americans would be perfectly safe in Paris, even if the army did occupy the city. For weeks Cora had taken this line with her parents as they'd begged her to return home.

It had been so hard to get across to them how it felt living here in one of the most beautiful cities in the world, where she'd grown even closer to Iris, who her parents had agreed was like family anyway. Now she had a new friend, Madeleine, who she'd met in a cafe in the early days of being in Paris, and she also regularly visited Francine – Iris and Evie's wise old friend from the last war. As she'd told her parents, she was far from alone here.

It had been so hard to listen to Evie in tears on the telephone, her father angry, raising his voice for once. It had been heart-wrenching to say no to their pleas, but she was twenty-three years old now, a fully grown woman who needed to assert herself. Making her own decisions was a huge part of that. She'd worked as a library assistant in New York, a waitress in Montauk and as an auxiliary nurse in her mother and father's medical practice to raise enough money to travel to France. On her return home, she planned to secure a place at medical school in New York. In the meantime, she needed a chance to grow, to become even more independent, find her true self before she got caught up in the intensity of medical school.

In addition – though she would never share this with her parents – there was a buzz of excitement amongst the young American expats. The German army were at the door of the city, history was in the making. Those, like her, who'd decided to stay, had had their interest piqued. Even if they didn't say it out loud, they were curious, they wanted to know how it felt to be at war. If she hadn't been told that Americans living in France would be safe, of course she'd have gone straight home, but right now, looking up at the swastika flying from the Eiffel Tower, she was conscious of being a witness to history in the making. She would never forget this day.

Pulling into the shadows as she heard the stamp of boot heels in the next street, she felt her heart thumping against her ribs with a mix of excitement and terror. She strained her ears, listening for more footsteps, then forced herself to take a succession of deep, steady breaths. Somewhere she heard a child cry. Her mouth was dry. She swallowed hard and leaned back against the smooth wall of an apartment building, drawing comfort from her belief that the city itself would somehow make sure she was safe. Paris had felt like a nurturing presence since that very first day when she'd walked from the railway station to Iris's apartment. She'd fallen in love with the ornate buildings, the wide tree-lined boulevards, the street cafes with their music and the murmur of conversation, all threaded together by the genteel – almost silent – progress of the Seine beneath the historic bridges. She'd never felt more instantly at home anywhere.

Parisians she'd spoken to had seemed stoic, confident that their beautiful city, having endured so many incursions and uprisings in the past, would see this one out and then be restored. Iris, who'd made the city her home after years of travelling the world on ocean liners, shared their optimism even though she'd been born and brought up in Liverpool. In the months they'd spent together, Cora had seen Iris slowly coming back to the person she'd been before her beloved Lucien had died. But now, with all this happening, she feared her aunt would be set back even further.

Cora felt her heart twist. 'Iris, I need to get back to Iris,' she gasped, setting off at a run, her feet hammering on the pavement.

Slowing her pace, she nipped in through the double door of the apartment building, the baguette still tucked firmly beneath her left arm. Not wanting to risk waiting in the lobby for the elevator, she started to run up the marble steps, glad that she'd worn her trademark slacks and sneakers this morning and not the tailored skirts and smart heeled shoes that Aunt Iris insisted she wear for her job at the library. Moving swiftly, she barely had time to observe what looked like a fine spray of bright red blood on the wall. A thrum of fear started in her chest, but she pushed through it, panting now as she reached the tall door to Iris's apartment. Pausing a moment to catch her breath, she glanced around her; the door was firmly closed, there was no sign of disturbance. She was sure that she'd find Iris in her favourite chair by the window, patiently waiting for her to return.

Cora clicked open the door. Normally she would have shouted out to let Iris know she was back, but once inside the apartment she knew immediately that something was wrong. There was an earthy smell, a body odour that Cora's sharp nose detected. She didn't need to hear the grunt of a laugh and the heavy male voices coming from the lounge to know they had visitors. She felt a terrible unease creep over her, but she mustered every scrap of courage and strode through to the lounge with an air of being the rightful owner.

'Where is Madame Becker?' she asked firmly in her best French, hiding the terror she felt at finding a red-faced German officer sprawled in Iris's chair with his legs crossed and leather boots up on a treasured antique side table, a full glass of Iris's best Bordeaux in his hand. It pleased Cora to see him startled by her sudden appearance: he shot forward in the chair, removing his feet from the table, slopping wine on the pale blue and cream Persian carpet.

Cora stood firmly, repeating her question.

She saw the soldier open his mouth to speak. He was still flustered, but then an answer came from behind her. A grey-eyed younger man with neat pale brown hair and an erect posture stepped out from a recessed area that housed Iris's cocktail cabinet. 'Madame Becker is no longer the occupier of this apartment,' he said authoritatively, and Cora knew she would have to be very careful.

She snatched a breath, lifted her chin, not high enough to appear arrogant but enough to let him know she meant business. She spoke clearly, 'I left here an hour ago to buy bread. Madame Becker was safe, waiting for my return. I can see that things have changed, and I need you to tell me where she is.'

She saw the younger man narrow his eyes and his mouth twitched with amusement or irritation, she wasn't sure which.

'You're American,' he said, starting to walk full circle around her, as if surveying her.

'Where is Madame Becker?' Cora repeated.

'What are you doing here, American girl? Don't you know we've taken the city; we are in charge now?'

'I need to know where Iris Becker is.'

'Iris?' the man smirked, repeating her friend's name.

Cora felt the hairs at the back of her neck prickle. Somehow she had to break this spell he was trying to weave.

She took a step towards him. Being tall for a woman, she could almost meet him eye to eye. 'You do realise that Madame Becker was married to a high-ranking German businessman, and she still has connections, important connections, in Berlin.'

She saw a waver in his dark grey eyes before he regained his composure. He tipped his head to the side. 'I will allow you to pack a bag, but I want you gone in five minutes, do you understand?'

Cora stood her ground, 'Yes, but I need you to tell me where Madame Becker is.'

She saw the glint of a smile in the man's eyes; she'd cut through somehow, not that it made her feel secure, but she could sense some stirring of admiration perhaps.

'Madame Becker is safe, at least for the time being. I cannot tell you where she is.'

Cora held his gaze for a few seconds, deliberately waiting for him to break eye contact first. The moment he blinked, she spoke again, 'I can see I will have to make my own enquiries... and just so you are aware, I believe Madame's nephew is now an officer in the SS.' Cora wasn't sure if that detail was true, all she remembered was Iris's consternation when she'd received a letter from Franz, Lucien's nephew, telling her how proud he was to have joined Hitler's army. Cora had met him once, years ago when she was in her teens. He'd been a smiley, tousle-haired young man with pale blue eyes who clearly adored his uncle. Her mother, Evie, had been entranced by him, they had got along swimmingly.

'Hey, Karl, maybe we should take this one in for questioning as well?' The gruff voice of the officer in Iris's chair cut through like a knife. She saw the younger man turn down the corners of his mouth as if weighing the situation. Cora felt a painful tight-ness in her chest and she inhaled deeply, desperate not to show her anxiety. Her mind was already calculating whether she could dodge past him, throw a side table in his path, run to safety.

'Nah,' the younger man replied after a steady silence, a glint of amusement in his grey eyes as he tapped into her discomfi-ture. 'We'll let her go for now, but if she's picked up again...'

Cora felt something shift in the air between them and knew she needed to get out of there fast. 'I'll collect some belongings,' she announced, turning on her heel, still feeling as if the young officer were breathing down her neck.

'You have five minutes,' he called as she retreated.

She headed straight to the guest room which she'd made her own during her time in Paris. Grabbing a leather holdall, she rapidly gathered up items of clothing and other belongings, pushing them in. With her heart racing, she scanned the rest of the room... what else, what else? The copy of *Gone with the Wind* which sat by her bed had been borrowed from the American library last week and she'd only read a few pages. Hastily pulling open the drawer of her bedside cabinet, with shaking hands she gathered soap, talcum powder and a toothbrush.

Her entire body felt tight as if from a blow. She was desperate to be out on the street, free from the threat of the officer's presence in the apartment. Passing by the open door of Iris's bedroom, she could see that it was neat and tidy as always; clearly she hadn't been given the opportunity to gather any belongings... Was it possible she'd gone out, maybe to find her, and would be back soon? Or, as the officer had implied, had she been arrested, taken from here forcibly?

Cora felt a jolt through her body at a bark of laughter from the lounge and the clink of glasses. She dodged into Iris's bedroom, quickly scanning the precisely placed items on her ornate dressing table. *What would Iris want?* Her breath caught in her chest, she only had seconds to decide, and her mind had gone completely blank. Then she saw the framed photograph of Lucien placed at an angle on the bedside table and she grabbed it. Next came the leather case containing Iris's precious ruby drop earrings and the matching necklace – she remembered that these had been gifted by her benefactor, Miss Duchamp. There were other jewels, she had only seen a few pieces, but they were in a hidden safe that even she didn't know the location of. *What else, what else?* The tortoiseshell hairbrush – Iris had had this forever and used it every day. She ran to the wardrobe and flung open the door. So many fine clothes and shoes... *what to choose?* Hearing the harsh sound of boot heels in the marble-tiled hall, she grabbed a paisley patterned shawl, and as her stomach squirmed with anxiety, came a click of memory... the peacock blue silk gown that Iris treasured! Yes, that had to come. As she slid it from the hanger and pushed it with the other items in her leather holdall, a voice called, 'Time's up, American girl.'

Aware that the young officer, the one called Karl, had come to lean against the door jamb, she zipped up her bag and exited the room without even a glance in his direction. Feeling his eyes on her as she walked and then the sound of his boots in the tiled hallway, she moved swiftly. Grabbing her serviceable blue cotton jacket and the red patterned headscarf that had been Evie's off the hall stand, she exited the door and closed it in his face.

Not until she was out on the street did she start to tremble, tightening her grip on the leather holdall which now contained all her worldly possessions. Her body felt taut, ready to run, but her eyes were fixed, as if mesmerised yet again by the swastika flag on top of the tower. When a shot of anger surged through her body, she was ready to move, but even as she turned away, she couldn't help but glance back one more time. The flag appeared lurid, casting a shadow over the city.

Audibly growling, she shouldered her bag and started to walk briskly, dodging her way through other straggling dispossessed citizens on the street. There was only one place she could go: to the small house occupied by the close French friend of Iris's from back when she was a stewardess on the White Star Line. Francine King was old now, but she was a tough cookie. She would know what to do.

CHAPTER 4

Weaving her way through narrow alleyways, Cora felt glad she'd practised this hidden route to Francine's house. Only once did she stop abruptly when she heard a deep German-accented voice from the other side of a brick wall. With her heart pounding, she pressed her back against the wall, praying that the soldier didn't decide to open the wooden gate right next to her. He was still calling out to whoever it was, some poor soul probably trying to get home. His French was poor, but she could just about make sense of it. Cora was so glad she'd honed her own language during her year in Paris, turning her classroom French into something that was much more fluent.

Still reluctant to move, not wanting to risk making any tiny noise, she heard the soldier strike a match and then the smell of tobacco smoke drifted over the wall. Come on, come on, she urged, impatient now to be on the move again. He must have picked up on her thought because in a few more seconds he sighed out a heavy breath and she heard his boot heel grinding out the stub of the cigarette, then he was on his way.

Cora exhaled carefully, her shoulders dropping as the tension seeped out of her body. With the leather holdall still clenched in her right hand, she moved stealthily at first, wanting to get deeper into the warren of narrow streets. Almost there, to the small, blue-painted door of the house where Francine lived. As she began to feel a sense of relief, she almost screamed out loud as a figure stepped out of the shadows. An elderly Frenchman with dishevelled white hair, asking for a light. '*Non, non*,' she said, explaining that she didn't smoke.

He shook his head in disbelief. 'Everybody smokes! Especially now the Nazis are here,' he called after her in rough French.

Tapping on the door at last, Cora stood panting. She almost fell into Francine's arms when she opened up. All the way from the apartment she'd held back the shock of finding Iris gone and now it hit her again.

Francine let out a gasp, reached out a hand. 'Come on, *ma chérie*, you need to tell me what has happened, I can see you are distressed.'

The moment Cora opened her mouth to tell the story, a lump formed in her throat and almost strangled her. In through the door, still standing with her bag, she swallowed hard, only able to gasp out three words, 'Iris is gone.'

Francine's eyes widened and then she brushed a wisp of silver-grey hair from her cheek. 'Let's try not to panic,' she said, taking the bag from Cora and reaching out to place a gentle hand on her upper arm. Cora forced herself to relax enough to breathe properly and then she was able to follow the older woman into the kitchen, where Francine beckoned her to sit at the white scrubbed table.

Cora nodded, slipping into the chair that over the last year had become hers when she'd visited with Iris. She had never been here without her aunt and the place Iris usually sat, the chair with the patchwork cushion, felt glaringly empty. It made her want to cry but she swallowed down hard, knowing that Francine had endured so much during the last war – her beloved husband, Sam, had been killed and one of her sons had suffered badly afterwards due to shell shock. They were at the beginning of this, what use would she be to anyone if she were already in tears?

As Cora told the story of what she'd found at Iris's apartment, Francine stood, resting one hand on the table, her mouth slowly forming into a grimace which accentuated the deep wrinkles of her face. She nodded from time to time and then as Cora told her about the young German officer, Francine shifted her posture – straightening up, placing her hands on her hips. Even though Francine was thin and often breathless, her stance made Cora feel reassured, as if she had real substance despite the natural frailty of her advancing age. It was exactly what Cora needed right now.

'I'll make some coffee,' Francine offered, turning to the small stove.

As the gentle rituals of the coffee-making proceeded, Cora began to regulate her breathing in an effort to get her racing mind to settle. It helped her, being here, triggering her back to all the other times she'd visited. Francine had often teased Iris with stories from before the last war, when Iris had been a young nurse stewardess working on a ship called the *Olympic* with Francine's husband, Sam, who'd been a bar steward. To Cora's ears it had seemed like a wonderful, romantic time and when Iris had described the luxury of the liner, it had sounded dreamy. So much had changed in the intervening years. But then again, maybe not so much, since they were once again at war with Germany, despite the optimists insisting that France would never be invaded because the Maginot line could not be breached... Paris had been taken.

Cora repressed a shudder at an image of Iris being dragged out of the apartment. *No, don't think like that. She might be back there already, marching those German officers out onto the street.* Even as Cora thought it, she knew it wasn't true – those men had known exactly where Iris was.

'She'll head straight here, if they release her,' Francine said, turning slowly from the stove with a pot of coffee.

'Yes, I know she will,' Cora exhaled, leaning back in her chair, starting to feel some more easing of the tension in her body. As Francine placed the coffee pot gently on the table, things began to right themselves a little.

As she lowered herself stiffly into her chair, Francine smiled and joked, as she always did, about her old bones not working any more.

'You're not doing so bad for your age,' Cora found herself saying, the words that Iris always came out with right before she pulled out her French cigarettes and offered one to Francine.

'Hmph,' Francine said by way of reply, 'wait till you're as old as me... then you'll know. I keep telling Iris she needs to be more careful about what she eats – she's been putting on a bit of weight, particularly since Lucien died. It doesn't pay to become too fond of your pastries when your knees are getting creaky...'

Francine chuckled and then started to cough as Cora, far too young to understand what Iris's oldest friend was on about, nodded politely as the older woman flicked a silver dolphin's head lighter and lit up her cigarette. As she took her first drag, she leaned both elbows on the table... 'I'm not sure what to make of this situation, but we must believe that Iris will be safe. The question is, do we need to take any direct action?' Her voice was husky with age and tobacco.

'I have no idea,' Cora said quietly. To steady herself, she reached across the table to pour the coffee, her hand shaking slightly until she got the rhythm of it.

'I don't think there's anything we can do immediately,' Francine sighed, using the flat of her hand to wipe away a small spill of coffee that had run down the side of the pot and onto the table. 'And if there's anyone who can take care of themselves, it's Iris. She's always been an independent person, in charge of things. So... let's try not to worry, tell ourselves all shall be well... especially since she was married to a German, and her nephew, Franz Becker, is in the army.'

'I told the officers that he was in the SS... so they were aware that Iris had contacts higher up.'

'Very good move,' Francine smiled, her rheumy eyes glittering with pride. 'And I have one or two contacts myself who might be able to find out about arrests that have been made by the Germans, I will make enquiries tomorrow.'

'You sound like a spy,' Cora said, gasping at the absurdity.

Surprisingly, when she glanced back to Francine, there was something about the way she tilted her head that seemed to confirm rather than refute the possibility.

Cora didn't pursue it any further, she didn't want to know what circles Francine moved in, what lengths she might go to.

'We'll need to send a telegram to your parents first thing in the morning, it'll only be a matter of time before the Germans start closing down all means of communication with the outside world,' the older woman said, tapping ash decisively from her cigarette into a blue-enamelled ashtray. 'Your mother and father will be frantic with worry once they hear that Hitler's army have taken Paris.'

Cora felt her heart squeeze with guilt, she hadn't even thought about that, but Francine was right.

Sleeping fitfully on a cot bed in the attic room of Francine's house, Cora's waking and dreaming mind conjured images of marching ranks of German soldiers, Paris on fire, bleeding bodies in the streets. Gasping awake with her heart pounding, she forced herself to think of Montauk beach, the feel of the surf on her bare feet, the salt smell of the ocean. But with that came more angst about her parents; they would be so worried and then, when she told them that she couldn't return home until Iris was found, she knew it would make things so much worse for them. But how could she abandon Iris, her faithful companion, her guardian? Adam and Evie would have to trust that her American citizenship would offer sufficient protection to see her through the coming weeks and months.

A loud rap on the front door and Cora shot up in bed. The sound of voices below, Francine and another woman's... she sighed with relief, it was her friend Madeleine. She could already hear her running up the narrow stairs.

'Cora,' she cried, 'Thank goodness, you are safe.' Her cheeks were wet with tears. 'I went round to your aunt's apartment and the Germans are in there already... I was going to go straight up, but a woman on the ground floor shot out of her door and told me the Nazis had taken the top flat. She said the soldiers in there were disgusting drunken creatures, one even pissed down the stairs... Sorry, madame,' the girl called over her shoulder, remembering that Francine would be able to hear her impassioned speech.

'That's all right, say what you want,' Francine shouted up. 'I'm making coffee... laced with brandy. Let's start how we mean to go on.'

'Ha, Madame is very spirited,' Madeleine said quietly, wiping a hand over her eyes to swipe away the tears.

'You look exhausted,' Cora offered gently, noting the grey smudges beneath her friend's eyes and the disarray of her usually immaculately coiffed bright blonde hair.

'It's so awful isn't it, seeing the Germans at every street corner and then we've been so busy at the cafe bar these last few days, clearing it, cleaning everything, boarding up the windows, not knowing what's going to happen. But now I've had a message from the manager, Jacques, he's saying we need to open again next week. The Germans are asking for drinks, for good times, nights out.'

Madeleine glanced away for a moment, held her breath. 'You should go home, Cora. Back to America. I would if I were you. These smiling Germans are saying everything is going to be fine, but there is too much danger in the city. As I was walking here, I saw some officers sitting at a cafe table in their shiny leather boots... they clicked their fingers for the waitress and as I went by...' she shuddered, 'the way they looked at me. There is so much behind those eyes, their politeness is fake, I'm sure of it.'

Cora scrambled up from the bed and put her arms around Madeleine. Her throat felt tight but when she spoke her voice was steady. 'I can't go home, Madeleine. Until I find out exactly what has happened to Iris, I can't go anywhere.'

She saw the disappointment in Madeleine's eyes.

'I'll be careful, I promise,' she murmured, pulling her friend close for a few seconds. Then, stepping back, she tried to lighten the mood. 'The first thing I need to do is look for a new job. The American library is closed now. Miss Reeder, the head librarian, she's staying on to look after the building, but most of the others packed up and left days ago, in the exodus south.'

Madeleine reached out a hand, not yet ready to let her concerns go. 'You should have gone with them.'

Cora took her hand, gave it a squeeze, glossed over what her friend had said. 'So I was wondering, given the cafe bar will be even busier when it reopens, how about asking Jacques if he'll take me on as well?'

Madeleine gave a dramatic sigh, 'It is so ridiculous that you choose to stay here, Cora, when you could go off to the American embassy and get safe passage home.'

'I can't leave, not until I find Iris,' Cora repeated gently, 'and as you know, Paris is my home now. I'm certainly not deserting my adoptive city in her hour of need.'

CHAPTER 5

MONTAUK, LONG ISLAND, JUNE 1940

Evie tore open the telegram with shaking fingers while Adam stood waiting, an anxious presence in the background. Gasping for breath, all she could initially see was Cora's name – the other words swam before her eyes. Direct memories from the last war jabbed at her like knives. Seeing the telegrams come to the hospital, and then the devastating telephone calls that could change life in an instant, like the one informing her friend Charlotte that her brother had been killed.

The voice in her head growled for her to pull herself together. Clenching her jaw, she made herself read every single word.

'Cora was... she is... safe.'

Hearing Adam groan with relief, she turned to see his still stricken face. He was fighting back a sob and she had to swallow hard to contain her own. Surely, they should both be whooping for joy, rejoicing, but the gaze they shared needed no words. They'd both lived through the last war, fighting together to save the lives of wounded men on a troop ship and in a military hospital. They knew that this was only the beginning – all this talk of the war in Europe being over soon, they'd heard it before and that conflict had dragged on, destroying a generation of young men, and leaving a terrible legacy of grief and pain. It was a hard, heart-breaking task indeed to be faced with the prospect of going through such agony again.

When they'd visited Paris and travelled out to rural Normandy when Cora had been in her late teens, Evie had tried to find the right words to tell her daughter about the reality of the last war. But with battlefields smoothed over, green with grass and wildflowers once more, she could see why Cora struggled to take in what she was trying to say. Though the girl was aware of Adam's work in New York with disabled army veterans, fitting them with prosthetic limbs, it didn't seem to penetrate that this was the reality of war. Did each generation need to experience the horror first-hand to understand what it meant? Evie had prayed that wasn't the case, that there would be some way of averting further conflict, but even as she'd thought it, she'd known that it was already too late. Hitler's rise to power had come on the back of the last war and now here they were again, the whole world poised for further escalation of the hostilities. And her only child, her darling Cora, was in Paris, thinking that she was safe because she was an American citizen.

'Crazy, it's crazy,' she muttered out loud, tears spilling from her eyes as Adam stepped towards her and tried to pull her close. Evie didn't want to be held, something bubbled inside her and she had no choice but to blurt it out. 'Why is Cora so stubborn, so bloody-minded? I've been trying for months to get her to come home. I know she's in her twenties now, a grown woman, but why won't she listen to those of us who have direct experience of war?'

Adam offered a wry glance and when he spoke his words were measured. 'Well, I know this might not be what you're wanting to hear, Evie... but you do know that she is very much like you.'

Evie gave an anguished cry and set her mouth. 'You always say that about me and Cora, and it's not helpful, Adam. Why is all this my responsibility? You haven't exactly been *firm* with her.'

'You know that's not true. I've tried to speak with her on the telephone many times... especially after Daniel stopped me in the street, almost in tears with worry about her.'

'Danny is such a lovely, kind young man. If only she'd accepted his marriage proposal, we'd be in a far different place right now... As if I haven't got enough to worry about with my brother Douglas's two boys having joined up. I can't believe this is all happening again, Adam, I truly can't. It feels like a recurring nightmare. Are we a doomed generation, forced to endure war after war?'

Adam was shaking his head. He made another attempt to embrace her, but she growled and stepped back, rereading the telegram, making sure she'd read and understood every precious word.

'I hadn't seen the final line... it says that Iris is missing,' she said, her voice flat, her heart squeezing with pain. Despite her recent anger with her closest friend, she and Iris were like sisters, the ties they had ran deep.

Adam came to look over her shoulder. 'So, if Iris is gone, then what about the apartment, where is Cora staying now?'

'It says on the line above,' Evie said, stabbing the paper with her forefinger, 'she's gone to stay with Francine.'

Adam groaned, 'I know she's a dear and trusted friend of Iris's, but she's an old woman, how can we be sure she will be able to keep Cora safe? She'll have to come back now,' he said, his voice clipped. 'Surely she'll see there is no other choice.'

Evie didn't reply, turning instead to gaze at the sea, her mind whirring. Knowing how her softly spoken husband was wracked with worry, she didn't say out loud what she knew instinctively to be true: Cora would not leave Paris. Even though they didn't share the same blood, she knew that Adam was right: she and her daughter shared the same headstrong spirit. Cora was quieter, more like Adam in some ways, but those wilful flashes and a strong tendency to resist well-meant advice were traits she recognised. Before she married, that was Evie Munro, through and through. Maybe personality was acquired, breathed in from those who reared you, or maybe that mysterious woman with dark red hair who flitted through Evie's consciousness had left her baby girl complete with all her own inherited qualities... ones that mirrored Evie's.

Strangely, over the last year, Cora's birth mother had appeared more vividly and more frequently in Evie's thoughts. It was always the same: the poor woman stooping down, leaving the blanket bundle and then that look in her eyes, the desperation, the shock as she turned and fled. Evie had tried many times to describe Cora's birth mother to her, but apart from the colour of her hair, she'd been unsure if what she was saying was accurate. The only thing she could be certain of was how beautiful the woman was. She'd described her as having a full mouth and high cheekbones, like Cora's, but she didn't really know, she'd only seen her face for seconds. Years ago, she'd added in, for Cora's benefit, that her mother had been weeping and she'd kissed her hand and pressed it to the blanket bundle before she'd run away. It wasn't true, but Evie had wanted Cora to know that she was precious, that her birth mother had loved her and hadn't wanted to abandon her.

As Cora had grown and become a teenager, she'd started to set herself apart from Evie, who had come to regret embellishing the story of her abandonment. It had begun to feel as if her daughter now thought of her birth mother as some beautiful angel, someone very special who must be found at all costs. Evie sighed heavily, trying to let go of the feeling that, although she had fed and clothed and nursed Cora through all her childhood illnesses, in her daughter's eyes it was only her birth mother who truly mattered. She had to fight to hold back the recriminations that kept running through her mind, especially since the onset of war: *If Cora truly loved me and her father, she wouldn't want us to suffer the agonies of anxiety and she'd come home right away.*

With that emerging thought came anger, pure vitriol – directed not at Cora but Iris, her so-called *friend*. Why hadn't she sent Cora home months ago? Any fool could see that the march of Hitler's army was unstoppable and that they would breach the Maginot line and enter France and then Paris would fall. It didn't make sense; Iris had always been the careful one, meticulous in everything she did. Now, Evie felt fury rise in her gut. *Just wait till I get the chance to speak to that so-called friend of mine.* Her body started to shake with a mixture of anger and fear... She'd heard the voice of Adolf Hitler on the radiogram and it had sent shivers of revulsion down her spine.

She used both hands to scrunch the telegram into a tight ball. 'I'm going to France,' she shot at Adam.

'You can't, Evie... you're British, your country is at war with Germany.'

'Well then, I'll get false papers. I'll wear a disguise, learn to speak French.' Her voice wavered, holding back a sob as she recognised the plan was ludicrous, unworkable.

Adam gathered her in his arms. 'She's safe for now, we have to trust that at twenty-three years old, with a good education behind her and those excellent language skills, she will look after herself, keep out of harm's way.'

'I know, but she's my only child, she's everything to me.' Evie started to sob into Adam's shoulder.

She could feel the sharp corners of the scrunched telegram in her hand and, as Adam held her, she squeezed the paper more tightly, until the creases dug into her palm. Drawing back at last she saw him fashion what was meant to be a reassuring expression and then he patted her upper arm.

With a single nod and a forced smile to indicate that she was OK, she stepped away from him, turning to gaze out of the window towards the shore.

She cleared her throat. 'I've only got two antenatal visits this afternoon... I think I'll go down to the beach for a quick walk before I set off. The breakers are coming in fast and furious, it might help me think.'

'I can see the maternity patients for you if you wish?' Adam said quietly.

She switched round, a furrow between her brows. 'No, definitely not, I need to keep up with my work.' Seeing Adam reel back a little, she reached out a consoling hand to him... 'Sorry, I'm on a knife's edge. I know, we both are.'

She kissed him on the cheek before turning on her heel and heading to the front door, which opened straight onto the wide, boarded porch that had a direct view of the ocean. Pausing for a few seconds to catch her breath, she drew in some salty air, then she ran from the house, her pale brown hair whipped back from her face by the stiff breeze off the Atlantic. As soon as she was on the sand, she shucked off her sandals and waded into the sea, grateful for the wind buffeting her body. She gulped in air, striving to keep back what always waited for her at times of trouble, that place of deep sorrow where she'd lost her first love and then endured a stillbirth. She dared not open that box again, but it was with her all the same in the crash of the breakers on the shore, the shells beneath her feet and the mournful cry of a lone herring gull in the sky above.

CHAPTER 6

Summer evenings in Paris used to be a time of expectation – music, laughter, slow promenades along the banks of the Seine. Now, as Cora walked to her new job at the cafe bar with Madeleine, she felt the hollowness of the city, as if its vibrant core had been ripped out. Cafes and bars had reopened and there were still people on the streets, but occupying soldiers mingled and dominated. It felt stifling, as if a heavy shadow were hanging over the whole city.

She wondered how things were at home in Montauk. At this time of day, she'd probably be on the beach with friends, chatting, drinking a few beers... it was hard to imagine, but life in Long Island was probably going on very much the same. For the first time since she'd moved to Paris, she really missed home. The weather-boarded house by the sea with its broad porch where she used to sit reading her book, her mom moving back and forth, never settling for long but always chatting, laughing. She felt the rift between her two lives widening, unstoppable, making her chest feel tight. Drawing a deep breath, she made herself imagine walking the beach with the sound of the surf and the cry of the gulls. She forced her mind to recreate the salt smell, catching the edge of her mother's laughter as she plunged into the water, her skirt gathered in one hand, her face thrown back to greet the breeze.

Cora smiled at the thought of Evie, as full of life as a young girl. None of her friends' mothers waded in the sea or foraged on the beach, none of them tipped back their heads to laugh out loud. When she'd been a teenager, she'd often been embarrassed by her mother's behaviour but the older she got, the more she grew to love Evie's earthy grasp on life. And right now, still frantic with worry about Iris and daunted by the grey-uniformed German soldiers clustered outside street cafes or walking in packs along the boulevards, it made the hairs at the back of her neck prickle. She yearned to see her mother's sun-bleached dishevelled hair bobbing along ahead of her as they set off for the beach.

The stamp of boot heels in the street behind her made her heart clench. She held her breath as a gaggle of German soldiers chased past and only then did she realise that the young men were laughing, running to meet a fellow soldier who was now greeting them noisily. Cora kept her head down as she walked past the group, still grinning and slapping each other on the back, engaged in some joke. The soldiers were young boys, they reminded her of her friends from college in New York – fresh-faced, joking with each other, not yet sure if they were boys or men. *If this war continues, they'll find out soon enough*, she thought to herself grimly, feeling the persistent tap of the bag containing her gas mask against her hip as she increased her pace. No more leisurely strolls to work at the American library for her, no more gazing into shop windows. Some of them were boarded up anyway and the tables outside the street cafes where she used to go for coffee were all crammed with German soldiers, officers by the look of their immaculate uniforms and distinctive peaked caps.

Ignoring a low whistle from one of the tables, she kept her

head down and increased her pace, grateful when she realised it was probably aimed at the woman ahead of her – dressed in a cobalt blue dress which fitted the curves of her body, she carried her gas mask in a specially fashioned silk bag decorated with red sequins. Typical Parisienne, Iris would have said if she were here, that tone of admiration for a woman who, like herself, loved to dress immaculately and had a confident personality. It felt good to think of Iris but with it came another piercing stab of anxiety which made Cora suck in a breath and quicken her pace.

As if sensing Cora's unsettled thoughts, the woman in the cobalt blue dress slowed her pace and then glanced over her shoulder. She offered a reassuring smile and blew a kiss. 'It will be all right, *chérie*, just stay strong. We will survive.'

Cora felt as if the kiss had brushed her cheek, and as she returned the smile it made her feel lighter, hopeful. Iris would have loved this woman's attitude; it would have made her laugh out loud. As the moment dispelled, Cora continued on her way, pulling her blue cotton jacket around her body to hide the creases on the new waitress's uniform which Madeleine had delivered. She had forgotten to press it with the flat iron Francine kept by the stove – no more laundry from Iris's serviced apartment, no more luxury. An ache of sadness gripped her as she thought once more of Iris's beautiful home with its fine furniture and treasured belongings, all of it left to be mauled by German soldiers. They were only 'things', Cora knew that, and she had at least been able to save a few special items for Iris and grab her own essentials. Except, of course, the leather-bound journal which she'd left beneath her bed. She still couldn't believe that she'd forgotten such a personal item. With a sinking feeling, she felt again the ache of loss she'd experienced yesterday. She'd been sure she had the journal in the side pocket of her leather bag, but it wasn't there. She'd gone over in her head those frantic moments when she'd scrabbled her few things together, but each time pulling out the journal from under her bed had not been a part of her recollection. Her cheeks flushed as she thought of some of the more personal entries, recording how she'd felt on leaving Montauk and what had happened on that final night when she'd met her first love, Danny, to say goodbye. How could she have been so stupid as to leave her most intimate thoughts lying around for that young German officer to find? She shuddered, imagining him propped up on her single bed, leafing through the pages.

She swallowed hard – at least she had her silver necklace with the spiral-patterned pendant. She would never take it off, especially now, with the unseen threat that hung over the city, seeming as if it were in the air she breathed. As she walked, Cora raised a hand to her breastbone, feeling for the shape of the necklace which she'd worn since she was a teenager. The embossed spiral pattern the only clue she had as to where in France her real mother might be. As soon as she'd arrived last year, she'd asked around and been told by a French friend of Iris's that the pattern was Celtic, almost certainly from Brittany.

Iris had taken her there last summer, in what now felt like a lifetime ago. They'd travelled by train from Paris to Rennes, and then Iris had hired a driver so they could explore some of the villages and travel to the rugged cliffs and beaches of the coast. It was frustrating that they'd found no clues to Cora's heritage, but she'd fallen in love with the landscape, especially the wild coastal area that chimed with her experience of growing up in Montauk. She'd seen similar Celtic spirals in the towns and villages, symbols inscribed on stone or fabrics. But, in her dreams, Cora had imagined that she'd find many other people with her dark red hair and one of them would know of a pregnant woman who had travelled to Southampton towards the end of the last war. Or even more fantastically, she'd see the woman herself, walking down the street. She'd only spotted one person with her hair colour of around the right age, a surly woman carrying a basket of lace – she'd been rude in her response and had hurried away laughing. How crazy she'd been even to ask; how could she have thought that in the whole of Brittany she'd stumble upon her birth mother quite by chance? Even with the distance of time it made Cora's face flush with embarrassment.

But then, after they'd got back to Paris, there'd been a ray of hope. Iris, sensing her disappointment, had sent a letter to the matron of Netley hospital in Southampton to double-check if any of the staff who'd worked there during the last war could remember anything that might be helpful. Months later, Matron reported that they'd recently received a letter from a Monsieur Duval of Saint Malo, Brittany. He was asking if anyone could remember a young Frenchwoman with a tiny baby visiting the hospital back in 1917. They'd lost all contact with her and were hoping to find some clue as to where she was and what had happened to the child. Iris had written to the address, but then a week later the Germans had occupied Paris. Now, even if a reply came, no one would be there to receive it... The not knowing irritated Cora but, compared with Iris's disappearance and what they were facing in Paris, the mystery of her birth mother had paled into insignificance. One day, she'd pursue it, but it was impossible to do so right now.

It was frustrating, but at least the trip to Brittany with Iris and their common goal had drawn them closer together. She'd always known Aunt Iris and understood how close she was to Evie, but during Iris's yearly visits to Montauk there'd been something formal, slightly aloof about her. Evie had often said that Iris could seem like a cold fish on the outside but once you got to know her, she was all warm scent and flowers. Cora had thought Evie had been exaggerating, as was her tendency. But Iris had loosened up a little once Cora had come to stay, then after their trip to Brittany, she'd seen her warmer, more open side. That's when they'd become intimate friends, confiding in each other, laughing together. Iris had told her stories of the old days when she'd been working on the wards with Evie, how mischievous her mother had been, even dancing the cancan in her uniform! Cora hadn't been surprised; it was exactly the sort of thing Evie would do.

She would have liked to have found out more about her aunt's past life, but each time she'd asked Iris had discreetly changed the subject. Cora had thought afterwards it was probably because of Lucien; she'd seen the way she gazed at that framed photograph of him, his loss was still very raw. Not only that, she'd remembered Evie hinting at some other tragedy that Iris had endured during the last war. But at least, having done military service, Aunt Iris was perhaps better prepared than most to cope with whatever she was dealing with now. There'd been no information whatsoever about her whereabouts. Francine had made enquiries, she hadn't disclosed who her 'contacts' were, but no news had come back.

Cora didn't know what she would have done without Francine. She could have stayed with Madeleine in her tiny apartment, but that wouldn't have stopped her unravelling with anxiety, especially since she couldn't call home or even send a telegram now. After the first few days, all contact with the outside world had been severed. Cora felt marooned on what seemed like an island run by the German army. All they could do was listen to war news from the British Broadcasting Corporation on Francine's crackly wireless, which she now kept hidden. Without Francine's constant reassurance that Iris was a strong woman who had survived one war and she would certainly rise to the challenge of another, Cora would have given in to despair. All she could do was to keep telling herself that Iris was alive, she had to be alive. It didn't make sense, it was her own rationale, but at least it gave her a way of coping. Especially now, with the guilt setting in as she imagined how frantic her parents must be without any communication from her.

Agitated by swirling thoughts, Cora picked up speed. She would do everything in her power to find Aunt Iris but right now she needed to keep her head down, develop new ways of living in this city which had come to feel like an alien place with mere flashes of the Paris she'd grown to love before the occupation. The outward appearance was very much the same but what ran beneath was tense, like a trap ready to snap shut. From what she could see on the surface, the German soldiers were polite, they smiled, they seemed to show some respect for French citizens and interlopers like herself. But the malign glint beneath the veneer that she had detected while speaking to the young grey-eyed officer in Iris's apartment told another story. Cora had not been reassured by the hint that Iris was safe *for now*, his tone of voice had made it sound like a threat. She needed to be clever and make sure not to trust a single German.

Even before she entered the cafe bar, she heard the roar of male voices from inside and a rousing cheer. She pushed open the door onto a sea of grey uniforms – the bar was packed out with German soldiers, many of them officers. Madeleine was behind the bar, frantically serving drinks to a clamour of men, all raucous, shouting, but seemingly good-humoured. Francine had told them both earlier that the Germans were under orders to be friendly and unthreatening, to ingratiate themselves with the French people so that a productive collaboration could be instigated. Wherever Francine had acquired her information, it seemed to ring true, at least for now.

Madeleine was red-faced and busy, a fixed smile on her face, but strangely this didn't seem too far removed from any other busy night with rowdy customers. In the next second, as she pushed her way through the crowd, Cora instantly bit back that thought as a sweating German soldier grabbed her around the waist and pulled her into his muscular body. He shouted something in her ear, his French was terrible, his breath stank of cognac, and she couldn't understand the words, but as his arm slid upwards and he tried to squeeze her left breast, she instantly got the meaning.

'Get off me,' she shouted furiously, wrenching free to the guttural laughter of the soldier's companions.

'This one is a real tiger... keep back, my friends,' the laughing soldier offered in broken English.

'Madeleine,' Cora shouted, raising a hand to show her friend she was ready to assist as she was propelled towards the bar by the press of German soldiers behind her.

Madeleine's eyes flashed a grateful welcome, but Cora could see she was guarded, already careful.

When Cora reached the other side of the bar, Madeleine thrust a white apron at her and muttered, 'Speak French, you're good enough to pass... Don't let them know you're American.'

Cora opened her mouth to counter with the fact that America wasn't at war with Germany, that she wasn't the enemy. But seeing the set of Madeleine's mouth, she knew it was best to follow advice.

The amount of beer and champagne and brandy drunk that evening was incredible. Cora couldn't help but notice the glint in Jacques's eyes as all the profits he'd lost over the last few weeks came back, all in one go. It felt topsy turvy, all wrong, seeing the bar benefit from the occupying force, going about their normal business when outside on the street soldiers patrolled the city.

Cora's work involved collecting and washing glasses, an endless supply. She remained silent, servicing the tables efficiently, not making eye contact, pretending that she didn't understand the language, when in fact the smattering of German she'd learned in high school was rapidly coming back to her. She was glad that she'd managed to borrow a German textbook from Francine; she would put every effort into mastering as much as she could so that she might be able to better understand any unguarded conversation. Who knows, maybe a drunken soldier might start talking about what had happened to a wealthy, fair-haired woman who had been taken from an apartment on the Avenue Rapp.

'More glasses,' Madeleine yelled from behind the bar.

Cora jolted from her reverie with a start, grabbing some empties off the nearest table and heading to the sink behind the bar to start the washing. It was a tight squeeze behind there with Jacques in and out delivering to tables and Madeleine frantically serving. It was chaos, and as the night progressed the bar became louder and louder. They had to call closing time, but it went beyond the curfew. A German officer gave Madeleine and Cora written permission to be out after curfew so they wouldn't be arrested on the way home.

When all the glasses were collected, the chairs stacked and the floor swept, Cora grabbed Madeleine's arm and pulled her out through the door. 'Come on, it's fine, Jacques will be too busy counting his money to pay much attention to whether there's enough shine on the glasses.'

Out in the quiet of the occupied city, the sound of their shoes on the pavement seemed to echo as they clung together like two abandoned children. Only when it was time for Madeleine to break away towards her own tiny apartment did they speak.

'Go straight home,' Madeleine whispered.

'What do you think I'll be doing?' Cora replied, her hushed tone breaking into a nervous giggle. 'Dancing the night away with a German officer?'

'Oh, you mean that one with the big red face who grabbed you when you first walked in?'

'Definitely,' Cora laughed, 'he's just my type.'

They hugged and then Madeleine murmured goodnight and kissed her on the cheek before she broke away.

'Goodnight,' Cora whispered back, aware of how incongruous it seemed, given they'd been laughing out loud. She supposed it would take some time before they knew what the rules were, how they were meant to behave in a newly occupied city.

She made herself brave as she walked on alone, aware of every step. She was almost back to Francine's, ready to turn down the short alley that led to the blue-painted door, when a deep voice shouted halt. A German soldier stepped out from the shadows; a rifle slung across his shoulder.

Cora's instinct kicked in; her body made the choice before her mind was able to catch up. She ran. Aware of the need to lead him away from where she lived, she leapt over a low wall and disappeared down a narrow passage she had only ever used in daylight. Sprinting, her heart pounding, she took a right turn, using nothing more than instinct to guide her. Pausing for a moment with her back pressed against a stone wall, she listened for the sound of boot heels, expecting to hear the soldier in pursuit. All she could discern was the sound of her own rapid breath, moving in and out of her lungs. Not wasting any more time, she walked softly, needing the safety of near silent footfall. Only when she could see the shape of Francine's blue door did she pick up speed, bursting into the house as if the devil were after her.

'Stop right there,' Francine growled from her armchair.

In the dim light Cora saw that she was pointing an ancient-looking revolver straight at her chest, her finger on the trigger.

'It's me, it's only me,' she gasped.

'*Mon dieu!*' Francine shouted, instantly lowering the gun. 'Don't be bursting in on me like that.'

Cora felt a ripple of hysterical laughter rising from her belly, it was crazy – having run away from a German soldier carrying a rifle to be confronted by an old woman with a gun.

She tried to hold it back, but the whole ordeal made it impossible for her not to blurt out a laugh.

'Where did you get the gun?' she called across the room, collapsing onto a dusty armchair, her mind and body still fired with adrenaline.

'Oh, it was given to me by a friend, a keepsake from the last war.'

'I'm assuming it's not loaded.'

Francine chuckled, pushing the revolver back beneath the knitted blanket that covered her knee. 'Oh, it's loaded all right. What use would be a gun be without ammunition?'

Cora gasped in horror, but then she started to laugh again, letting it all out this time.

CHAPTER 7

After a fitful sleep and dreams of wandering the streets of Paris searching for Iris, only to be confronted by an angry German soldier pointing his rifle at her chest, Cora woke with a gasp, so agitated she fell off the cot bed with a clatter onto the wooden planked floor.

'Cora,' Francine shouted up the stairs, 'are you all right?'

'Yes,' Cora slurred in reply, rubbing both hands over her gritty eyes, aware of how heavy her body felt, how muzzy her head. As if last night in the bar, *she'd* been the one downing glass after glass of champagne.

'I have fresh croissants from the bakery,' Francine called again, in a bid to entice her down, as if she knew that all Cora wanted to do right now was crawl back onto her bed. Her body craved sleep.

'I'm coming,' she croaked, tempted now by the smell of fresh coffee.

Still in her full-length white nightgown, she grabbed a clip from the top of an upturned wooden box that served as a bedside table, pulled her shoulder-length, wavy hair into a loose knot and clipped it into place. Descending the stairs in bare feet, she padded onto the stone flags of the warm kitchen, drawing in the smell of croissants and coffee, feeling it soothe her troubled soul.

'You look tired, *ma chérie*,' Francine said, turning from the stove and indicating for her to sit at the table. Cora slipped into her chair, taking a deep breath to stop herself from yawning. What good would she be if all she could do was sleep? Was it enough to simply adapt to the occupation? Surely she should be planning something, joining forces, thinking about resistance.

As if reading her conflicted thoughts, Francine placed a gentle arm around her shoulders and planted a kiss on her cheek. 'You look like a beautiful angel in that nightdress,' she smiled. 'I'm glad you have come to stay with me and brought your blessing to my home.'

'A beautiful angel that you almost shot last night,' Cora smiled. 'How come you have a gun, Francine? I'm living here under the same roof, I think you need to tell me a little more about that.'

Francine made a noise in the back of her throat, 'It's tricky, *ma chérie*, you might have to accept that now the city is occupied, it makes sense to keep a firearm in the house.'

Cora tipped her head to the side, considering for a few seconds, 'Yes, I understand that, but who is this friend of yours who gave you the gun?'

Francine twisted her mouth before she spoke. 'He is an honourable man who fought and was injured during the last war.'

'Are you able to tell me anything else about him? Is he someone who might have other guns? Could he be turning up here under cover of darkness?'

'He is no threat to anyone except the German army... I can't give you any detail, so you will have to trust me when I say that he is a good man but after what happened to him in the Normandy trenches during the last war, he hates the Germans.'

'What about Americans, is he all right with Americans?'

'Yes, of course... especially the ones I hold dear.'

Cora opened her mouth to ask another question.

'No, that's it, I can't tell you any more. I've been sworn to secrecy.'

'Mmm,' Cora grinned. 'With all these secrets and guns, I'm beginning to wonder, Francine, if you are an actual spy.'

Francine placed the coffee pot firmly down on the table, as if drawing a line, 'Stop asking questions and pour the coffee.'

Cora giggled and reached for the pot, savouring the smell of the delicious liquid as it flowed into her blue-patterned cup. She sighed with contentment as Francine placed a warm croissant in front of her.

'Eat up,' she urged, 'before it goes cold... Don't be like your mother, Evie, and let it go stone cold as you talk on about this and that.'

'Ha,' laughed Cora, knowing this to be true. 'She does that at home with her toast and her coffee, she's chatting on and jumping up and down, doing all kinds of things while she's supposed to be eating her breakfast, while Dad sits there with his head down, reading the paper, slowly and efficiently eating every morsel on his plate.'

'Mmm, those of us who lived through the last war, we always eat up.'

'I never thought about that... let's hope this one doesn't upset the food supplies.'

'I think it will, and quite soon,' Francine added as she carefully lowered herself into the seat opposite. 'So, let's savour our breakfasts, before the Germans start their rationing.'

'Do you really think it will come to that?' Cora asked, through a delicious mouthful of pastry.

'Yes, I do,' Francine replied, matter of fact as ever, 'And I think there's every possibility that this will be much worse than last time around. After all, the Germans have taken the city very decisively and already it feels as if they are here to stay. It won't only be food either, they'll be rationing other things like petrol, so they can send it to their army.'

Cora paused, a piece of croissant in her hand, it felt as if the invading army would be unstoppable. And so far, no news of America joining the war effort... Surely it wouldn't be long before they did. With that came the realisation of the precariousness of her position here in Paris. All right for now, but once America declared war, she would have to disappear quickly.

'Hopefully there'll be news about Iris soon,' Francine said, disrupting her thought pattern.

'Yes, I hope so,' she sighed, making herself chew and swallow the fragment of croissant.

'Iris is safe, I feel it in my bones,' Francine declared, slipping a cigarette from her pack, and flicking the silver dolphin's head lighter.

Cora nodded, making herself believe that was the case. Then reaching out, she ran a finger over the silver lighter Francine had placed back in the centre of the table, next to the ashtray.

'My husband gave it to me for our twentieth wedding anniversary,' she said with a smile. 'I've used it every day since, and all this time has ticked by. But in my head, I still see Sam's handsome face, his thick head of hair and that look in his eyes, how pleased he was to give me this surprise, this gift that he'd picked up in a department store in New York.'

'In New York?' Cora said, picking up the lighter now, feeling the weight of it in her hand.

'Yes, he was on turnaround, in the days when he worked as a bar steward on the transatlantic crossings. He always went into the city to see the sights, have a cocktail in one of the bars – he loved New York. As did your Aunt Iris... she always liked her clothes and the face cream and cosmetics she picked up. She was very smart, very beautiful, a real heartbreaker.'

'But she only married when she was much older...' Cora mused.

'Maybe she did, but she found true love before then... He was an American, a stowaway, and they met on the ship. She tried to give him the cold shoulder, but he was very handsome, very charming and it was one of those things, you know, it was pure instinct. She said she felt as if they breathed the same breath.'

Cora didn't know what Francine meant, she hadn't felt anything like that when she'd been dating Danny. It had been interesting, nice to explore that side of life, but nothing earth-shaking, nothing memorable, even on that last night when they'd pushed towards increased intimacy as they'd said good-bye. She shuddered, instantly plunged into anxiety over the indiscreet entries she'd left in the journal beneath her bed.

She cleared her throat. 'So, what happened to the stowaway?'

'Oh, he was killed in France during the last war... so tragic, they'd only just been reunited at Netley hospital. He was shot and fatally wounded somewhere out in the wilds of France or Belgium. He fell with many others that day, part of the whole generation of young men who were lost, last time around.'

Cora felt her heart squeeze with sympathy for Iris. 'That is so sad... and she has lost Lucien as well, and she is grieving again.'

'Yes, she is,' Francine sighed out a lungful of cigarette smoke. 'But at least she's known love like that. She's fortunate like me, some never find it. If you are lucky, you will find it one day, Cora... and if you do, grab it with both hands, don't let it go.'

Sensing a waver in Francine's voice, Cora asked softly, 'Do you still miss Sam?'

Francine shrugged, dabbed at her moist eyes, 'Yes... even after all these years, I still feel his presence – not as strongly as I used to, but I hear his voice, he talks to me sometimes. It's like I've always said: the dead are with us, they don't go till we do.'

'I hadn't thought about it like that,' Cora said, tipping her head to one side as if to let the thought settle. Wondering if Iris held that view, if the voices that came to her were from both of her lost loves.

'I've started *Gone with the Wind*,' Cora offered, attempting to lighten the conversation. 'Have you read it?'

'Oh yes,' Francine beamed, breaking into a laugh, then lowering her voice: 'I won't tell you the ending, it will spoil it completely, but it is a very romantic book, very passionate. I'm hoping one day to see the film. I don't think it will come to Paris, not while this war is on.'

'Another good reason for pushing the Germans back to where they came from,' Cora quipped.

'Oh, if only war were so simple, *ma chérie*,' Francine called, reaching for another cigarette, 'but we will get rid of them one day, I'm sure of that.'

'Well, I was a bit put off when I started the book, only a few pages in and the characters are talking about war. I'm not sure if I want to read about armed conflict now that I'm caught up in one.'

Francine smiled. 'You must keep reading. In *Gone with the Wind*, the war adds drama, it's a backdrop for tragedy and loss... but also for love.'

Cora felt sceptical, tragedy and love didn't seem to fit together in her head, but she was willing to give the book another chance. 'And when this is all over, Francine, let's go and see the film together in the best cinema in Paris.'

'Yes, we will do that my young friend.'

Cora felt relieved to see Francine smiling, she worried that with her own anxieties playing out in her head – laughing one minute, anxious or distracted the next – she wasn't always easy company for the older woman. It felt as if she needed to find more purpose in her life and it was hard to do that now amidst the uncertainty which overshadowed the city. There was one thing she could do, however. She hadn't told Francine, but she'd found the key to Iris's apartment in the side pocket of her bag. She was going to walk back to Avenue Rapp, see if she could establish whether the German officers were still there. If she could be sure it was empty, then she would go in to rescue her journal. It niggled at her constantly, knowing she'd left her most personal jottings to be found.

As Francine smiled at her across the table, she saw the light in her eyes, her strong spirit. It made Cora feel that if an older woman like Francine could be so resilient, she could get back to some version of that free and easy young woman who'd arrived in Paris last year, bewitched by the city's beauty. She returned Francine's smile, starting to feel a warm surge of energy through her body. The thought of breaking into Iris's apartment, reclaiming her own property, made her feel good, as if she were fighting back.

CHAPTER 8

As Cora walked through the streets with the sun on her face, her secret mission occupied her mind and body. Her pace was brisk, her heart beating in time. The city appeared to have regained more of its colour, its vitality. For the first time since the occupation, she sensed a version of normality. The shops, cafes and restaurants were open, no shortage of food or drink yet. People seemed to be going about their daily lives. The German soldiers were like tourists, thrilled to be in Paris, smiling and appreciative, walking around with guidebooks in their hands, snapping photographs of the Eiffel Tower, the Champs-Élysées, all the famous landmarks. It was easy to lapse into a false sense of security, until you reminded yourself that the city had been taken by force by these uniformed visitors, and all the young Frenchmen who had joined up last year at the beginning of the war were maimed, dead or held in German prison camps, far from home.

Passing by a street cafe, Cora saw a line of officers occupying the front row of tables. An older, more authoritative man with hair greying at his temples was sitting with his legs crossed, the sheen on his black leather boots glinting in the sunlight. He was scrutinising his newspaper as the others chatted and smiled, summoning a nervous-looking waitress who approached the table. As a couple of young soldiers passed, they saluted. The senior officer narrowed his eyes, nodded as they marched by his table, almost in formation. Two Parisian women were standing chatting on the pavement, dressed in their finest, hair neatly coiffed, silk hats placed just so. One of them had a white fur stole draped over one arm, something of her effortless elegance reminded Cora of Iris.

As Cora mused, a shout and the sound of breaking crockery came from the cafe tables. The young waitress must have dropped a cup and saucer. The older officer leapt up, throwing back his chair, he was shouting as if a heinous crime had been committed. The girl stood frozen, a hand clasped across her mouth, then, with a sob catching in her voice, she apologised profusely. The officer pursed his lips, wiped down his uniform with his serviette, then slumped back heavily in his chair, flicking his newspaper with irritation.

In that moment Cora witnessed the mask of the occupying army slip and it sent a chill through her. It was right there, the rawness which lay beneath the veneer of normal life carrying on as usual. The presence of the German soldiers in Paris was anything but normal, real danger lurked beneath the surface, like a shark basking, waiting for prey. The two Parisian women chatting on the street corner fell instantly silent and hurried away with a fearful look in their eyes, their high heels tapping a staccato rhythm on the pavement. Cora felt as if a cloud had scudded across the sun; a shiver ran down her spine as she picked up her pace, the need to revisit Iris's apartment stronger than ever. She longed to enter what had been a safe, private space and take back something of her own.

As she approached Avenue Rapp, the closeness of the Eiffel Tower was a clear signal that she was almost home. Seeing once more the swastika flag at the apex of the tower, drooping now without any breeze, Cora felt her stomach clench. What if this went on for months, or even years, what if the French people never took Paris back?

She stayed close to the buildings, keeping in the shadows. The street was almost deserted, so much quieter than normal, which felt ominous. A shiny black Mercedes was parked smartly in line with the pavement, a trademark swastika mounted on the bonnet. Cora sucked in a breath, drew back as far as she could at the sight of a group of German officers outside the famous art nouveau building. The officers were laughing, calling to each other, one with an impressive camera guiding the others to pose in the lavishly decorated doorway of the house. They jostled together for a few moments, pointing at various bits of the trailing vine and Adam and Eve sculpture. The man taking the photograph became impatient, calling for them to stand still, then smile. Again, exactly like tourists. But after what Cora had witnessed at the cafe, she wasn't fooled.

With relief she saw the officers pile into the black Mercedes and drive off, no doubt making their way to another Parisian landmark. From her position in the shadows on the opposite side of the street, Cora had a good view of Iris's apartment block, its outward appearance unchanged. She'd expected to see some difference, maybe a flag or other symbol of occupation. From the exterior, no one would know that at least one of the apartments had been occupied by soldiers. *What was she doing? Surely it was madness to think of going in there, not knowing who she would find?*

In the second she was about to turn and make her way back to the cosy safety of Francine's house, she saw the heavy wooden door of the apartment block open and two German officers stepped out laughing, one lighting up a smoke. Cora recognised the younger officer, Karl, who had delighted in intimidating her, alongside his thickset sidekick with the round face. They were walking away now, so the apartment would be empty.

An urge – a cross between fear and excitement – struck the pit of her stomach. Without interrogating it, she ran swiftly across the avenue, pushing open the door and slipping into the once familiar ornately tiled entrance hall. The white marble stairs beckoned, she inhaled deeply and ran, her soft-soled sneakers near silent on the steps. Only mildly breathless, she reached the top, already pulling the heavy metal key out of her pocket. It slipped easily into the aged lock with a satisfying click. She was in.

Pausing to steady the rapid beating of her heart, the now alien smell of the place assaulted her. When she'd lived here with Iris the apartment had been fresh, well aired with an underlying spritz of citrus. Now it was musky with stale sweat cut through with an overtone of sour wine. Glancing into the normally pristine lounge she saw complete disorder: food scraps on plates, discarded wine bottles, broken glass on a side table and debris on the Persian rug and, most tellingly of all, a poster of Adolf Hitler taped to the ornate gold-framed mirror above the fireplace. A feeling of disgust mingled with the thrill of breaking in spurred her on to complete her business. Stepping briskly towards what had been her bedroom, she glanced into Iris's room. The drawers and wardrobes had been turned out, the bed was unmade, stained with what looked like spilt coffee. All of Iris's ornaments had been swept off her dressing table, some lay smashed. For a moment, Cora couldn't understand it, but then she realised – they must have been looking for a safe. They would know that an apartment as opulent as this was bound to have jewels or currency stashed somewhere. From what she could see, they had found nothing, Cora didn't even know where the secret safe was herself.

A shiver ran through her as she pushed open the door to her own room. The pungent smell of a male body met her, but her single bed had been left tidily made up with what looked like hospital corners. She swallowed hard, spotting a pair of cream silk camiknickers she must have left behind strewn on the floor. With one swift move she stooped down and picked them up. Was that the front door opening? She strained her ears, listening for the sound of footsteps, holding back raw panic. No, she could hear nothing but the steady tick of the bronze ormolu clock in the hall. She fell to her knees and reached under the bed for her precious journal. Her hand met nothing... and even before she lifted the bed cover to double-check, she knew with a sickening dread that the journal was gone.

Still clutching her silk camiknickers, growling with agitation now, she jumped up from the floor. Feeling as if someone were breathing down her neck, she moved fast. It wasn't worth spending any more time searching, the young officer, Karl, would have read all her most intimate thoughts by now anyway. She had risked coming in here for absolutely nothing. The urgent need to escape, to be back on the Avenue Rapp, free as a bird, spurred her to run out of her bedroom towards the hall-way. Two paces from the door, she heard the sickening sound of a key in the lock and she froze, her raspy breath seeming loud. There was discussion, consternation at the other side of the door and she could make out from her rudimentary grasp of German that the two men were querying whether they had locked the apartment behind them. Cora had seconds to act. She slipped behind the coat rack, knowing that the door would swing open any minute now. Her heart thumped so hard against her ribs that she was sure they would be able to hear it. Then, as the door started to open, she spotted the camiknickers she'd been holding in her hand right there on the marble-tiled floor where she must have dropped them. Her painful heart squeezed even tighter.

With the sharp sound of leather boots in the hall, the men walked in. Her heart was hammering so hard it was painful, every muscle in her body felt tight. She couldn't bear to look, aware she would know by the tone of their voices if they found the discarded silk underwear. She could hear the men murmuring as they closed the door. They weren't moving and she imagined they'd seen the camiknickers, they knew there was someone in the apartment. Then Karl called out to his companion and the sharp tread of boots sounded on the tiled floor. Cora opened her eyes, peeped from beneath the sleeve of Iris's full-length wool coat that was, thankfully, still on the stand. She watched as Karl's booted foot caught the light silk camiknickers and pulled them along two steps. Her gut twisted, it would take one single glance down for him to see them. She knew already how whip-sharp he was, he'd know instantly that she was there, in the apartment. He'd slowed his pace now, one more agonising step, still dragging the silk with him. Then two steps from the lounge doorway, she saw her underwear slip from his boot. Slowly she let out a long-held breath.

Go on, go on, she urged in her head, willing them to enter the living room, needing a few seconds to make her exit. Her heart was steadying now, her body poised to make her move. Thankfully, they hadn't bothered to relock the door.

That's it, they were gone from the hallway. She moved in a sequence, as if performing a dance. A sidestep out from behind the hall stand, three tiptoed steps to collect her camiknickers and then a light-footed bound to the door. She blocked her ears to any sound from behind her, left the door wide open in her wake and as she raced down the stairs she felt elation run through every bone of her body. Especially when she heard a shout from the top of the marble stairs, a deep German voice calling after her. Too late, far too late... she was running free and there was nothing they could do to stop her.

Only when she was far enough away to feel the warm glow of relief did Cora slow her pace to a brisk walk. Pushing a hand in her pocket she felt the silky softness of the camiknickers against the hardness of the iron key – someone must have been looking out for her while she was in the apartment. She reached a hand up to the spiral-patterned necklace; maybe it was her birth mother. Recovering an item of her clothing felt like winning a prize, something to offset the pain and humiliation of losing her personal jottings. She would have been exultant if she'd managed to rescue the journal as well, but at least she'd had the guts to go in there, to take something back. She wouldn't tell Francine what she'd been up to, she didn't want to worry her.

'Where have you been?' Francine asked as soon as she was in through the door.

'Out for a walk, getting some air...' Cora tried to say.

'Mmmm,' Francine offered from her armchair, narrowing her eyes, the knitted blanket over her knee. Cora hoped she didn't have the loaded revolver under there again.

'You look like my sons used to when they'd been up to no good... so you might as well come clean.'

Cora heaved a sigh and then started to smile when she noted the playful twinkle in Francine's eyes.

'I've been on a mission... to rescue these,' she laughed, pulling the silk camiknickers out of the pocket of her slacks.

Francine tipped her head to one side. 'So, you've been back to the apartment, have you?'

Cora nodded, lowering herself into the armchair.

'That seems like a big risk to take, for such a small reward.'

'Probably,' Cora replied, knowing she might as well tell the whole story. 'But I went to find something else, a journal that I'd left behind.'

'Oh, I see now,' Francine murmured, 'but even so, to risk who knows what for some scribblings.'

'It was personal stuff, diary entries.'

Cora saw the immediate understanding in Francine's eyes, but now that she'd spoken the words, the whole escapade did seem a bit far-fetched, even to her. Those moments she'd stood concealed behind the hallstand could have gone drastically wrong at the drop of a pin. But knowing she'd done it, she'd held her nerve, it, felt like an act of defiance. It gave her a buzz, thinking back over it.

'You have hidden talents, Cora. It takes courage to do something like that... you would probably make an excellent cat burglar.' Then dropping her tone, '*But*... it could all have gone horribly wrong, so don't you ever take a risk like that again without discussing it with me first. Do you understand?'

The steely tone of Francine's words was unmistakable. 'Don't worry, I won't,' Cora said instantly.

'So, we know where we stand then, don't we? From now on, if there are any missions you feel like undertaking, you speak to me first and we work together.'

'Yes,' Cora said, intrigued. What did Francine mean by 'missions'? On top of the mystery surrounding the gun, a sense of things being not quite what they at first seemed was beginning to emerge. Seeing the glint in Francine's eye, she knew she wouldn't get far with further questioning right now but as her friend rested back in her armchair and smiled, it seemed to Cora as if an unspoken deal had been made. A pact.

It felt good to find shared understanding with an older woman such as Francine who had so much experience of life. She'd learned a great deal from Iris, and of course from Evie, and it made her feel guilty now, that she hadn't been more understanding of her mom. She knew in her heart that Evie fully understood the instinct that burned inside of her to find her birth mother. And that her quest to find the woman who had willingly abandoned her was bound to be a difficult issue. Now that all communication with the outside world had been cut by the Germans, Cora yearned to speak to her mother, to tell her how much she treasured the memories of growing up in

Coney Island, then in their precious family home in Montauk. Why hadn't she said all these things before she left for France?

Not that she would ever fully abandon the search for her birth mother, but now her tenure in Paris and her very existence were threatened, she knew those most important to her had to be Evie and Adam. She so wished she could tell them that now. In a way it might have been better if Evie had come right out and said how Cora's actions had made her feel, but in the time before she'd left for Paris, all they'd ever done was dance around the issue, offer snippets but not too much detail. Despite Evie's fearless manner, there was a vulnerability there as well, and the last thing Cora had wanted to do was cause her any distress. Evie's life had been tough. On their last trip to Scotland, three or four years ago, she'd confided that she'd given birth to a son at the beginning of the last war. She'd been young, unmarried, and the father of the baby had drowned in a storm while fishing for herring. Even the telling of it had made Evie tremble, Cora had been able to see how real it still was to her. Then she'd taken Cora to see the grave of her stillborn son, a tiny mound of earth that marked the final resting place of little Martin Munro. He had a headstone looking out to sea, Evie had given her yellow roses to lay on the grave... It had made Cora cry so much; she would have loved to have had an older brother.

Lost in her thoughts, Cora must have sighed audibly, because she saw Francine lift her head. Feeling suddenly very weary after her adventure in the apartment, Cora settled back in her armchair. Francine's voice broke through gently, 'It's hard isn't it when thoughts and regrets from home come at you, and there's nothing you can do to resolve them.'

'Yes,' Cora sighed. Then, 'Hold on a minute, how did you know what I was thinking about?'

Francine smiled and shrugged. 'I've been dealing with the troubles women endure for a very long time, *ma chérie*. It's easier than you think to tap into thoughts running through someone else's mind.'

Is it? Cora thought as she rested her head back against a soft cushion, letting her mind drift, feeling the heaviness of her limbs as she entered a contented state of pure drowsiness. She was safe here with Francine, a woman who could read thoughts, understand things that were never made clear, who knew more about the world and its joys and its woes than anyone Cora had ever known.

CHAPTER 9

Three sharp knocks at the front door made Cora gasp awake. Groggy, as her eyes focused, she saw Francine slip the ancient revolver down the side of the chair and lever herself up. Having already been confronted with the weapon head-on, Cora's heart didn't even miss a beat.

Francine shouted for whoever it was to come in and the door creaked open. A woman, perhaps slightly younger than Francine, with grey hair and dark eyebrows drawn together over a thin nose, entered first, closely followed by a heavy-set man with dishevelled greying hair and a scruffy dark beard. His expression was unreadable, he was a bear of a man with a pronounced limp, using a walking stick with a rounded knob of a handle. They both paused, looking to Francine.

'This is the young friend I told you about, the American.'

The man grunted; the woman looked sceptical.

'We can trust her,' Francine said firmly, 'She's family.'

The woman sniffed, came close, looked her up and down.

'If Francine trusts her, that's good enough for me,' the man said, his gravelly voice a low growl.

Cora was wide awake now, but she had no idea what was

going on. All she knew was that she needed to act, or she might be facing an interrogation. Mustering her best French, she fully introduced herself, repeating Francine's words, assuring them that she could be trusted.

The man's mouth turned down in an exaggerated fashion, he waggled his head from side to side. 'Her French is good, for an American,' he said at last, 'she gets my vote.'

The woman shrugged and offered the shadow of a smile intimated only by the deep wrinkles at the corners of her dark eyes turning up ever so slightly. 'All right, all right... let's get on, there's work to do.'

While Francine made the coffee, Cora sat with the two guests, introduced as Estelle and Bertrand, at the kitchen table. The woman did most of the talking from the start and had an air of being in charge. Bertrand lit up a freshly rolled cigarette with the dolphin's head lighter and then rested back in his chair, his eyes narrowed against the smoke, listening.

Once the coffee was poured, the dynamic around the table changed. Francine led the discussion, she was authoritative but thoughtful, paying attention to not only the detail of what she was saying but also the reaction of her guests. Cora's mouth dropped open when it became rapidly apparent that these three had formed their own small group of resistance to the German occupation. Bertrand had a radio transmitter hidden in his home. Estelle, it seemed, had worked as a typesetter and could produce and print posters, maybe even fake documents in the back room of her house. Cora's heart started to beat faster, it seemed incredible that these three older people had rallied together so quickly.

Once there was a pause in the complex plans the three of them seemed to be making, Cora put down her coffee cup and spoke out. 'Can I ask how, or why, did you all get together and think about defying the German army so soon?'

Bertrand started to chuckle, a deep rumbling sound in his

chest, but when his voice came it was more solemn than she expected. 'If you'd lived long enough to fight these bastards in the trenches once already, and you'd lost your closest friends trying, you'd be there with us right now.'

'Of course, the first war... and is that why you have a limp, were you injured?'

Bertrand grimaced, then nodded. With sudden tears shining in his eyes, he shrugged his shoulders, 'I was one of the lucky ones, if I'd been one step closer, I'd have been blown up by the same shell that killed my friends.'

'There was a reason why you were spared, Bertrand,' Francine said, reaching out a hand to him. 'You are here, and you can help the next generation fight again, this time around.'

Bertrand ran a rough hand over his face, then he pulled out his tobacco pouch to roll another cigarette.

Estelle was frowning, she opened her mouth as if to speak but then thought better of it. Francine got up slowly from her seat at the table and put an arm around her shoulders. 'My friend here, she lost both of her sons at Verdun... one of the longest, bloodiest and most brutal battles of the last war.'

The woman gave a single nod as she sat straight-backed, breathing deeply.

'I'm so sorry,' Cora spoke softly, respectfully, 'I was born right at the end of the last war so I don't remember it, I can't even imagine how awful it must have been... and the way that your Sam was lost as well, Francine, on that passenger ship torpedoed by the Germans. It's easy to see why it is so important to all of you, but why do this now, why not wait a while to see how things are going?'

Bertrand coughed on his cigarette, then stubbed it ruthlessly in the glass ashtray. As he pulled out another smoke and reached for the dolphin's head lighter, Cora sensed the unmistakable tension around the table, she felt as if she'd thrown a stone into smooth water.

After Bertrand had taken his first drag, he cleared his throat and looked directly at Cora... 'On the day the Germans entered Paris, I walked to Les Invalides – I have an old friend from the last war, so badly wounded he is bedbound. He lived there in the hospital until the Germans shipped all the sick and disabled veterans out. Afterwards, I went to a small square close by, somewhere to sit for a while, think about the world. Two German soldiers were there with pickaxes and shovels, destroying the statue of a French general, a hero from the last war. They jeered at me as they hacked it to pieces, leaving only the pedestal covered with debris. I knew then that their onslaught would be remorseless... the grudge they bore from the last war was hard as iron, bitter. After they'd gone, I took a piece of the stone and pushed it in my pocket. When I looked up, a retired colonel, another French ex-military who I'd chatted to before was there. He pressed a hand to his chest, like this...' Bertrand repeated the gesture. 'We need to act now,' he said, 'I know other veterans who are ready to join, maybe we can collect military intelligence, smuggle it across the Channel to the British.'

Cora felt an ache deep in her chest, a moment of realisation. 'And are you able to do that, right now?'

Bertrand gave a firm nod and smiled. 'Yes, it's working well so far. And my retired colonel has organised routes for the information to flow, we can even receive requests for specific details... We are not alone, there are other small groups of resistance, a whole network of them.'

'That's very impressive,' Cora breathed, starting to feel a connection with this bear of a man when she saw the warmth in his eyes.

Estelle leaned forward, her elbows on the table, 'It's crucial we work as hard as we can in these early days,' she said, her frown deepening. 'The Germans are relaxing in Paris, riding high, they think they're untouchable. We are currently catching them off guard... but as the weeks and months go by, it will become much harder.'

'Yes, I agree,' Francine was nodding, 'So we'll have to stand our ground, take it as it comes... After all, we're doing this for the next generation, our children and grandchildren – at least mine are currently safe in America.'

Estelle pressed her mouth into a firm line, looked directly at Cora. 'You're American, why aren't you over there as well?'

Cora felt her chest tighten, 'I should be, you're right, I can't bear to think what my parents are going through, knowing I'm in an occupied city. But at the time, most of my American friends were so confident we'd all be safe, and I'd got used to the idea of the Germans coming through Paris. When it did happen, I was so shocked... especially when my mother's friend, Iris, disappeared from her apartment.'

'So you thought you might be able to find her, then?' Bertrand offered, his voice rough but kindly all the same time.

'Yes, I did, *I do*. Only I don't know where to start.'

'We've met Iris Becker, in happier times, here at Francine's table,' Estelle said, 'and we are aware of her disappearance. Bertrand used to work for the police, so we have contacts there, but no news yet.'

Cora felt her heart twist, 'So do you know if she's alive, is there that at least?'

Bertrand slowly shook his head. 'I'm afraid there's no way of knowing... but the chances are, given she has family contacts in the German army, that she is safe and she will be released at some stage.'

'Is there nothing else we can do? What if *I* go to the police?'

'No, definitely not, you'll only draw attention to yourself if you do that,' Estelle drew her brows together in a sharp line and spoke firmly.

Cora heaved a sigh, rested back in her chair.

'It's a waiting game, I'm afraid,' Francine offered, 'there is nothing more we can do for the time being and, like I've said before, I feel in my bones that Iris is safe... so no more going back to the apartment, stirring up those German officers.'

Bertrand coughed on his cigarette, suddenly interested. 'You did what?'

'Don't encourage her,' Francine warned. 'They didn't clap eyes on her this time round, but it was a very close call. We don't want to be looking for another missing person, do we?'

'You need to do as you are told,' Estelle's voice was strict, her eyes narrowed.

Cora swallowed, 'I will, I'll follow orders from now on, don't worry.'

'She's sounding like she's part of the group,' Bertrand chuckled.

'Well, I do have a French mother,' Cora offered, her eyes bright, still trying to win Estelle over.

Estelle narrowed her eyes, 'Yes, but your mother is in America, so—'

'No, I mean my birth mother. She is French and she left me this – look...' she said, pulling the necklace out from inside her blouse, 'I'm a foundling, my birth mother abandoned me in Southampton a few weeks after I was born.'

'Well, well,' Estelle murmured, a slight catch in her voice as she took hold of the enamelled pendant. 'This is a very unusual necklace, the spiral pattern reminds me of the Celtic influence somewhere like Brittany.'

'Yes,' Cora gasped, feeling a stab of excitement, 'I've been told that before... Soon after I came to France, to search for her, a friend of Iris's said that too. We went to Brittany but found no leads. I was going to go back, but with Iris missing and this war, well...'

'It's all been put back, hasn't it,' Francine added.

Estelle let go of the pendant, her expression unreadable, 'You have no choice, you'll have to wait now till this mess of a war is over... No one will want to talk to a young American strolling around Brittany looking for her long-lost relatives.'

Cora nodded. 'Yes, I'm aware of that, but if anything comes up along the way...'

Estelle shrugged, then with a glint of warmth in her eye she added, 'You don't seem to have done well with the women in your life do you, Cora? You came to France looking for your birth mother and then you lost Iris as well.'

'I guess... I guess I hadn't really thought about it like that... it feels as if I'm forever searching.'

Francine reached out across the table to pat Cora's hand, 'One day, your people will be found. This will all be over, and families will be reunited.'

'Yes, we have to believe that don't we,' sighed Cora. 'I'm one of the luckier ones; at least I've got my adoptive mother and father waiting for me, safe at home in Montauk. But it's so agonising when I can't even send a telegram to let them know I'm safe.'

Bertrand cleared his throat, flicked ash from his cigarette, 'You could send a letter.'

Estelle tutted, 'No, no, Bertrand... have you not heard, the Nazis have stopped the mail as well.'

He rolled his eyes at Estelle, leaned forward on the table, 'Yes, my friend, I have heard about that... Have you not heard that there is now a route for letters to be smuggled south to the free zone and sent from there?'

Estelle pressed her mouth into a firm line. 'No, I have not.'

Cora felt her heart squeeze tight, 'So, can you send one for me?'

'*Mais oui*,' he said, leaning back in his chair with an expansive smile.

Cora leapt up from her chair, 'If I write it now, can you take it straight away?'

Bertrand laughed, 'Whoa, little one... I will have to make

some enquiries first. It will take a couple of days... so get the
letter written and I'll collect it next time I'm here.'

'Thank you,' Cora breathed, her throat tight with emotion
thinking about what she would write.

As she sat back down in her chair, Francine reached out a
hand to her and murmured, 'I have notepaper and envelopes, I
will bring them for you when our meeting is over.'

Bertrand added, 'There are no guarantees how long it will
take, this route is only just being developed... it could take
months to get letters out to America, but my comrades are keen
to make it work.'

'I understand... but at least I can write it and it will stand
some chance of being delivered. Knowing that makes me feel so
much better.'

Glancing across the table, Cora thought she saw a sheen of
tears in Estelle's eyes, then the woman sniffed, cleared her
throat and signalled a shift back to the business in hand. 'I have
the camera,' she said, pulling it out of a canvas shopping bag. It
was a shiny, newish-looking Leica. 'One of the Germans was
foolish enough to leave it unattended on the table of a street
cafe on the Champs-Élysées. The place was crowded with
soldiers, all clicking away, reading their guidebooks. At our age,
Francine, we're so invisible, that I didn't even have to run. I used
my fake limp and while they were all jumping around, calling to
the patron to find the lost camera, I slowly disappeared out of
sight with it tucked in my bag.'

Bertrand gave a slow, deep rumble of a laugh.

'These Germans, they are so distracted being tourists, we
could probably strip off their uniforms and they wouldn't even
notice: "Oooh, let me get another shot of the Eiffel Tower... oh
no, why am I in my underwear?" he chuckled.

Cora joined in with the laughter.

'So, we need to get pictures of key sites, starting with their headquarters,' Francine interjected, neatly bringing them back to the business of the day.

'I can use a camera,' Cora offered, before the discussion had even begun.

Estelle was instantly shaking her head, 'No, we can't risk you doing that, you're too obvious, you stick out like a sore thumb.'

'Yes, but she's American, she's a tourist too,' Bertrand reasoned, between drags of his cigarette.

Francine exchanged a wide-eyed glance with Cora, she was weighing it up, but clearly she had her concerns.

'I can do it. I know I can... tell me where and when.'

Francine exhaled slowly, muttering, 'When Iris gets back, she is going to kill me.' Then she cleared her throat, reached for a cigarette. 'I think we should let the American have a go.'

Cora was grinning, already reaching for the camera which Estelle had deposited in the middle of the table. 'I used one of these back home, it's a Leica, a standard 35mm,' she said, flicking the various levers and checking the lens. 'They're fairly straightforward to use.'

Bertrand offered an admiring glance as if to say, *See, she's right for the job.*

'All right, then, I'll be guided by you two,' Estelle said, only mildly grudgingly. 'I know that we oldies struggle with these new-fangled portable devices, back in our day you'd need a big box of a camera and a black sheet to cover your head.'

They all laughed together.

'Right, so what do you want me to do?' Cora asked.

'We don't want you to do anything yet,' Estelle spoke forcefully, 'We'll let you know when the time comes. All we need to know right now is if you'll be ready to act.'

'Yes, I will,' Cora nodded, feeling the same thrum of excitement mixed with fear she'd experienced earlier in the day when she'd broken into Iris's apartment.

Later, after Bertrand and Estelle had had another cup of coffee, exchanged some gossip about rationing and then left, Francine brought the writing paper, an envelope and a brand-new pencil. 'I need to go out and join the queue for meat, so I'll leave you to it,' she said, placing a gentle hand on Cora's shoulder. 'Write well, *ma chérie*, and when you're finished leave the letter under my lighter, ready for Bertrand to collect.'

Cora hadn't held a pencil since her last entry in her journal... she fought back a flashback of the young German officer's face and the rush of humiliation that accompanied it. It felt a little easier now that she'd been back to the apartment, at least she'd had the guts to try and retrieve her property.

Now, ready to begin, her thoughts felt like an act of defiance in themselves. She already imagined those who would carry the hidden letter across the new border – the haphazard, imaginary line that lay between the occupied zone in the north and along the west coast and the free territory to the south.

It was rare to be alone in the house without the reassuring presence of Francine in the background. She sat with her pencil poised, blank. Then, startled by a loud spit from the stove fire, then a yowl from a cat in the alley outside, her mind came alive, and she knew exactly what she needed to say. And with the soft scratch of the pencil on embossed paper, she began to write.

Dear Mom,

I want you to know that I am so sorry for all the worry you and Dad must have had with me staying on in Paris. It might be hard to believe, but all is well here, even with the Germans in the city! I am safe with Francine, sleeping in her attic room and enjoying coffee and croissants every day.

The city is strange, the Germans are EVERYWHERE – so far, they are mainly sightseeing or sitting at cafe tables. It was daunting at first, seeing a swastika flag flying from the Eiffel

Tower, military vehicles and soldiers in the avenues, but it's surprising how quickly we are all getting used to it.

My only real concern is for Iris, as you will know from the telegram (the Germans have stopped all means of sending them now, by the way), she went missing from the apartment on the first day of occupation. There is no news of her yet, but Francine keeps saying she feels in her bones that Iris is safe (I'm getting used to Francine's instincts, I won't argue with that!). Please stay calm, I am perfectly fine here... I will find a way of getting back to America just as soon as Iris turns up.

Francine is a wonderful support, but I miss you and Dad so much and I need you to know this one thing. It is very important to me. I sensed you were upset when I left to look for my birth mother; it felt as if there were a wall between us. Now with Paris an occupied city, everything has changed here, and it has made me realise that you and Dad are so special to me. I think about you and our house by the sea every day and imagine walking the beach, listening to the sound of the waves.

Once Iris is found, I will do everything I can to get out of France and return to Montauk. I miss you both so much.... I don't know when or even if you will receive this letter, but know this, it is sent with all the love in the world.

I listen to Vera Lynn on the wireless as often as I can with Francine, singing about us meeting again, even if we don't know where or when... I know you love your radiogram, so keep tuned in, we will be together again some sunny day!

With love, as ever,

Cora x

She toyed with the idea of mentioning the hope she had of receiving news of her birth mother via the letter Iris had sent to the contact in Saint Malo. But recalling the stricken look on

Evie's face a few days before she left for Paris, the final time she'd mentioned the subject, she decided to keep quiet. The hope still burned inside of her that there could be some contact from Brittany, and maybe it would be passed on from Iris's apartment to Francine's address, or simply left there on the table in the hall, ready for her to collect when the occupiers of the apartment moved on. But with those two German officers, she knew it was a very long shot.

She sighed, then read the letter through one more time before folding the stiff notepaper and slipping it into the pristine white envelope. Picking the pencil back up she wrote the address of the house beside the sea in Montauk in bold letters, then kissed the envelope before carefully placing it beneath the dolphin's head lighter in the centre of the table. She wanted it to be gone now, today, and prayed it wouldn't be too long before Bertrand confirmed its dispatch. Glancing at it again, she pulled it out and gave it three more kisses, one each for Evie and Adam and the other for safe passage through a troubled land.

CHAPTER 10

At work in the bar that evening, Cora was already making close observation of the German soldiers who crowded the place. It was easy, once they'd had a few drinks, they were all garrulous. She was pleased that in her spare time she'd been studying German and by hearing the language spoken all around her, the rudimentary learning she had from school had grown rapidly. She was increasingly expert at deciphering at least some of the conversations and committing them to memory. Francine had asked her to report back with anything that might be of significance for the Resistance group.

Slightly distracted, as she strained to listen in on a heated discussion between two officers, Cora almost dropped a glass while clearing away. One of the officers at the table grabbed her wrist – 'Hey, watch it, waitress... unless you want me to take you aside for special training.'

Cora remained expressionless but polite, and once he knew he wasn't going to get any retaliation his grip slackened, and he turned back to his conversation. She quietly slipped her arm free, feeling the impression of his hand there for some time afterwards. The soldiers weren't all hostile, some were quiet and polite, even pleasant. But she'd remember this one, she'd be wary of him in future.

Madeleine had been very smiley tonight and Cora had noticed a handsome fair-haired young officer, one of the nicer ones, paying her special attention. At first Cora thought *well, why not, if it's no more than gentle flirtation.* But then she remembered how these things went – one thing could lead to another and then Madeleine might find herself in a compromising situation. But her friend looked so happy, it had been weeks since Cora had seen her smile like that. She was tempted to leave well alone, but then she saw a rough-voiced friend of Jacques's who'd come to help wash the glasses, glancing sideways at Madeleine. He'd noticed the flirtation as well, and he didn't look happy.

Cora clenched her jaw and picked up her tray of empty glasses. It felt as if the moment you forgot you were walking on eggshells, things started to crumble around you. She would have to warn Madeleine right now, try to calm the situation. Slipping past Jacques's friend, she came up close to her and murmured her warning. Cora's heart squeezed with dismay when her friend shrugged her shoulders and played down the concerns. It put her on edge, seeing Madeleine continuing to chat and laugh with the young soldier.

Later, when Cora didn't see any alteration in Madeleine's behaviour, she was further troubled by a table of officers who were cracking jokes about the soldier and the barmaid and pointing at Madeleine. They shouted out to the young man chatting at the bar and he turned with a sheepish smile, his face flushed.

'Hey, Romeo, you'd better watch yourself, these French girls can be trouble.'

Cora saw Jacques's friend lift his head from behind the bar, his eyes narrowed as he clocked the officers making the joke and then he glanced to Madeleine again, just as the young soldier whispered something in her ear. With horror, Cora observed Madeleine reach up to stroke the soldier's face.

Something clicked inside her then, she knew the situation was escalating. Walking quickly, she dodged behind the bar. 'Excuse me,' she murmured, slipping past Jacques's friend at the sink. She tugged at Madeleine's arm, pulling her to the far end of the bar. 'You have to stop talking to that soldier right now, people are noticing,' she whispered, her tone urgent.

'Let them notice, I'm not doing anything wrong,' Madeleine muttered angrily.

Exasperated, Cora repeated her warning, dropping her voice to spell out what the consequences might be for behaviour that might be construed as fraternisation with the enemy.

Madeleine stubbornly set her mouth and dismissed Cora's concern. She had no choice but to withdraw from the situation and pray that the young man, who had shifted his attention to a fellow soldier, had at last lost interest.

Cora felt her stomach clench into a tight knot for the rest of the shift. She couldn't wait for her work to end so that she could speak properly to her friend on the walk home.

'What was up with you tonight, grumpy?' Madeleine joked, linking her arm at the end of the evening.

'You know what it was,' Cora replied, trying to keep her voice light until they were out through the door.

'I think you're making a great deal out of me chatting to a nice young man.'

Cora pulled her out onto the street, made her walk a few paces before she replied. 'Even Jacques's friend noticed, he's sure to report back to Jacques and to goodness knows who else.'

'Well, that washer-upper left ages ago, and I've just seen Jacques, he didn't say a word to me about anything.'

'Maybe not yet, but he will if this carries on. You need to be much more careful, Madeleine.'

Madeleine was huffing now, starting to pull away from

Cora. She walked on ahead a little and then turned to say something. Before the words were out of her mouth, the sound of running feet came rushing toward them and Madeleine was grabbed by a heavily set man and punched full in the face, three times. Cora felt a spray of blood hit her cheek. Her friend was screaming, Cora was hitting out at Madeleine's assailant. She couldn't see him properly, he had a cap pulled down low over his eyes, but when he shouted, 'Bitch, collaborator, German whore,' as he ran away, she knew he was French.

Throwing herself down beside Madeleine, Cora ripped off the white apron she was wearing to hold against the bleeding laceration above her friend's left eyebrow. All the while, jumbled, soothing words were pouring from her. With her heart hammering against her ribs, she could hardly breathe. But she'd been raised in the house of a doctor and a midwife, she didn't have far to reach inside to know how to manage a casualty. Many of her father's patients had turned up raw and bleeding at the door of their house by the sea in Montauk.

Applying steady pressure to a deep laceration above Madeleine's eye seemed to be slowing the flow of blood. She pulled away her apron, 'The bleeding seems to be under control now, but I think you might need stitches,' she said, using the calm voice her mother had when dealing with emergencies. Feeling Madeleine's body tighten, she followed up with, 'You're going to be fine, I promise.' She could only hope her friend wouldn't realise that she was only playing the role of a nurse.

Madeleine took a deep, shuddering breath and sobbed, 'I was only talking to that German soldier, he was so nice... he reminded me of my brother.'

'I'm so sorry,' Cora's voice quavered, in tears herself, remembering that Madeleine's brother had gone to the Maginot line as soon as war had been declared. Nothing had been heard of him since the German advance. Cora was needled with pure anger knowing the attack had been perpetrated by a fellow French citizen. It was all she could do to keep her voice steady. 'You did nothing wrong, Madeleine, nothing at all. It's the world that's messed up right now, not you.'

Cora felt the slackening of Madeleine's body, either her words had calmed her, or she was in shock, about to faint. Panic shot through her, all thought of how Evie had treated her casualties completely gone from her head.

'You have to walk, Madeleine, I need to get you some medical help,' she urged, pushing an arm around her, helping her up from the ground, making her walk. 'I have a friend, Chris, he's a doctor, and he works nights at the American hospital. He will be able to treat you.'

Cora was clutching at straws, Chris wasn't a friend as such, he was a subscriber to the American library who had regularly visited to borrow novels of the literary greats; F. Scott Fitzgerald had been a particular favourite. He'd made Cora promise to keep in touch, and in the spirit of American expats in Paris sticking together, he'd told her that if she ever needed anything, to come straight to the hospital. That time had come much sooner than she thought, she was desperate now to get Madeleine into a clean, surgical space, where people knew exactly what they were doing.

It was an ordeal to walk through the deserted streets, supporting Madeleine, dragging her into the shadows whenever they spotted a sentry. All the while her friend was pressing the white cotton apron to the deep split above her eyebrow.

Every muscle in Cora's body ached by the time the American hospital emerged from the gloom. She'd only ever been to this quiet suburb once; she remembered its pleasant tree-lined boulevards where she'd walked with a work friend from the library, and they'd sat on a bench to eat a picnic lunch and discuss the works of Franz Kafka. Coming here at night, dragging her injured colleague, felt like a grim contrast.

Grateful to find a wheelchair waiting in the doorway of the

hospital building, she assisted her friend to sit. 'You're safe now, Maddy,' Cora gasped, almost coughing on the strong whiff of carbolic that assailed her nostrils. When a white-uniformed nurse met them in the corridor, Cora saw her frown, 'This is a military hospital now,' she said. 'We're only taking casualties of war.'

Cora stiffened. 'My friend was attacked by a German soldier, I think she qualifies, don't you? Can you tell me where to find Dr Chris Anderson?'

As she walked in the direction duly pointed out by the dumbfounded nurse, Cora mused on how easy it was to bend the truth. Even though it had been a French thug who had punched Madeleine, the conversation with the soldier had been the cause of the attack. Cora was surprised at how nimbly her mind flipped information around, made it justifiable to tell a white lie. What was that poem by Emily Dickinson about never knowing how high we are, till we are called to rise. More like never knowing how adept we are, till we are called to lie.

Chris was busy with a screaming wounded soldier when she finally located him within the warren of corridors and wards full of groaning patients. Directed by a nurse to a wooden bench, gratefully she slumped down, pulling Madeleine's wheelchair close.

'It won't be long now, my darling,' she whispered to her friend, her mother's voice again from years ago when Cora had fallen from a tree and gashed her scalp, waiting for her father to come home so he could suture the wound.

'You're just like me, always an adventurous spirit,' Evie had murmured, pulling her close as they'd waited for Adam, starting to tell made-up stories to distract her. Cora felt that comfort now, even though this time, she was the one doing the supporting.

Chris appeared at last in his blood-spattered surgical gown, a cotton mask suspended beneath his chin. His cheeks were flushed, his eyes red-rimmed with grey smudges beneath. 'Sorry to keep you both,' he offered, attempting a smile that didn't have the energy to move beyond a grimace. 'As you can see, we're packed out with casualties... I can't wait for these Germans to be pushed back out of the city.'

Having seen the number of polished, well-trained, well-fed German soldiers who now lounged at cafe tables and inhabited every corner of Paris, Cora was confident that Chris's wish would not be fulfilled in the near future. But she bit back her reply and instead nodded in support.

'We'll soon have this laceration sorted,' he murmured, after a thorough inspection of Madeleine's injury. 'I'll keep the stitches small, try to make sure you don't have a prominent scar.'

Madeleine nodded and then started to hiccup with a sob, too exhausted to form tears and properly cry.

After the work was done and Madeleine was resting full-length on the bench with a blanket for comfort, Chris brought two cups of weak coffee and lowered himself beside Cora for a brief respite.

'I miss going to the American library,' he sighed, offering a weary smile, 'and now the only book I have is *The Great Gatsby*, I'm having to read and reread it and I've got some thumbprints of blood on the pages, hope the library won't mind.'

'Well, I'm not working there anymore, there's only the director left to oversee things, but I'm sure the staff will understand, given the circumstances.'

'Have you any idea when it'll reopen?'

'I honestly don't think it will, Chris, not for years... you should think about going home to America, as soon as you can.'

A stubborn jut of his chin told her that he wasn't about to take that advice on board. He dropped his voice to barely above a whisper, 'I've heard that a big push is coming from the Brits, they're going to be back on French soil in weeks.'

Cora was slowly shaking her head, 'I have a French friend,

an older woman, she's able to get information from across the Channel. The British army were pushed back to Dunkirk, they need to regroup, think through their strategy, there's no sign of them coming back yet. And the Nazis are pounding British cities with bombs, it's terrible over there.'

Chris heaved a sigh.

'It's only a matter of time before our lot join in, I suppose. We won't stand by and let this carnage continue without offering military support.'

'That's why it's even more important for you to get out of here soon, get back to America so you can volunteer your services for the war effort.'

'But what about you, my favourite librarian, surely you must leave too?'

'I can't,' Cora sighed.

He knotted his brow. 'Can't or won't?'

'Can't,' she said emphatically. 'My aunt, guardian, whatever you want to call her... she's gone missing. She's my mom's best friend, I can't leave Paris without knowing what's happened to her.'

'I don't think your mom would advise you to stay, even if this woman is close. She'll choose you every time, you're her daughter.'

'I know,' Cora groaned, weary after the ordeal of the night, almost in tears at the thought of Evie upset, desperate for news. 'It's just that I've got close to Iris as well and I'm the only family she has here. I'll give it a bit longer, but if no more news comes through, I might think about going home, that's if I can still get safe passage.'

'That sounds reasonable, I should probably be thinking that way as well. Come and see me if you decide to take it any further, maybe we could go together,' he offered.

'Dr Anderson, you're needed in theatre – another amputation,' an urgent voice called down the corridor, the words echoing emptily against the green-tiled walls.

'Hold that thought,' he gasped as he jumped up from the bench, running up the corridor, shouting back over his shoulder, 'I'm not ready to leave yet, there's still too much work. Stay safe, Cora.'

'And you,' Cora called to his rapidly retreating figure. Placing a gentle hand on Madeleine's blanket, she was glad to feel her stirring, it was time to be on the move. They were both exhausted and it would take ages to get her injured friend back through the streets.

'Come on, Maddy, time to go home... you can stay with me at Francine's tonight,' she murmured, helping her up from the bench, steadying her with an arm around her shoulders.

'I'm so sorry, Cora, you warned me but still I managed to drag you into this.'

'Stop right there,' Cora's voice was gentle but firm enough for Madeleine to understand that there was no recrimination on her part. 'I'm glad that I was with you, I can't bear to think what might have happened if you'd been on your own. And what's more, we're all in this together... Americans, French. All in the same fight.'

As they made their slow progress back through the city, Cora saw the sun rising above the elegant buildings, casting the first warm rays of light upon the world, and she knew, at least for now, that she was doing the right thing by staying on in this beautiful historic city which had seen so much and had weathered so many other uprisings. *You'll come through again, I know you will*, she whispered to the city and its people.

CHAPTER 11

Cora slept badly, curled on a blanket on the floor beside the cot bed where Madeleine had rested fitfully, crying out in her sleep. Holding back a groan, she straightened her stiff back, gazing down to her friend who now lay more comfortably. One eye swollen shut and navy-blue bruised, the black stitches on her brow a brutal reminder of the violence of last night. Cora shuddered, feeling the impact of the attack again. Gently she adjusted the soft, pale blue blanket which Francine had brought last night to make Madeleine more comfortable.

Still in her nightgown, she descended the stairs tentatively, aware of every creak of wood that might disturb her sleeping friend. Francine was hunched over the table reading a leaflet, a cigarette with a length of grey ash grasped between two fingers. She looked up as Cora stole to the breakfast table, 'How is she doing?'

Cora blew out a breath, 'It's only now when the bruising has come out that I can see how badly injured she was. I can't really remember exactly what happened, her attacker was on us in seconds, it was so vile.'

'The poor girl,' Francine sighed, stubbing out her

cigarette, 'It comes to something, doesn't it, when our own are attacking our own... and for what? I'm glad she had you there, to get her to the hospital. God knows what might have happened to a young girl like that if she'd been left lying in the street.'

'Shall I make some more coffee?' Cora asked, feeling overwhelmed, needing to be actively engaged in a task.

'Put the kettle on, I'll make the coffee when it boils... I need to speak to you about something, Cora.'

As soon as she lowered herself into her chair, Francine reached for another cigarette and flicked the silver dolphin's head lighter. She was frowning now, a deep line etched between her brows, but when she spoke her voice was crystal sharp, 'You can't go back to the bar, Cora, not after what happened last night, and when Madeleine is recovered, she definitely shouldn't.'

Instantly Cora was ready to make a case for carrying on as normal to show they wouldn't be beaten by the brutality of one man, but when she saw the intensity of Francine's gaze, she knew that it would be unwise to argue. So many times, she'd defied the advice of others – her mother, her father and Danny had all tried to dissuade her from travelling to Paris. Maybe it was time she started taking heed, particularly to someone like Francine who had lived through so much.

'You're probably right,' she sighed.

Francine's face slackened with relief. 'I'm so glad you are able to see sense on this issue, *ma chérie*.'

Cora shrugged, 'It makes me feel nauseous, even the thought of going back to the bar... there'll still be a bloodstain on the pavement.'

'Madeleine was lucky to get away with superficial injuries, it's a good job you were there with her, it could have been far worse.'

Cora winced at a flashback of the attack, her right hand was sore, she must have thrown a punch at the man... she couldn't quite remember, it had all happened so fast.

'Best to try and put it out of your mind,' Francine said, getting up to brew the coffee. 'We're only at the start of all this... we need to save our strength and not dwell too much. Madeleine is safe, and that's all that matters.'

Cora nodded. There was no choice, they had to keep going, for all they knew there was probably much worse to come.

When Francine returned to the table with the coffee pot, she brought a leaflet in her hand. 'Rationing!' she spat. 'Just as I thought, they're going to introduce rationing... you know why, don't you, so they can take the best of our food and wine for themselves and ship the rest to Germany.'

Even before Cora could reply, Francine thrust out a hand, counting off on her gnarled fingers.

'Coffee, bread, cigarettes, meat. They will leave us to starve.'

Cora reached across the table to take the leaflet. 'It doesn't specify here exactly what—'

'Pah! They'll go in gently at first, small cutbacks on bread or sugar, a silken glove concealing an iron fist. Then they'll chip away at us, bit by bit... We'll be smoking dried grass in no time.' Francine scrunched the leaflet into a tight ball and aimed it at the open door of the stove. 'Dried grass, bay leaves, oregano,' she muttered, a glint in her eye, starting to chuckle.

Francine slipped a cigarette out of her pack and lit up. After the first drag, she leaned in towards Cora. There was something almost conspiratorial about the gesture.

'Now, Cora... I want you to think about this carefully, especially after what happened to Madeleine last night, but are you ready to go out with Estelle's camera, take some photographs around the city?'

Cora felt a stab of excitement. 'Yes, I'm ready,' she answered quickly, making Francine laugh and shake her head.

'Such a hothead American, I'm not sure we will be able to keep up with you.'

'So where do you want me to go, what do you want me to do?'

'There are two hotels – the Crillon and the Ritz, they've been taken over by the Nazis to serve as headquarters. We need photographs of vehicles, people going in and out. If any one of us could easily use these new-fangled cameras we'd do it ourselves, and we certainly don't want you to take any undue risks, but we need some snaps of officials, high-ranking officers, that kind of thing. We've had word that a particularly influential officer is due to visit Paris today. If he is spotted, it might be of significance for those higher up the network. Not that we ever get feedback as to whether the snippets we provide are any use, but it feels good to be doing something, don't you think?'

'Yes, definitely.' Cora felt almost gleeful, she had to temper her reaction so Francine wouldn't think she'd be indiscreet, put herself at risk.

Francine leaned in closer, dropped her voice, 'So, I need you to go out this morning, like a tourist with the camera.'

Cora felt a glow in her chest at the thought of being trusted with a mission. She started to smile.

'You must stay hidden... Your mother, Evie, she is fearsome... I don't want to be the one trying to contact her to tell her that her daughter has gone missing in action.'

'I'll be careful, I promise,' Cora grinned, taking a sip of her coffee then reaching for a piece of baguette, slathering it with butter and jam, needing to get through her breakfast quickly so that she could be off out on her assignment.

Quietly slipping into her best blue slacks and a smart white blouse, she grabbed her tortoiseshell-rimmed sunglasses, and after a quick check of her still-sleeping friend, she tiptoed back downstairs, eager to be off.

'Will you check on Madeleine for me?' she asked, as

Francine handed her a small grey rucksack that contained the camera.

'Yes, I will look after your friend, I'll make her some breakfast as soon as she wakes.' She thrust a spare roll of film into Cora's hand. 'Put it in your pocket,' she ordered, 'and remember: no taking chances, don't stay too long in any one place... Do you need directions to the hotels?'

'No, I know where they are, and I have a good map, for future use.'

'Don't write anything down,' Francine added, tapping her forehead, 'keep it all up here.'

Shoving her feet into her sneakers, she barely had time to lace them, impatient as she was to be off. She almost ran down the short alley that led to the street, standing for a few moments to breathe the air, she tipped her head back to gaze up to the blue sky. Removing the rucksack, she pulled out the Leica camera to check it over. It was in good order, and she was tempted to string it around her neck so she'd begin to feel like a real tourist. But no, best to keep it hidden in case she saw someone she knew, and they started asking questions.

The impressive colonnaded facade of the Hotel Crillon gave nothing away as she stood on the Place de la Concorde observing it. She'd walked by many times but had never really stopped to study the huge building in detail. Taking cover behind a large, ornate stone fountain which stood to the front of the hotel, she did some surveillance, all the while pretending to take snaps of the fountain, like any other tourist in Paris. When a shiny black Mercedes sporting a swastika flag pulled up outside the hotel, Cora turned from taking yet another snap and slipped closer to the hotel. She found cover behind a lamppost and stood with her back to the hotel as if she were taking a photograph of the square. Swiftly spinning in the opposite direction when she heard a car door opening, she took two snaps, one of a short bespectacled officer and another taller man. A burst of adrenaline coursed through her body, making her heart sing.

'Ah, you have a Leica, good camera,' a German officer said as he passed in front of her, moments later. She held back a gasp, glad that she'd instantly turned to face away from the hotel and he was only passing by. Dodging back to the cover of the fountain, she hid, breathless, her head spinning with a mixture of fear and excitement.

After pausing long enough to recover, she walked at a leisurely pace towards the Ritz Hotel, stopping regularly to hold her camera, pretending to take snaps of historic buildings and statues.

At the Ritz she was glad of another ornate lamppost that gave her cover as she listened for activity at the entrance to the hotel, all the time gazing across to the Vendôme Column sporting its statue of Napoleon. It provided a good focus for a tourist and from a distance it took time to frame a pretend shot in the lens. Nothing moved outside the hotel for over ten minutes, Cora steadied her nerves and took a stroll towards the column, then back again. As she approached the hotel once more, she saw a flurry of movement at the entrance: a car had pulled up. By the way the driver leapt out to open the door and then stood to attention, she knew this had to be a person of importance. She was determined to get a picture. Back behind her lamppost, she was glad of a slowly scudding cloud that obscured the sun and cast her in shadow. Turning to take a picture of the view down the street, she shifted her focus in seconds to catch a snap of the German officer who had exited the car. Her heart lurched as she clicked the shutter, it seemed unbearably loud to her heightened senses. Quickly slipping the camera from around her neck, she shrugged off the small haversack and pushed it inside. She felt a wild, leaping elation, her legs were weak as she put her arms through the straps. She was done now, sure that the photograph she'd taken would be meaningful. The thrill of the activity sent tingles up and down her spine, it was exhilarating.

As soon as she turned to walk away, a man in uniform stepped in front of her. Blinded by the sun which had emerged from behind the cloud that had given her cover when she needed it, she didn't recognise him at first, but when she pulled her sunglasses down to the tip of her nose, she became instantly aware of who it was.

'Ah, I thought it was you, Madame Becker's young friend, the American girl,' grinned Karl, the younger of the two soldiers who had occupied Iris's apartment. He linked her arm as if they were old friends, her heart clutched with fear, but she made herself smile, desperate to distract him from any thought of searching her. The camera in the rucksack felt very present as it rested against her spine. But even though her heart was thudding, she maintained an outward appearance of calm as Karl began to pull her along with him as he walked towards the hotel.

He paused abruptly, making her halt, turning with a fixed smile, a glint in his eye.

'I must say, I've had many hours of happy reading from the journal you so kindly left beneath your bed.'

Cora felt a stab of pure fury, she had no control over her temper now, it blazed out of her. 'My journal is *private*, you had no right to read it!'

'Oh, but it is so well written, especially your thoughts about that night with, what's his name, your beau? Danny... that's it, lovely Danny.'

She felt her hand ball into a fist, but she knew if she retaliated, he might arrest her and then, inevitably, the camera would be found. Swallowing hard against a dry throat, she pulled her arm free. 'It was improper of you to read my journal, you are not a gentleman,' was all it felt safe to say.

'Oh, but I am a true gentleman, especially when it comes to

dealing with young ladies who have fire in their eyes,' he smiled. 'If only you would allow me to get to know you better, you would soon realise that I am very aware of how to treat a lady.' He moved his clean-shaven, angular face close enough for her to smell his sharp-scented cologne. 'Maybe, if you want news about the lady of your apartment, Madame Iris Becker... we could come to some sort of arrangement. And who knows, maybe you would grow to enjoy spending special time with me. After all, what is it they say about Paris being the city of love.' The smirk he gave told Cora all she needed to know about his offer of assistance.

She toyed with the idea, wondering if agreeing to what he was suggesting might be the only way she could get any information about Iris. Then she saw his too bright eyes, the set of his mouth and she knew that she would get nothing from any kind of liaison with this man. And furthermore, it might compromise the work she was doing with Francine's group. 'Well?' he asked, an impatient edge to his voice, glancing past her to nod to a fellow officer.

She tapped into his need to have an answer and stayed silent, expressionless. *Breathe, just breathe.*

He reached out to tuck a stray strand of hair behind her left ear. The intimacy of the act made her stomach clench so hard she felt physically sick, but she held his gaze.

'Captain Hesse, you are needed urgently,' an officer called from the door of the hotel.

The spell was broken. He took a step back, offered a small bow, spoke rapidly, 'Farewell, no doubt I will see you around the city, and if you change your mind and decide that you do want news of Madame Becker, leave me word at the Hotel Crillon reception.' As he walked away, he called over his shoulder, 'You are safe here for now American girl, but when your country enters the war... that will be a whole different matter.' Cora stood her ground, not displaying any of the giddy euphoria of relief which surged through her. Watching his retreat, hardly daring to breathe, she didn't feel secure until he was in through the door of hotel. Only then did she snap into action, striding rapidly towards Francine's, yearning to be safely home.

Bursting in through the door, she heard Francine shriek, 'Who's there?' from the kitchen. 'Sorry, it's only me,' she called, so glad her friend hadn't been sitting in her armchair with the gun at the ready. Still agitated, she pulled the rucksack from her shoulders, walked through.

Madeleine was slumped in a chair, her elbows on the table, supporting her head with both hands. 'How are you doing?' Cora asked, making a physical effort to temper her voice, discreetly slipping the bag next to Francine's chair.

Madeleine groaned, 'I want to cry but it hurts too much,' and when she lifted her face, Cora felt her stomach clench afresh at the navy-blue bruising around her closed eye which extended right down her cheek. The wound was bright red and angry, punctuated by the black silk sutures.

'That looks very sore,' she said, wanting to reach out to soothe the rawness of it, but knowing that her touch would only cause more pain. Instead, she put an arm around Madeleine's shoulders, 'I wish I could give back to that brute of a man what he did to you.'

'He must be no more than an animal,' Francine muttered angrily, rising from her chair abruptly, taking the rucksack with her. 'I'm going to make your friend some fine oatmeal porridge since she can't chew anything yet. Do you want some?'

'No, thank you,' Cora said, shaking her head, the thought of eating anything after her encounter with Karl making her queasy. Seeing how indisposed Madeleine was, Cora knew to leave her sitting quietly, but there was one thing she needed to ask. 'Francine feels it would be best if we didn't return to work at the bar, what do you think about that?'

Madeleine made a noise, a strangled sob, her voice was

throaty when the words came but her fierce intonation was clear, 'I never want to see that place again... once I'm able to travel I'll head south, to the Loire, I have family there.'

'That's good, so good,' Cora breathed, 'I'll send a message to Jacques, he might struggle this evening, but I don't think he'll have any problem filling the positions, women are looking for any work they can find.'

'I would have liked to see that young officer again, though,' Madeleine sniffed, her voice suddenly small.

Cora gave her shoulders a squeeze, 'There'll be others, you wait and see.'

Madeleine was sniffing louder now, then a single tear escaped down her bruised cheek. It made Cora sob and then she started to cry.

'Look at you two girls,' Francine offered, turning from the stove, 'One in too much pain to shed tears, so the other is doing it for her.'

'Yes, that's true,' Cora hiccupped, dabbing at her eyes but knowing that she wasn't only crying for Maddy, these were also angry tears for what Karl had said about the private words she'd written in her journal. In her head she'd known that was exactly what he would have done once he'd found her journal, but to see his gloating face...

In the next second, she thrust away those thoughts. He'd seen it all now, and from what she could remember, they were naive scribblings, nothing compared to what had happened to Madeleine.

She thought of her mother, the way she straightened her spine, jutted her chin when something bad came at her. Cora did the same now, the stubborn part of her determined not to let Karl Hesse have the last word on this. He was a malicious, worthless individual. Rather than give him the satisfaction of upsetting her, she would force herself not to care about the journal, not to give a damn if he'd read it.

CHAPTER 12

Iris could tell she'd lost weight by the slackness of her skirt waistband. Hungry, disorientated, unable to sleep on the thin prison mattress in her cell, she knew that if something didn't change soon, she would struggle to recover. With only a slit of light from a window high up on the wall, she barely knew if it was day or night. For the first three days, she'd kept track, then as the gnawing hunger in her belly overrode her other senses, she became lost, adrift in time. Maybe she was still in Paris... she didn't feel as if she'd travelled far, but then that first day she'd been very drowsy, as if she'd been drugged, so who knew?

The door was locked, her scant food and water brought twice a day. Most sickeningly of all, she was required to use an unscreened commode in the corner of the cell. The stench of it still made her gag. If Iris had been a weaker person, she would have already broken, but she drew on every morsel of her past life – the love she'd had for Jack and for Lucien, Evie, Francine and Cora. It was the niggling anxiety for Cora that kept her on edge, maybe helped hold her together. That and the flashes of memory which came when the cell darkened and she lapsed in and out of consciousness. A recurring image from her early life as a nurse stewardess on the giant White Star ship, the *Olympic*, became a lifeline for her. Up on deck, leaning over the side to watch the clean, white cresting wave as the vessel cut through the water, she imagined her hair blowing back from her face, the smell of the salt ocean. It sustained her, kept her alive. That and feeling the closeness of her first love, Jack Rosetti, as they danced to the strains of the first-class orchestra on that one special night when she knew he might be the love of her life. And then, when she was travelling as a first-class passenger, the evening she met Lucien, again on a transatlantic crossing. She remembered his smile, his kind eyes at a time when she'd thought she'd never find love again.

These memories became her world, they kept her adrift, prevented her from sinking to the depths of despair. She had to believe that she would be released eventually, but for now she was staying afloat, lying flat on her back in the ocean as she did when her hospital ship *Britannic* hit a mine and capsized during the last war. Day after day in her prison cell, she tipped back her head, imagined the feel of the sun on her face, felt the hope of being saved.

A tap at the door. She glanced to the slit of light; it must be morning. Weak as she was, she pushed herself up and sat at the side of the bed, pulling her stained blue linen skirt as straight as she could and using her fingers to quickly brush her tangled hair back from her face. The reinforced door clunked open, a sound that set her teeth on edge. Her heart missed a beat when she saw the tall slender frame of the German officer who supervised her captivity. He removed his cap to reveal his thinning black hair as he clicked his heels and gave a small bow. It felt increasingly absurd to Iris, to be treated so despicably but with such a show of meaningless respect.

The officer cleared his throat, 'Madame Becker... I have news. We have made extensive enquiries and you will be pleased to learn that we can now corroborate your story.'

Iris felt a stab of disbelief. She straightened her back, certain that this was some cruel trick.

The officer offered a reluctant smile. 'We have, at last, managed to trace your late husband's nephew, Franz Becker. He has been able to confirm that you were married to Lucien Becker.'

Iris could have collapsed with relief, but still she didn't trust this pale-faced man. It could be a trick to disarm her, then they'd start asking questions again about her contacts in Paris, things she knew nothing about. She'd told them over and over that the reason she'd stayed on in Paris was that it had been her home for twenty years, and she'd been married to a man with French and German heritage.

'We still need your late husband's nephew to formally identify you in person before you are released. But we have checked your marriage papers, and all appears correct. However, given you were a British citizen before you married, we think, for your own safety, it would be much better for you to leave France right away. After all, despite your nephew's credentials and the fact that you have lived in Paris for many years, it is best that you have passage to a neutral country. My superior suggested Portugal, but your nephew told us you have friends in America, and he asked as a favour that you be shipped there. Given that Lieutenant Becker is a highly respected officer, true to our cause, we have been able to give the special dispensation required.'

Iris swallowed hard, nodded; she still couldn't bring herself to trust this man who had treated her so callously, but if what he was saying was true, the news he brought offered such hope she had to grit her teeth to stop herself breaking down in tears.

She straightened her back, looked him in the eye, 'Will I at least be able to wash myself and comb my hair before my husband's nephew arrives?'

The officer pressed his lips together, considering the

request. 'Yes, I believe that will be acceptable. I will have a bowl of hot water, some soap and a comb sent.'

'Thank you,' Iris croaked, starting to feel dizzy. She gripped the edge of the mattress to steady herself. She'd lost so much during this time of imprisonment; she wasn't prepared to lose another shred of her dignity.

Later, the hot water and other items were brought to her by a very young, blond-haired guard with wide blue eyes which openly showed his shock at seeing a seemingly respectable older woman in captivity. Iris felt a bubble of hysterical laughter rising through her chest. The soap was carbolic, the same she'd used throughout her nursing career to scrub her hands and clean surfaces. It made her feel as if she were scrubbing up for an operation, but it felt so good to use the rough flannel against her sticky, crusted skin.

The silk blouse that she'd peeled off was filthy, but she sat with it across her knee and meticulously sponged every stain that she could see, anything to make herself decent, proper, to face a relative of Lucien's who she remembered with fondness as a smiling, fair-haired boy with a lightness of spirit. Before she combed through every tangle of her matted hair, she dipped and wrung the flannel again to scrub at her itchy scalp. Only able to imagine how it would feel to slip into a deep bath, to massage perfumed shampoo into her hair, to reclaim her broken body.

Glancing into the small hand mirror which the young guard had handed over, she hardly recognised the sunken-cheeked woman with dark smudges beneath her eyes. But she made herself smile, just for the hell of it. And when the knock came to the door to announce Franz's arrival, she stood up from the bed, lifted her chin and offered a greeting.

The tall, broad-shouldered man who stood before her bore little resemblance to the gangly teenage boy she remembered, but once he removed his cap, she recognised the boy she'd known in the man who stood before her. He was so like Lucien, especially his eyes, it almost took her breath away.

'Franz,' she said as kindly as she could, 'it is so good to see you again... even in these unusual circumstances.' He opened his mouth to speak but nothing came. Instead, he cleared his throat. He seemed at a loss for words and looked uncomfortable as he stood before her. Then she saw it, he had Lucien's eyes, but whatever light had shone there had been extinguished. He shifted from foot to foot, ill at ease, like a man who needed to get something over with.

'Yes, this is my uncle's widow,' he said, his voice clipped, already turning on his heel without a fond word.

'Franz?' Iris called again, her voice weak, faltering.

She saw it then, in the heave of his shoulders as he struggled to keep his emotions in check. In that split second, she understood, he couldn't let any of his comrades see that he was moved by the plight of this British woman who had been the wife of his German uncle. It heartened her, knowing that he still had some connection even if he couldn't express it, that all memory and warmth of past times hadn't been completely extinguished by the boy's inculcation into Hitler's army. She could see him now as that gangly teenage boy in his short pants, laughing with Lucien as they sat on the grass in the shadow of the Eiffel Tower on a summer's day with a selection of food from a picnic basket spread on a blue-and-white checked cloth. The memory of that one perfect day, the pop of a champagne cork and the red strawberry juice that she'd mopped from the boy's chin with a white linen serviette... it brought tears to her eyes now. A yawning gulf had opened between them in the years that had followed, a gulf that now seemed unfillable.

In the end Iris was relieved when Franz left the room with the sallow-faced officer. She hoped that the war would go well for the young man. If he hadn't come to identify her, she would probably have ended up going to some prison camp... people died in places like that. She was grateful to him but also very troubled, she'd seen first-hand the changes that war wrought on people. She would probably have walked by Franz in the street and not recognised him. Yet, there was still that link, a bat squeak of connection with the past which in the end had saved her life.

'Your transport is waiting; everything has been arranged. You will be travelling to Lisbon in Portugal, and you will be required *not* to make contact with any friends or family in France... Make no mistake, Madame Becker, we are fully aware that your allegiance is bound to be with the country of your birth, England, so we cannot afford to take any chances,' the officer announced as he stood blank-eyed before her. Then, almost as an afterthought, 'You will be booked into a hotel room where you can bathe and your nephew has left some money for new clothes to be bought, please supply us with your size and the required items will be delivered.'

As Iris took her first wobbly steps out of the cell, she knew that she was escaping by the skin of her teeth. Still not quite believing what had happened, she felt a thrum of sensation in her chest. *Was this real? Was she being released?* She swallowed hard to keep back the tears, she didn't have enough energy to expend on weeping, not if she were to keep putting one foot in front of the other as she began her walk to freedom.

Once out in the air, breathing freely with the light of day hurting her eyes, she knew she'd made a huge step closer to safety. All those weeks of captivity had weakened her body, her head was spinning. Forcing her broken mind to start piecing things together, she knew her priority was to stay calm, follow orders and make sure once she arrived in Portugal, to secure a passage to Long Island, straight to Evie. And as soon as she was out of occupied territory, she would send a telegram with news of her arrival and to ask after Cora. *Where was Cora?* A painful stab of fear, her first pure sensation since she'd been dragged into that cell... as her brain thrummed back into life, she was beginning to feel reborn to all her worries and sorrows, during captivity she'd made herself think only of the things that sustained her. And if Cora hadn't turned up, then what about Evie and Adam? They must be enduring an agony of waiting. The thought of a reunion with Evie when she felt partly responsible for the disappearance, if that's what it still was, of her only child, felt very daunting. If it hadn't been for their long history and the depth of their understanding, she would probably have opted to go somewhere else, alone, to recover first. But she had to be with Evie, no one else would do. Thinking of her now, standing firm on the porch of the house by the sea, turning with a cheeky smile, it was all Iris could do to hold back the emotion.

'I won't cry for anyone else,' she murmured to herself, determined her captors would not witness her tears. 'I'll only cry for Evie.'

CHAPTER 13

The evening rhythm of the house with the blue door was winding down with the lighting of a candle, the gentle pop of a wine cork and the setting of the table. Their meal had been carefully prepared by Francine and had used up the last of the beef and the vegetables. Cora was hungry and she ate quickly, her belly still rumbled a little. But the easing of her body with the first glass of wine and the murmur of conversation at the table covering their usual topics – books they'd read, films they'd seen – had made her feel content.

'Cheers,' she called, reaching across the table to clink Francine's glass before taking another sip. 'Mmmm,' she sighed, 'this is a nice one, is it the last bottle of Bordeaux?'

'Yes, I'm afraid so, *ma chérie*... Bertrand has contacts, he should be able to get me some more, but supplies are much reduced and more expensive.'

Cora swirled the deep red wine in her glass, drawing in the aroma, then she took another sip.

'Nice, hey,' smiled Francine, the lines of her face deepening. 'I always save the best till last.'

Cora smiled back, hoping to bolster her, aware of how much

weight she'd lost recently and how out of breath she was at times. The war seemed to be chipping away at her friend bit by bit. She knew how close Francine had been to Iris, she never really spoke of it, but the sorrow she carried seemed to have visibly increased in the last few weeks. It made Cora's heart ache, she wished she could do more to help, but Francine was so darned independent. If she dropped a teaspoon on the floor, she'd struggle to pick it up herself, rather than have Cora do it for her. Cora respected that, of course she did, and she was proud of Francine's spirit, but given her friend was often so short of breath, was it worth her pushing herself so hard?

Even as she thought it, she knew that she'd be the same herself – that's if she lived long enough to grow old. Who knows what might happen with the war, so many young people were dying, it was unbearable to think about it. At least she'd heard that Madeleine had left Paris. She'd felt sad when she'd heard the news via Francine; she had many happy memories from before the war of making friends with Madeleine, talking in a cafe, both sipping their coffee, reading their books. They'd shared so much laughter. She'd seen her briefly before she'd left for the Loire; her wound had healed well but it was still a bright red, angry mark. That wasn't the worst of it though. Madeleine's spirit was broken, her voice flat, her eyes glazed, she was a shadow of her former self. At least Cora had been able to reassure Madeleine that her scar would fade. 'Look, she'd said, tracing the mark on her upper lip, all scars fade in time.'

Madeleine had offered a fleeting smile and then she'd started to cry, their final intimacy a shared hug with her friend sobbing on her shoulder. She'd seemed less burdened once she'd pulled away and dried her eyes, but Cora knew that her friend would go through repeated loops of grief before she was able to leave some of her demons behind. She sighed heavily, just thinking about Madeleine. She hoped that one day, when all this was over, she'd be able to find her again.

When the embers of the kitchen stove had burned low, Cora pushed back her chair and started to clear the table. Francine got up stiffly from her seat and tried to assist but Cora insisted this time, 'No, I'll do the washing-up, you go and sit, finish your wine.'

Francine took a breath, her eyes bright, weighing it up, then for once she assented and picked up her wine glass, making her way carefully to her armchair in the front room.

Cora liked to help with the chores, the swoosh of her hands in the warm, soapy water cleaning the plates, the gentle clatter as she stacked them on the wooden draining board... it all helped her to relax as her mind went over the day. When she'd been out with her camera, she always needed to settle herself, push away nagging thoughts of whether she'd been seen, whether anyone had followed her. Despite that, the buzz of the missions still exhilarated her, and she was getting so much better at snapping her pictures. When Estelle had got the early ones developed some had been blurry, indecipherable. 'Camera film is precious,' she'd told Cora, 'You need to do better.' Estelle never dressed things up, she always came straight out with it. So, Cora had asked if they could get her a book, or some tips about using a Leica. Two nights later, Bertrand had handed over a handwritten list of essential points. He never said where it had come from or who had provided it but with a wink he'd whispered, 'Once you've practised this, you'll be snapping like a fashion photographer... even Estelle won't have any issues.'

Cora took on board all the advice, making sure to practise without the film in the camera. She was pleased when there were no more comments from Estelle. And when a photograph had shown an unexpected visit by a high-ranking German officer, Estelle had shrugged her shoulders and almost smiled.

'High praise indeed,' Francine had whispered with a mischievous grin.

It made Cora smile to herself, thinking back over the past

few weeks. Time was ticking by in this bubble of existence that she knew could pop at any moment. Their survival here at Francine's was contingent on not being caught. So, here she was, an American in Paris, out by day dodging around German soldiers, taking risks on the street with her camera, coming home to spend time with an elderly woman who sat with a gun concealed under a blanket. *Me with my camera, her with her gun.* It made her start to laugh, the sheer ridiculousness of it. As unlikely as it was that Francine would be identified as a member of the Resistance, still she felt the need to be able to defend herself in the event the German army came knocking at her door.

'What were you giggling at, through there?' Francine asked when Cora came into the front room once the kitchen was straight.

'Oh, the absurdity of life,' she said, lowering herself into the deep red brocade armchair in Francine's front room, the one that had become hers during her stay. She closed her eyes for a moment, feeling a little sleepy now.

'You all right?' Francine murmured, then with a sudden yowl of a cat in the alley and a clatter of something falling over, she shot forward in her chair, whipped out the gun.

Cora's heart nearly jumped out of her chest. 'It's a cat, only a cat,' she gasped, leaping up from her chair, her eyes wide, breath coming quick.

'If it does that again, I'll shoot it,' Francine quipped, leaning back in her chair, pushing the revolver beneath the blanket.

Cora began to feel a tickle of laughter in the pit of her stomach, 'I know you won't, you're such a big softie when it comes to cats and dogs.'

Francine smiled as she pulled a cigarette out of her pack, 'Yes, of course I am, especially for dogs... Years ago, I had a Jack Russell called Barney, he had a brown patch over one eye, the cutest little dog ever. Such good company once the boys had left home and Sam was away on the transatlantic crossings. He ran out yapping and going crazy every time Sam came home, carried on doing it for months after he died, every time there was a knock at the door...'

Cora let her talk without interruption. She knew when Francine was wistful, when her mind was reaching back through time. As soon as she saw her start to smile, she knew she was coming back to the present.

As her friend puffed on her cigarette, Cora rested back in her chair, breathing in the now familiar tobacco smoke. She'd tried to smoke when she'd been younger, just to be like the others but she'd coughed and spluttered, never liked it. Now she was getting used to the smell, she felt at ease with it, maybe she'd have tried again if it hadn't been for the rationing of tobacco. She certainly didn't want to end up smoking dried grass, which is where Francine had said they'd all end up.

Once Francine stubbed out her cigarette, she leaned forward, as if she were going to say something. Then, changing her mind, she pulled out the gun and pushed it down the side of the chair before pulling herself up to stand.

'Can I get you anything?' Cora asked, seeing how stiffly her friend moved.

'No, that's all right, I just need to show you something.'

Rooting in her skirt pocket, Francine pulled out a small key looped on a red ribbon. Her eyes were shining brightly, Cora was keen to know what was going to be revealed.

Tutting as she struggled to securely fit the key into a locked drawer of the chest of drawers beneath the window, Francine then muttered with satisfaction as the key turned and she could slide the drawer open. Pulling out a blue silk drawstring bag, she slowly made her way back, pausing by Cora's chair.

Cora glanced up expectantly, as Francine undid the drawstring and pulled an expensive looking necklace out of the bag, letting it dangle in front of her, glinting in the lamplight.

'Wow,' gasped Cora, never one to wear necklaces or know much about jewellery, she knew instantly that this was no fake item, this was the real thing. And by the way the stones flashed in the light, she knew they were almost certainly real gems. Cora was mesmerised by the lightning sparkle of what looked like a diamond choker, and when Francine offered it to her, she reached out a hand to feel the weight of it.

'Wherever did you get this?' was her first question, as Francine slowly made her way back to her chair.

'Oh, it's not mine, it's your Aunt Iris's,' she said, easing herself back down into her seat, waiting to catch her breath before she spoke again. 'I've been keeping it safe for her for many years.'

Cora wondered why she hadn't simply given it back to Iris, but then, knowing Iris's apartment was currently occupied by soldiers, she supposed it made sense to spread these things around.

'She first gave it to me in 1914, at the start of the last war. It had been a gift from her benefactor, Miss Duchamp.'

'Oh, yes, I know who you mean, the bad-tempered spinster, the one who gave her the apartment. She was one of Iris's first-class passengers, wasn't she?'

'Yes, she was, but once Iris got to know her, she found that underneath all that bluster, Amelia Duchamp was a kind and generous person. This was the very first item Miss Duchamp gave Iris, it was a thank you for all her years of service on the liners. Even though the war had only just begun, Miss Duchamp was sure she wouldn't be crossing the Atlantic again.'

'How would she know that?' Cora asked, knotting her brow.

Francine smiled, 'Once you get to a certain age and you feel your body changing, starting to tire more easily, if you've got any sense you listen to it and you adjust your life.'

'Is that what you should be doing, Francine?' Cora pushed, smiling to ease the impact of her words.

Francine sighed, 'Probably... but now with this war, there isn't much ease for anyone, and if I can do anything at all to help, I will.'

'Please try to rest more though, Francine.'

'Oh, all right Nurse Cora,' Francine tutted, 'just like your mother and your aunt... Anyway, as I was saying, Iris gave the necklace to me for safekeeping before she went to work at Netley hospital and then on the hospital ship *Britannic*.'

Cora was enjoying the feel of the necklace in her hand, she'd never handled real diamonds before.

'It's quite something, isn't it?' Francine smiled. 'Iris did her best to turn it down, she was concerned that with the ship in turmoil due to the declaration of war and all the passengers agitated, Miss Duchamp wasn't her usual self. From what your aunt said, she was in a terrible state, but you know Iris, she calmed her down, got her settled and then Miss Duchamp produced this necklace. Iris was shocked, she thought it seemed far too extravagant. But still Miss Duchamp insisted and then, as Iris always said, once she'd seen it glinting and gleaming in the light for long enough, she was mesmerised by the diamonds and there was no going back.'

'I can understand that...' murmured Cora, still entranced by it herself.

'I never told Sam about the necklace, I didn't want him worrying about me with a fortune in diamonds stashed in the house. I thought I'd tell him after the war... but then, well...' her voice wavered, tears shone in her eyes.

'I'm sorry, Francine,' Cora soothed, motioning to get up from her chair.

'Oh I'm fine, just a sentimental old woman,' Francine said, clearing her throat, 'Sam was the love of my life. I still feel his presence, hear his voice... some days it's a comfort, others it's unsettling, but like I've always said... our ghosts live with us, we simply have to get used to them.'

'Yes, I suppose that's true... I'm not sure if it's the same thing but I sometimes feel that way about my birth mother, I've no idea if she's alive or dead, but she feels like a ghost to me. I have this sense of her with me, but I've never seen her, so I can't even imagine her. All I know is that she has the same red hair as me.'

'That must be hard for you, Cora.'

Cora shrugged, 'Like you say, we have to get used to it, hey.'

'We have no choice, *ma chérie*.'

Cora slipped the necklace back into the blue silk bag and pulled the drawstring tight. 'Do you want me to put it back in the drawer for you?'

'That's all right, I can do it later, when I get my old bones moving again... I can't believe it's still here, with me. I've said to Iris so many times she must take it, put it with her other jewellery. She's always said no, you keep it, Francine, it's been with you so long, it's at home with you now. I had it for years with me in Southampton, I had it before Sam was killed... and then when the boys came home after the war and they decided to settle in New York, I came back to France, first to Calais and then to Paris and I brought it with me.'

'Did you ever tell the boys about it?'

'No,' Francine chuckled. 'I think by then, I'd got used to it being a secret and, once again, I didn't want them to worry that their mother was carrying around a fortune in diamonds. So, they have no clue to this day.'

'I suppose there's no need for them to know,' Cora said, not sure if that was the case... what if something happened to Francine and Iris was still missing. She didn't even know why she was thinking it, but now that she knew Francine had the necklace it troubled her as well.

She'd met Francine's sons once in New York when she was at college, they were both tall with a thatch of fair hair, very much like their father was the way that Aunt Iris had described them. She had fond memories of the day she'd spent in Central

Park with them and their wives and children... three boys and two girls from what she could recall. Cora couldn't work out if Francine's grandchildren would be too young to be called up if America joined the war, and she didn't want to ask, life was difficult enough without adding extra anxiety.

'The thing about the necklace, though,' Francine continued, leaning forward in her chair, her eyes shining. 'It helped me and your Aunt Iris so much after Sam and then Iris's first love, Jack, were killed in the war. If we were sad, we used to have a few drinks and then we'd take out the necklace, try it on, tell stories from the glory days of the White Star ocean liners – the *Olympic,* the poor old *Titanic* and the *Britannic*, the hospital ship your mother and father and Aunt Iris worked on together. Your Aunt Iris ended up in the sea when it was blown up by a mine. She was rescued by a fishing boat.'

'I didn't know about that,' Cora gasped, 'Iris never told me much about the war.'

'Well, your mother was on board the *Britannic* as well, did she never say anything about it either?'

'No,' Cora said, feeling forlorn, as if she'd been left out of something. Then suddenly aware that there were probably many things she didn't know about her mother or her Aunt Iris.

'They'll tell you all their stories, when they're ready, don't you worry about it. Those two are still spring chickens compared to me,' Francine laughed, shifting her position in the armchair to make herself more comfortable. 'Now, make an old woman very happy by trying that necklace on and then let's have the last of the wine, to celebrate old times.'

There was no way Cora could refuse, so she jumped up from the chair, pulled out the necklace and gazed into the mirror above the fireplace. Unless absolutely necessary, she never removed her spiral-patterned necklace, so she fastened the diamond choker over the top of the thin silver chain. Even the most expensive jewels in the world could never be so precious as the simple necklace her mother had left for her. Nonetheless, feeling the weight of the diamonds against her skin, seeing the ice sparkle, sent a trill through her body. She was fascinated by how it changed her appearance.

'You look like a princess or a very rich lady, you could easily pull it off,' Francine said. 'If you had one of your Aunt Iris's silk gowns and your hair done up, a young woman like you with your elegant neck and high cheekbones... you were made to wear expensive jewellery. Who knows, maybe your birth mother was an aristocrat?'

'I very much doubt that, Francine, she was after all seen depositing me herself on the shores of Southampton Water. If she'd been rich, she'd probably have got a servant to do it.'

'True,' Francine said, 'but it adds so much mystery and romance, doesn't it, having all the possibilities. You can be what you want to be, in your head.'

Cora hadn't really thought of her situation like that, it was a positive way of looking at it, but still she longed to know exactly who had given birth to her – rich, poor or somewhere in between.

When she glanced back to the mirror, she saw the silver scar where her cleft lip had been repaired, she noticed the slight distortion of her top lip. Instinctively, she ran a finger over the line, it made her think of Evie, telling her to be proud of it, telling her it was her special mark. Unexpected tears pricked at her eyes at the thought of Evie – she'd heard her voice so clearly in that moment, as if she were in the room.

'Don't you worry, Cora, like our ghosts the living speak to us as well sometimes, they're always with us. You'll see Evie again soon enough,' Francine said softly.

How did you know was on the tip of Cora's tongue, but she didn't want to dispel the magic by putting it into words.

Instead, she slowly unhooked the necklace, slipped it into

the blue silk bag and handed it back. 'You're quite something, aren't you, Francine?' she said.

Francine shrugged her shoulders, pulled down the corners of her mouth. 'Aren't we all, in our own way.'

In the next moment Francine was beckoning for Cora to sit back down. 'The real reason I've shown you the necklace, Cora, is that we can use it to our advantage. If, for example we need to get Iris out of a German prison camp, we can use it as a bribe. I have a contact who can sell it for cash, many a German officer would want an exquisite piece of jewellery like that for his wife.'

'That's good to know,' beamed Cora, 'and how apt it would be if she was saved by her own necklace.'

'How apt indeed,' breathed Francine 'but somehow, I don't think we're going to need it for Iris, I feel in my bones that Iris is safe, if not already then it will be so in due course. I would know if she'd come to any harm.'

It all sounded fantastical but right now, after Francine had tuned in when Cora was thinking of Evie, she was ready to believe that it was indeed true. And at least she could feel reassured that, if required, Francine had the means to raise what would probably be a substantial lump sum of money from the sale of the necklace.

For the rest of the evening, they sat in companionable silence, murmuring light conversation, feeling completely relaxed with each other. Later, when Francine started to yawn, she pulled her revolver out and opened it to check that the chamber was still fully loaded. Used to it now, Cora showed no surprise; she got up from her seat, assisted Francine out of hers and then they both said goodnight. At the sound of a gunshot somewhere out in the city, they both froze for a few moments, listening.

'Just a random shot, probably an inattentive sentry. It's nothing, all fine,' Francine shrugged, 'Make sure you get plenty of sleep, I hope you haven't forgotten you're out on a special mission for us in the morning.'

'I haven't forgotten,' Cora yawned, kissing Francine on the cheek, 'Goodnight, Francine.'

'Goodnight, *ma chérie*.'

CHAPTER 14

As Cora and Francine chatted at the kitchen table over a meagre breakfast of bread with a thin smear of butter and the last scrapings of strawberry jam, Francine ran through an imaginary list of what potential breakfast foods they might be having in future... 'Maybe we could eat baked acorns, crush them up and mix them with water. Or soap, can we eat soap? Oh no, that's rationed as well.'

Cora started to laugh and Francine joined in, 'How about pigeons, maybe we could chase them around the city catch them in a net—'

Tap, tap, tap. Three firm knocks on the door. For a moment they were both rendered silent, exchanging a wide-eyed stare. Until Francine realised that it would be Bertrand and Estelle arriving for the meeting. Today was the day of the special mission. Francine, visibly biting back more laughter, dispatched Cora to open the door.

Estelle came in with her brow knitted in a scowl, 'Whatever is going on in here, I'm sure the Germans will be able to hear you two halfway to the Eiffel Tower.'

Cora pressed her lips together, unable to speak in case she

burst out laughing again. As soon as Bertrand came through the door, he smiled broadly and grabbed Cora into a bear hug.

Estelle repeated her question, 'Well, what's going on?'

Francine shrugged and simply said, 'We have gone completely mad, please come and join.'

Bertrand coughed loudly to disguise what Cora knew was a bout of laughter. They all accepted that Estelle did have a point, they shouldn't be making any extra noise that might draw attention to the fact that people were meeting in groups. But the heightened tension that ran through the city and collected at every street corner had to have an outlet somewhere. That's what Cora thought at least, not that Estelle would ever agree.

Once the coffee was brewed and they were all gathered around the table, they were calm, focused on the mission. Estelle went through every detail then warned Cora to be extra careful with this one, the German tanks they were asking her to photograph definitely did not fit with her cover as a tourist.

Walking through the city on her way to the assignment, Cora saw some well-dressed women strolling along in their tailored skirts, high heels and hats angled just so on the side of the head. It made her think of Iris again and with that came thoughts of Evie and Adam still waiting for news. With a shrug of his shoulders, Bertrand hadn't been able to give any clear idea of how long it would take her smuggled letter to get through. It could be weeks, it could be months. She thought it was way too soon for it to have been delivered, so she visualised her mother's restless pacing up and down the beach, back and forth with the changing of the tides and her quiet, patient father, sitting in his well-loved armchair, pretending to read the newspaper, making out that he was sure everything would be fine, when all the while his heart was breaking.

Thinking of it made her own heart clench, she had to count her steps as she walked to get it out of her head so she could refocus on the task in hand. The camera in her rucksack tap-tapping against her back, the spare roll of film in the pocket of her slacks. *Think, focus,* she repeated in her head, unable to fight off more thoughts of Iris as she passed close to the Avenue Rapp. Still there was no news, it made her feel helpless not being party to any information whatsoever, and every time she raised it with Bertrand or Estelle they repeated the same thing: 'Be patient, as soon as we hear the faintest whisper, we will let you know.' They didn't understand how close she'd become to Iris, she was like an aunt, a friend, a mother, all rolled into one. Iris had gone missing from the apartment in June, the summer had passed already, surely there should have been some news by now.

'It's better being no news than bad news,' Francine had said last week. 'For all we know she could be back in Southampton or at home with your mother in Montauk.'

Cora had acknowledged it might be possible, but still it niggled at her, ground her down and at night dreams came of Iris distressed, calling for help.

'You're being melodramatic,' Francine had told her the last time they'd talked about it. 'I've known Iris a very long time, she's tough and she's not due to die just yet.'

In the end, all Cora could do was draw strength from the notion that one day she would come here with Iris, they would walk down the Avenue Rapp together and take back the apartment.

Moving briskly, she made herself feel confident in her white cotton blouse and cream slacks. Feeling the weight of the camera in her rucksack sent a ripple of excitement through her body. Over the summer she'd completed numerous missions. Francine had impressed on her the importance of the material they were sending to those higher up in the Resistance network who were able to make the relevant images available to the British army.

Once she was closer and she could see the tanks lined up, she felt the now familiar tingling of the tiny hairs at the back of her neck. She inhaled deeply, making herself calm, the whole process so well practised, it felt rehearsed. Not that she would ever become complacent, particularly on an atypical mission such as this. The vehicles looked solid, daunting, and she knew that she'd struggle to get close enough for a clear image, they were bound to be carefully guarded. Estelle had told her to go for a long shot, do what she could without taking too much of a risk. Pausing to gaze over to the tanks and gauge the distance, she was still weighing up her options when she heard the scrape of boot heels behind her and a voice shouted, 'Halt!'

Cora felt the shock like a punch. She froze, horrified. Trying to calm herself, she fixed a smile on her face and turned to see a broad-shouldered German soldier motioning with his rifle for her to stand facing the wall.

Her heart was beating a painful, staccato rhythm. She knew even before she felt the soldier grasp the rucksack that the camera would be found and, by his aggressive bearing, she was sure he would easily work out that she was here to take photographs of the tanks. He grunted with interest as he roughly pulled the bag from her shoulders. In the few seconds it would take him to open it and discover the Leica, she knew she had to act.

As soon as her arms were free from the straps of the rucksack, she twisted round, knocking him off balance as he bent to unfasten the bag. Running faster than she'd ever done in her life, she hurtled away, beginning to feel exultant.

When she heard the crack of gunfire, for a few moments it didn't connect with the searing pain in her right shoulder. Another two shots and then shouting voices, the sound of running feet in pursuit, hammering against the pavement. Still she ran, the pain increasing in intensity, feeling the warm seep of blood through her white blouse.

The soldier's boots drummed ever louder in pursuit – more than one pair now. She had moments to survive. Glancing from side to side, she spotted a narrow slit of an alley. Running past a few yards, she then U-turned and hid behind a parked car for a few seconds. Her breath caught as she became aware of blood seeping down the back of her blouse, soaking into the waistband of her slacks and dripping onto the clean white stone pavement. She counted to three, then used her remaining strength to run into the opening of the alley. Dizzy now, she supported herself with both hands on the rough plastered wall, leaving bloody prints, moving as quickly as she could, knowing it would be moments before her pursuers saw the blood, discovered her route.

At the sound of echoing German voices, her body tried to rally but she had no strength left, she was light-headed, drained. Maybe she was dying.

Lying in the alleyway, holding back a groan at the searing pain of the gunshot wound, Cora tried to pull her useless arm into a more comfortable position. A sharp pain stabbed through her body from back to front and she almost screamed out loud. But she had to get up. If she stayed here, she would be found and arrested or she would bleed out and die.

She thought of her mother and father, of Iris and Francine... she felt sorry that if she did die, they would all be so sad and then Francine would feel guilty, having got her into this mess.

Spurred on by the dire need not to die, she wrestled her body into a kneeling position, bowed over on the hard ground, as if in an act of penitence.

The thud of boot heels around the corner.

She used all her might to try and push herself up, one hand against the wall, she felt as if her heart were about to burst with the effort, flashes of light in her eyes, then a sickening, deep strike of pain in her back which took her breath and caused her to collapse back onto the unforgiving ground.

The boot heels were louder now, the German soldiers were close. She gritted her teeth, ready for what was coming.

A scraping sound, wood on stone, hands pulling at her. Then she blacked out.

'Wake up.'

An insistent voice called, squeezing her hand. Why couldn't they leave her alone, she was so tired, more tired than she'd ever been in her whole life.

'Wake up,' there it was again. She groaned, tried to turn on her side but a pain, sharp as a knife, stabbed through her shoulder.

She shouted out, struggled against it, then she heard a man's voice, she couldn't make out the accent or what he was saying. Where was she?

With sickening dread, she recalled what had happened. She must have been captured by the Germans... she couldn't let them know she was awake. Once they sensed a response from her, she would be interrogated. Maybe they'd already developed the partially used film in the camera and they knew she was a spy. The word shot back at her, *spy*, that's what she was. All the time she'd been swanning around Paris, clicking photographs, it had never occurred to her so starkly. Her head was reeling, screaming now, telling her to wait until the voices of those watching her went quiet and then get up, start to move. She had to try.

Another squeeze of her hand, a man's grip, almost painful.

'Cora, wake up,' the voice said.

How did they know her name? She'd been careful not to carry her identification card.

'Cora,' again, and this time she was sure she recognised the voice. A feeling of dread – she imagined Karl standing over her, his eyes burning. Her body shuddered. She had to attempt an escape, but her eyes were so heavy she couldn't open them.

A smell of carbolic, then a woman's voice. 'She seems to be shivering, maybe it's a rigor.'

'Check her temperature again, let's make sure she isn't spiking a fever and when she's due her next morphia injection, give her a shot of penicillin as well. I got the bullet out cleanly, but the wound is deep, she will be prone to infection.'

Then it clicked. She knew the speaker... it was Chris, her lovely American doctor friend, fan of F. Scott Fitzgerald and *The Great Gatsby*. The last time he'd come to the American library they'd talked about how Fitzgerald had served during the last war and what he'd said thereafter about it being the war to end all wars.

'The war to end all wars... haha,' she murmured, prompting a response from the woman, who she could only imagine was a nurse in a white uniform. 'She's just said something about a war to end all wars, does that make any sense to you, Doctor, or do you think she's delirious?'

A short laugh, Chris's laugh. Then his sweet voice, 'Yes, it makes perfect sense.' Followed by the cool, reassuring pressure of his hand on her forehead. 'You get some sleep now, Cora... we will continue our F. Scott Fitzgerald discussion later, when you're fully awake.'

She tried to speak but she was way too sleepy. Instead, she made a vow to herself – if she survived the war, she would never forget this moment of feeling reborn, being given another chance at life. Slowing her breathing to counter the niggling pain in her shoulder, she drifted deeper into her cocoon of sleep. So happy to be safe with Chris.

Later, when she woke, she became aware of someone holding her hand. When she opened her eyes she found

Francine, her face pale, stricken, sitting beside the bed. She offered a shaky smile, then dabbed at her eyes with a white handkerchief. 'I'm so sorry, I should never have got you involved with this. It is not your fight, you could have been killed. It is all my fault.'

'No, please don't cry,' Cora croaked, 'of course it's my fight, Iris is missing at the hands of the Germans.'

Francine sobbed, dabbed harder with her handkerchief. 'You must go home now, Cora, back to America.'

'No, I can still work with the Resistance, I want to help.'

Francine was shaking her head, calm, pragmatic. 'You cannot, Cora. We've had word from the Resistance sympathisers who rescued you, there were several soldiers in pursuit, any one of them might be able to recognise you. And it's only a matter of time before they plaster posters bearing your image and description on walls and shop windows throughout the city. The Nazis will be desperate to get their hands on you, they will hurt and humiliate you, make an example.'

Cora felt her breath catch. She opened her mouth to speak but no words would come.

Francine was patting her hand now, rallying. 'You are safe here, in the hospital, but we can't leave you for too long. There's bound to be someone who'll turn you in... So, I'm already speaking to Estelle and Bertrand: you will go to a safe house for recovery, there are hidden rooms, places that no one can find. We are planning to get you out through Calais, across the Channel somehow, then on a transatlantic ship back to America. It will be risky, but escape routes exist, particularly for a young woman who can speak fluent French. We might have to alter your appearance a little, but don't worry, it won't be permanent.'

Cora held back a sob. 'But what about Iris, there's no sign of her being found yet?' she pleaded. 'What will happen to her if I leave Paris?'

'We are all here for Iris, you need to hand it over to me,' Francine said firmly, 'and as I've said before, Iris is strong, I feel in my bones that she is safe.'

Cora knew she had no choice but to agree, her position in Paris was completely untenable.

In two days, she was moved in an ambulance to the attic room of an apartment in Montmartre, her head and face bandaged to disguise her features and distinctive hair colour. Already she had a false identification card and bore a new name... Simone Devereux. 'You must only speak French, from now on, only French,' Francine had impressed upon her.

When Francine visited to bring Cora's belongings from the house, and to say farewell, they both shed tears. The crying settled with the wine Francine brought in a flask, and by the time her old friend was lighting up one of her now precious, rationed cigarettes, they were chatting with the same ease they'd had from the day Cora had turned up with her bag, evicted from Iris's apartment.

Later, Francine interrogated her regarding her fake identity. No smiles now, this was an exacting business. If she was stopped by the Germans she would have to instantly rattle off her name, address, date of birth... all the information on her new identity card. She needed to pass fully as a French citizen, someone moving to Calais to help with the running of a lodging house for visiting German officials.

'You are not to get involved in any of the undercover work in Calais,' Francine stressed, 'I've made it clear to my contact that you are only passing through, they *cannot* use you in any way.'

Cora smiled, as if she would be tempted to jump straight back in, after the toll her injury had taken on both of them. Francine had lost even more weight; her lined face was pale and drawn with dark blotches beneath her eyes. Cora reached out to take her hand, 'And you must promise me, Francine, that you will step back a little now, you will rest up.'

Francine offered a wry smile, her eyes suddenly alive, 'Well, I've had to accept a lift to come and see you here, so it looks like I'm trying to do as I'm told. But as for stepping back... you do know that I am the perfect operative, don't you? As an old woman with a shawl, I can move around the city and be completely invisible. Even if I'm standing right next to a German soldier, eavesdropping on a conversation, they don't see me as a threat. The best they can offer is to tell me to move on. And that's when I start pretending to be stone deaf, hobbling, taking my time to stagger away. Last week one young German almost carried me, all the while continuing his conversation with a fellow soldier. I got some advance information on what was coming next with rationing, just by pretending to be frail. It is a superb cover, and I don't even need to wear make-up or a wig, I simply dress old and threadbare.'

Cora listened wide-eyed. 'I hadn't even thought about that,' she smiled, feeling some reassurance.

'And naturally I will have my revolver close,' Francine added with a glint in her eye.

Cora sighed. 'I do wish you wouldn't keep that gun; can you not give it to Bertrand?'

'Pah, Bertrand has bad eyes, he's a poor shot.' She reached out to pat Cora's arm, 'Don't you worry about me, I will be careful.'

When it was time for Francine to leave, more tears were shed. Cora clung to her friend; they wouldn't see each other now probably for the duration of the war.

'I'll see you again when this is all over,' Francine said, before they pulled apart. 'And don't worry, I'll pass on your goodbyes to Estelle and Bertrand. They've both been worrying about you.'

'I'll miss Bertrand so much,' Cora said, 'and Estelle as well, in a way.'

'Estelle was very upset,' Francine said, lighting up another cigarette.

'Really?' Cora laughed.

'Yes, it's hard to believe but she does have a heart underneath all that tightness, she keeps it tucked away, that's all,' Francine started to laugh and then she was hacking with a deep, rattling cough. Cora patted her on the back with her good arm.

'I'll be all right,' Francine gasped. 'At this time of year, when the weather turns, I always get like this.'

Once her cough had settled, Francine stepped back, her face ashen, tears shining in her eyes. 'So, this is it then, until we meet again.'

'I suppose it is,' Cora said, a wobble in her voice. She hadn't realised until this moment how close they'd become. With a shaky voice Francine began to croon the words to Vera Lynn's *We'll Meet Again*. It made Cora feel even more upset, thinking about the mention she'd given to the song, in the letter she'd sent to America. She didn't have the heart to join in.

Watching Francine go, seeing how thin she'd become, how hunched her posture, Cora felt a niggle of unease. Her friend always presented strongly, but maybe all this rationing and the stress of war was taking much more of a toll on her than anyone realised.

'Please look after yourself, Francine, try to get more rest,' she called, her voice tight.

In the weeks it took for Cora to become strong enough to begin her journey along the escape route, she was fully confined to her attic room with nothing but a tiny skylight to let the light in and allow her to see out over the rooftops of the city. Each day she paced up and down the length of the room to strengthen her legs and she did arm exercises. The pain in her shoulder was excruciating at first, but gradually she regained full movement and made it strong again. She only had one small mirror in the attic so she couldn't see the healing wound, but she could reach with her good arm, trace the outline of the sutured hole where the bullet had entered. Still, in dreams, she felt the searing pain of it, heard the clatter of boot heels chasing after her, woke slaked with sweat, gasping for air. She knew she had to be patient, it would take a while for the flashbacks to reduce.

Meals were delivered three times a day and her commode and wash bowl emptied by a silent, grey-haired woman who barely made eye contact. Cora didn't want to compromise the woman's safety, so she never asked questions, she simply let her get on with her tasks. The days were long, so Cora broke them up into chunks – washing and dressing, bed-making, meals, exercise, then, when she had enough light, she read her copy of *Gone with the Wind*, imagining herself as a Scarlett O'Hara figure, preparing to march through the burnt-out and blasted landscape wrought by the American civil war. Even though she'd read most of it once before, Cora was still anxious for the love affair with Rhett Butler to be the one that mattered to her heroine and not wrongly placed with the weaker, passive figure of Ashley Wilkes. On the day she finished the book and had to deal with Rhett disappearing into the sunset, she shed a tear. Why couldn't all endings be uncomplicated, happy?

The next day, word came that she would be moving soon. The silent woman brought her a pair of sharp scissors and spoke at last, to tell her to crop her hair short to alter her appearance. As she stood in front of a small fly-spotted mirror, she felt the sadness of losing her wavy red locks, but her hair was so distinctive it was important for her to do the deed. As soon as she had the first few chunks cut, it was easy, she hacked at it mercilessly. As more red curls fell to the floor, she thought of Evie, glad that she wasn't here to witness the destruction of what she'd always called Cora's crowning glory. Tough as she was about other things, her mother would probably have been in tears. When all that remained was a crop of curls clinging close to her scalp, she put down the scissors and ran a hand through it. It made her feel light, unencumbered. She was pleased by the way it elongated her slim neck and made her look like a chic, edgy, modern French woman. 'You are Simone Devereux,' she told her reflection.

She checked through the black canvas bag of belongings she'd been given, all items befitting poor Simone Devereux, a shop worker from Paris, down at heel and out of work and supposedly heading to work as a maidservant in a boarding house. Cora picked up the dog-eared French paperback provided as reading material, tempted to replace it with her copy of *Gone with the Wind,* but it would look suspicious for Simone to be carrying a book written in English by an American author. The evening gown and the jewellery she'd rescued from Iris's apartment had been left behind at Francine's, they would be impossible to explain if she ended up being searched; at best they'd think she was a thief, at worst they'd know she was a spy. It made her sad to leave the rubies behind though, there was history attached to the jewels. Iris had told her they'd also been given to her by Miss Duchamp, they'd been of great sentimental value to the elderly woman, a gift from her fiancé, a Frenchman who'd had been killed last century during the Franco-Prussian war. Iris had said that Miss Duchamp had never recovered, never found another love to replace the one that she'd lost. It made Cora sad to hear the story, but she'd thought to herself that maybe Miss Duchamp should have tried a bit harder to work her way out of her grief. Maybe Cora was being ungenerous, but her naive perspective told her that most things could be overcome.

Cora fastened her bag, took a deep breath, the black gaberdine mac and matching beret lay on the bed, ready and waiting.

She felt a stir of unease; after being confined for so many weeks it felt daunting to be going back out into the world. Catching her harried reflection in the mirror, she was sure she'd never had that faint frown line between her brows. She stepped closer, scrutinising her reflection. Her face was thinner than it had ever been, her green eyes the only part of her former self she fully recognised. Green eyes, like Scarlett O'Hara... she wouldn't forget her promise to Francine. When the war was over, she would take her to the most luxurious cinema in Paris, they'd sip champagne and recline in plush velvet seats to watch Vivian Leigh and Clark Gable in *Gone with the Wind.*

CHAPTER 15

The first stage of Cora's journey began huddled in the back of a van, wrapped in a musty-smelling blanket, hidden behind a pile of requisitioned leather – old boots and shoes, belts and bags en route to Germany to be used in the manufacture of army uniforms. As they rattled over the cobbled streets, Cora clutched her canvas bag, praying they wouldn't be stopped for inspection and the dishevelled, nonchalant-looking driver of the vehicle had his wits about him. She'd practised, whispering out loud exactly what to say if she was stopped but she wasn't sure how she'd explain her presence hunched behind a pile of scrap leather in the back of a van. As she began to turn stories she might use over in her head, she tapped into the thrill she'd had out on operations before she got injured. Having escaped and survived a gunshot wound, she realised that, with that experience behind her now, she felt stronger.

She still hadn't found out who had dragged her to safety. Francine probably had some idea but as she'd said, the less one knew the better. She remembered a scraping sound, like a door opening over stone and then a sensation of being moved. She would probably never know, but she owed everything to those who had risked their own lives. Rattling along now in the back of the van, it felt as if she were on another mission and a nub of a thought began to form in her head – she had a false identity, if she were heading to Calais, why couldn't she make use of being undercover and continue her work for another Resistance group? Then the promise she'd made to Francine that she would stay safe stopped that thought dead. 'Calais is of great strategic importance, it is full of German soldiers,' Francine had said, 'Even though I lived there in my younger years, I'd never risk working in such a dangerous environment.'

Boarding a northbound train in the early morning, Cora kept her head bowed as she walked, clutching her ticket ready for inspection. Demurely dressed in her worn gaberdine mac and with the black beret pulled right down over her ears to conceal her red hair, she slipped into a seat beside a pink-cheeked older woman, strands of bleach blonde hair poking untidily from beneath her blue felt hat. The woman glanced up; she was knitting what looked like a pair of men's socks. Cora nodded in her direction but didn't speak, Francine's voice in her head telling her to keep her head down, read a book, only speak when spoken to.

Cora took the tattered paperback out of her bag. As the train built up a head of steam and then lurched into heavy, grinding movement, she felt her stomach clench as the conductor entered the carriage and shouted for *tickets please*.

The abrupt-mannered man gave a grunt of satisfaction as he clipped her ticket and thrust it back into her hand. Only then did she realise she'd been holding her breath. Resting back against the seat, she started to relax a little but when the train lurched and began to slow, there were anxious cries at the low rumble of aeroplanes overhead. A baby started to grizzle and the woman next to Cora paused her knitting, muttering a prayer.

A man's loud voice from the other side of the carriage broke through the murmur of consternation. 'There've been a number of catastrophes with British planes accidentally hitting the wrong targets or jettisoning their bombs, especially if the sky's cloudy.' His words sent a ripple of panic through the passengers. Cora glanced out of the window to see broken cloud in the sky. She clutched her hands tight together as if in prayer, kept her head down. Still the heavy, threatening drone continued overhead.

If these were allied planes overhead, she tried to make sense of what they hoped to accomplish. Then she recalled what Bertrand had said about British planes bombing the French coast and northern towns at sites where the Luftwaffe had built airfields or landing grounds. The allies were terrified that the Germans would advance across the narrow English Channel, so they were bombing whatever they could. Unfortunately, sometimes their bombs fell off target and innocent French civilians were caught up in the mess. It made Cora's gut twist at the horror of lives lost needlessly.

The carriage door clunked open, sending a ripple of fear through the passengers. 'It's all right, they're German planes,' the conductor called, almost jubilant, as he came down the aisle.

A collective sigh of relief and the woman next to Cora started to click her needles again. Cora mused on the precariousness of their situation, always listening, gazing up to the sky, wondering if this time they were going to be in the wrong place at the wrong time. Dropping her shoulders, making herself appear relaxed, she turned back to the opening page of her book and began to read. The words weren't quite stringing together properly but it helped to calm her as the train chugged on, heading north out of the city in a cloud of smoke and steam.

Time slipped by as the dog-eared pages were turned one by one. Cora was fully absorbed now in the tale of unrequited love, almost oblivious to the clack of the knitting needles next to her, the wheedling cry of a small child somewhere behind and the persistent cough of an elderly man with white hair and a walking stick across the aisle. Even the drone of more planes overhead didn't cut through, not until the train lurched to a grinding halt once again and the woman beside her cried out in alarm.

The sound of these aircraft seemed louder than last time, passengers were shouting, children crying. 'They're British planes,' a man's voice screamed from the rear of the carriage, 'We need to get out.'

Panic ricocheted through the carriage. They were all up from their seats, trying to struggle out into the aisle. The pink-cheeked woman next to Cora let out a strangled sob and Cora reached out a hand to her. 'Stay calm,' she said, overriding her own spiral of terror, knowing they were all stuck, with the door of the carriage not yet open. When the first bomb fell, it shook the carriage so hard it felt as if the train would topple over. Sheer panic now. 'Get off, get off,' screamed the voice of a man. Then a rush of air as the carriage door was opened at last, all the passengers surged at once shouting and screaming. The elderly man with white hair banged his stick hard on the floor and shouted orders, his shoulders back, almost standing to attention. 'Stay calm, no pushing, file out in an orderly fashion,' pointing with his stick to the carriage door. 'Those closest to the exit, you move first.'

Remarkably, the passengers followed his orders and the evacuation began. When the next bomb fell and the whole carriage rattled, children screamed, but all the adults stood their ground. The woman next to Cora was sobbing, struggling to push her knitting needles into her bag. Cora assisted her then, taking her arm, helped to lead her out, their turn next.

Boom! Another explosion rocked the train as she reached the door of the carriage. The air filled with grit, Cora put her arm across her nose and mouth, pulling the woman along now as she huffed and puffed behind. The white-haired elderly

gentleman who'd organised the evacuation of the carriage
following along next, his head held high, full of dignity.

As soon as Cora stepped down from the train, she turned to
reach up and assist the woman and that's when the explosion
hit the train. Thrown away, Cora lay winded, her ears buzzing,
grit in her mouth. With her hearing distorted by the blast, she
couldn't tell if the planes had gone or not. She struggled up
from the ground to a sitting position, trying to get her bearings.
Injured passengers lay groaning, spattered with blood. The
woman who Cora had assisted lay on her side, facing away,
completely still. Cora hauled herself up from the ground, grabbing her bag, stepping over debris to reach her fellow traveller.
The woman's bleach-blonde hair was soaked in blood, there was
no rise and fall of her chest, and when Cora pulled her onto her
back, she saw that half of her forehead had been blown away by
shrapnel. A ragged, gaping hole oozed white and grey blood-
stained matter. Cora bit back her horror, straightening up,
glancing around, looking for others, those she could help. The
white-haired gentleman who had saved many lives with his
clear instructions lay spreadeagled by the remains of the train
carriage he had evacuated, his body twisted at an odd angle, his
walking stick still clenched in his hand. Men and women were
shocked and weeping, calling out for loved ones.

The dazed train driver and conductor were doing their best,
trying to organise a response for dealing with the casualties but
then the rumble of heavy trucks heading towards them, made
everyone freeze. Cora knew it was probably the German army,
she daren't risk having her papers scrutinised, being asked questions. She needed to act quickly, the trucks would be with them
in minutes. With all eyes watching the approach of the vehicles,
Cora stepped back, started to run in the opposite direction,
making for the cover of a small copse of trees. She had to run
fast, or she would be seen.

Breathless, she threw herself down behind a tangle of brambles, the leaves dried, changing colour but still clinging on and enough to provide cover. She watched as German soldiers jumped down from the trucks, shouted orders, hurried to assist the wounded. As time went by, they started to clear some of the debris and hours later as Cora began to feel numb with cold as she lay perfectly still in her place of concealment, the last of the trucks drove away. Left with the sound of the breeze rustling the leaves and the cry of some crows circling in the sky above, she felt the rumble of hunger in her belly.

Only now did she feel the dawning reality of her situation. Being immersed in her book, she'd no real idea of how far the train had travelled towards Calais. They were out in open country, that's all she could remember. She couldn't even recall how many stops there'd been before the train was hit. She felt disappointed with herself, what kind of an undercover agent would lose all contact with her environment?

Still shocked, she felt a shudder run through her and she held back a sob for the poor woman and the elderly man, all of those who'd died. Looking out to the scene of the bombing, apart from the shattered remains of two carriages, there was no other sign that people had lost their lives. And now she was stranded, probably far away from Calais, with no food, no drink and she was beginning to shiver with cold. Pulling her beret further down over her ears, she rooted in her bag to check if the small flashlight supplied by Francine was still there, she'd need it later, when it grew dark. The wind was rustling the dried leaves now, the light already dying. Her nerves in shreds at the crack of twigs behind her, she wished that she had Francine's revolver.

Standing rigid, waiting for the tread of army boots, she hardly dared to breathe. Counting to ten before she made a run for it, she almost screamed when a huge hare bounded out of the undergrowth, more scared than she was. With a rush of relief, almost giddy with it, she randomly chose a direction and started to walk. Quickly at first, with a feeling of someone on her shoulder, breathing down her neck. But then, after she found a narrow, stony track to follow, she slowed her pace as dusk fell.

She waited till it was fully dark before she used the flash-light, knowing the battery would not last long. By the time her wristwatch told her it was twelve midnight and the stony track had not revealed any sign of habitation, she could walk no further. Finding a tree with a broad canopy for cover, she put down her canvas bag and nestled like some woodland creature with her back against the rugged trunk. The flapping of wings above, a bird roosting in the branches, made her startle with alarm. She grabbed her bag and hugged it with both arms, holding it fast, her only friend in this unknown wilderness.

She never thought she'd be able to get any sleep at all, but she must have blacked out. She woke very cold, blinking against the autumn light, her breath misting in the air and her back stiff and damp with the moisture that had soaked up from the ground. She'd loosened her grip on her bag and she was covered with brown, red, and gold autumn leaves. She scrambled to her feet, brushing stray leaves and dust from her mac, grabbing her bag from where it had fallen. Stamping her feet, she moved her arms to try and warm herself up. Another crack of twigs somewhere behind her in the thicket of trees. Too exhausted to react this time, she waited calmly as a deer ambled by, glancing at her, unperturbed. It made her want to laugh, she was covered in dust and leaves, she probably smelt like the earth.

Starting to walk once more along the rough track, she felt her belly rumble for food. Thrusting both hands into her coat pockets to keep warm, she found a small package – a biscuit wrapped in paper. Maybe the silent woman who'd brought her clothes had placed it there. She snapped it in half, hungrily consuming her first rationed portion as she walked, swallowing the crumbs against a dry throat but so grateful for the sustenance.

The sky was grey and overcast but thankfully it wasn't raining, maybe soon she would find a house and she could ask for help. Feeling cold and very hungry, her mind wouldn't properly work on what story she'd tell the occupants of the house; she'd have to make up something on the spot. She was out of Paris though, that was good, none of these people living out here would have heard of a search for a young American woman. And, of course, she was now Simone Devereux, travelling to work in Calais. As she marched on, putting one foot in front of the other, she made herself go over every detail of her situation. She was sure now the train hadn't reached Amiens before it was hit, so she must be south of there, hopefully heading towards it. She'd visited Amiens with Iris last summer, a sunny day in early June. It seemed idyllic now, thinking of the light and the open views of green fields through the window. And then, when they'd arrived in the city, she'd been shocked to see the still gaping holes and ruined buildings, damage caused during the last war.

Bertrand had fought in the trenches, he didn't talk much about it, except to tell the story of how he'd rescued a 'wet behind the ears' British soldier who'd got himself caught on the wire. He'd told it so calmly, as if scrabbling out of his trench and risking his own life to save another soldier had been the easiest thing in the world. He'd made out that he only rescued the young lad because he was shouting out, making a racket ... but that was Bertrand, playing down his courage. Once he'd dragged the wounded man into his trench, he'd fed him neat brandy, made him cough and splutter, then he'd tucked the soldier up in his own blanket, let him sleep it off. They'd stayed friends after the war had ended, writing letters and the lad had visited, newly married to a pale-faced British girl... with a baby already on the way.

Cora sighed heavily as she trudged, it felt now as if one war had bled into the next without any light in between. She even imagined she could hear the heavy rumble of planes overhead again. But when the noise grew loud, she realised, with a gasp, that the planes were real. When the first bomb fell, the ground shook. She was out in the open countryside, no shelter. All she could do was lurch to the side of the road, huddle down on her knees with her hands covering the back of her head. She counted backwards from ten in her head as the earth shook and more bombs fell. At last, there was a gap, and the drone of the engines had gone. Her whole body trembled as she stood, swaying on the spot, unable to walk until she collected herself.

As the grey light faded once more, she checked her watch; it would be dark again soon and still no food or shelter. Around the next bend, she found the shattered remains of what must have been a farmhouse, probably caught in the bombing. Large chunks of masonry lay asunder like the building blocks of a petulant giant. Fresh earth had been churned up from beneath the surface. The sound of some creature stirring amongst the ruins sent another shock through her body. A loud snort and a terrified, white-eyed horse trotted by, dragging its reins, shying when it saw her, starting to canter away from the broken remains. Cora felt a stab of unease, she glanced around, spotting another horse, chestnut with a white blaze, lying dead in a pool of blood.

She stared around her numbly. Apart from the horse and a few hens that were pecking for food amongst the debris, there was no sign of life. Hungry as she was, she knew the sensible thing would be to scrabble amongst the ruins, look for the remains of any food. But this felt like a graveyard, and she couldn't bring herself to scavenge for morsels in a place that might contain corpses. Standing for a few moments, saying a private prayer, she was about to move on when she thought she heard the mewing of a cat. There it was again, louder this time, the creature was distressed.

She angled her head in the direction of the sound, waiting. When the cry came again, her heart clenched. That was no cat, it was the cry of a baby, loud and clear, piercing her soul like an arrow.

CHAPTER 16

Cora was fully alert now, actively listening for the next cry, shifting her position in accordance with the direction, moving closer and closer to the remains of what must have been a farmhouse. She was fearless, she had a mission. She would risk anything, endure any hardship to find the child.

The next time the cry came, it was weaker and her heart squeezed as she bit back tears. Then, as if they were already linked by an unseen thread, the baby cried once more, with gusto this time.

Cora scrabbled over a large chunk of fractured masonry, scraping her hands, heedless of her bloodied palms. 'Where are you, baby, where are you?' she whispered. The light was fading, she daren't think about what might happen if she had to leave the infant undiscovered till dawn. It was all right, she could still see, she had time.

Another sound and she knew she was getting closer. Two more steps then she gasped, holding back a scream. A bloodied arm poked from a pile of rubble, drained of life. The fingers of the hand were delicate, it was a woman – probably the child's mother. A strange instinct guided her to the gold ring on the woman's finger. Knowing how precious her own spiral-patterned necklace was, she slipped the ring from the woman's hand and pushed it into her pocket. Her eyes were searching now for any other signs of human life – dead or injured. There was nothing. Within seconds, the baby's cry came again and immediately she refocused on her task.

Taking a few more steps through the rubble, she saw what appeared to be the scraped and dusty corner of what might be a wooden crib, poking out of a pile of debris. She was there in seconds, listening carefully, needing to be very sure of where the baby lay so as not to hurt it. 'Hello, hello,' she murmured gently, 'I'm here to help you.' Needing to say some words to steady herself and hoping that the sound of a human voice would prompt some response from the child.

When the next cry came, she knew that she'd been right about the wooden crib. 'I'm coming,' she called, grasping the crib, starting to wriggle it free. Another cry from the baby, much weaker this time. Cora's heart lurched in her chest, what if she was too late? She had no choice but to be bold. With her bloodied hands, she used all her strength to remove some of the larger pieces of debris. Still the crib was stuck, and the baby had gone silent now.

Seeing a length of wood, a discarded spar, she dragged it out from a pile of rubble. Working on pure instinct, she shoved one end beneath the largest stone trapping the crib, using it as a lever. Nothing budged at first. Then, desperate, she used all the strength in her arms and laid her full weight on it. Something shifted. Spurred on, she took a deep breath and, as if her life depended on it, she pushed down with all her might. 'Aaargh!' she cried, angry now, and with a final heave the piece of stone lurched to the side, taking the weight away from the trapped crib.

Panting now, steadying herself, she knew she needed to move delicately. Carefully she grasped the crib, puffing hard with exertion, and edged it free. At the first snuffling sound, her heart leapt with joy. One more move and a dusty shape appeared. Cora felt tears stinging her eyes.

The crib was free now. She took out her flashlight, got down on her hands and knees and slowly, slowly, moved a dust-covered cot blanket. The pale light of the flashlight beam showed her a tiny baby, probably only weeks old. The child was moving its arms and legs freely. She reached in further, ran a hand over the soft body and tiny limbs, checking for injury. 'You seem to be OK,' she whispered soothingly. 'I'm going to move you now, is that all right?'

The baby snuffled in reply and Cora reached in with both hands, pulling the swaddled bundle towards her. Settling back with the small body resting against her chest, she was aware of the thud, thud of her own heart as she ran a hand over the downy, dusty head. The baby blinked opened its eyes, snuffled again then sneezed loudly. Cora rooted in her pocket for her handkerchief and wiped the grime and mucus from the baby's face. Alarmed to see blood come away on the handkerchief, she wiped again, ever so gently. It was nothing more than a scratch on the child's cheek, but it brought more tears to Cora's eyes. Her heart was full, the experience binding her back to the past, to herself and Evie in the moment she was found. Placing her cheek against the infant's head, she breathed in the unmistak-able baby smell as her freely flowing tears made clean tracks down her dusty cheeks.

As she stood up with the child, something fell away from the shawl. It was a feeding bottle, still full of milk. Nimbly, she stooped to pick it up, knowing she would need every drop to feed the baby as soon as she found a sheltered place to stop. Pushing the bottle one-handed into her bag, she slung it across her shoulder, nestling the child in the crook of her arm. She'd sometimes gone out on calls with Evie to visit the newborns of Montauk, she'd seen how her mother handled them, so she wasn't too worried about the position of the child. It was the sheer tininess of the creature that overwhelmed Cora as it squirmed against her body, nuzzling at her chest, rooting for breast milk.

'We're going to struggle with that, I think,' Cora said softly, 'but when we find shelter, I'll give you the contents of this bottle and then hopefully we'll be able to find you more milk from a cow.'

The baby seemed to settle at the sound of her voice, as if they already had an understanding. At least, thank goodness, this little one wasn't like she'd been when Evie had found her in the long grass, screaming blue murder. Life was so strange, one foundling discovering another... all part of the process of war, she thought, but nevertheless it did seem remarkable. As soon as she identified a suitable place to feed the child, she would check the nappy, find out if this was a boy or a girl. Shifting the weight of the baby against her, she walked back through the shattered gateway to the farm, passing the splintered remains of a wooden gate and what had once been a horse's head carved into the stone post. Back on the narrow track as darkness began to fall, it was even more daunting now, facing the end of the day out in the open, with a tiny baby to consider.

She hoped to see the lights of a farmhouse, or at least find a barn where she could shelter, but it seemed as if the bombed-out farmhouse must have been the only habitation for miles around. All she could do was trudge on, feeling some comfort in the warmth of the baby's body nestled against her.

CHAPTER 17

MONTAUK, LONG ISLAND, OCTOBER 1940

Evie couldn't settle, even though she'd been down to the beach once already, something niggled deep inside her today more strongly than ever. The waves were breaking hard on the shore, the roar of the sea as she walked barefoot filled her senses, helped block her wandering thoughts. Still no news of Cora, it tore at her inside, most of her energy spent each day trying to keep her anxiety at bay. Adam wandered through the house distracted. For the first time in his medical career he was forgetting small details, regularly they received telephone calls for prescriptions that should already have been done. If he was challenged, he simply shrugged his shoulders, seemingly untroubled. Never able to voice his thoughts about Cora, it made Evie want to scream with frustration when he had so little to say. He loved their daughter so much and he knew more than anyone how precious Cora was to Evie, but still he walked silently, pale and distracted. It made her want to scream out loud.

She'd started wringing her hands as she walked the beach, an image of desperation, a wreck... that's what her mother would have called her. If only she had a single all-consuming task to work on, but her days went by in a series of individual visits to patients. When she used to gut fish all day long during the herring season, her mind could never wander, and it helped her to stay calm whatever else was going on in her life. She still had her knife, it was tucked away in her old leather medical bag in the box beneath her bed, maybe she could start whittling wood with it. Do something, anything, to try and relieve this perpetual agony. Without the pills that Adam had given her to take at night, she wouldn't be sleeping at all.

What was that? It sounded like a baby. Instantly her body was on alert. When it came again, she realised it was the lone cry of a herring gull overhead, buffeted by the wind. But she couldn't shake off that unsettled feeling, a whispering shift that took her back through the years to Netley hospital, finding Cora, feeling the squirm of her small body against her own as she screamed and kicked her way into her world.

Still not able to shake that restless feeling, Evie stood facing the wind, feeling it strip her hair back from her face. She opened her mouth and screamed out loud, like some ancient spirit of a woman keening for her lost child. She screamed until her throat felt raw. Then, hearing a shouting voice above the wind, she turned to see Adam running towards her, a piece of paper flapping in his hand.

Her heart clutched with fear, she knew it was a telegram.

She daren't look at his face, terrified to see his expression. If bad news had come from France, she didn't want to hear it, she felt as if at the first mention she would set off at a run along the beach, maybe throw herself into the water.

She could hear Adam's voice more clearly now, but the words were snatched away by the wind. In seconds he was beside her, doubled over, gasping for breath. He held out the telegram. She couldn't take it from him, he would have to tell her, she could not read it for herself.

As soon as he was able, he choked out some words... 'It's Iris, she's safe in Portugal, she has passage on a ship to New York.'

Evie felt pure anger surge through her body. 'Iris!' she spat, ripping the telegram from Adam's hand, her eyes scanning it. 'What about Cora, there's no mention of Cora!'

Adam tried to put his arms around her but she pushed him away, unable to bear his touch, blaming him for not being able to break the news more carefully. How had he not been able to see that she was going to think the telegram was about Cora, and he already knew how furious she was over Iris's failure to send their daughter straight home once the declaration of war had become inevitable. What was wrong with him? Why couldn't he be more attuned to her needs? And what about Iris? She'd always been her closest friend, why hadn't she acted in her best interest? More furious now than ever, Evie ripped the telegram into tiny pieces and let it fly in the wind.

CHAPTER 18

As Cora walked in the dark, guided only by the beam of her sputtering flashlight, it began to rain. She tucked the sleeping baby inside her gaberdine mac, grateful that she'd at least found a sheltered spot to feed the child with milk from the bottle and check the nappy. It was a girl; she'd found a girl. And thank goodness, apart from the scratch on her cheek, the infant was uninjured and able to suck greedily from the bottle. Cora knew she couldn't walk much further, she couldn't even remember how long it was since she'd had food or drink and with all the adrenaline that had surged through her body as she'd searched for the baby, she was exhausted now, almost on her knees. If it hadn't been for the small, warm body tucked into her coat, she would, at this point, probably have slumped beneath a tree and closed her eyes, sat there in the rain until she got so cold she couldn't feel anything anymore.

Instead, she willed herself to take one step after another, each one jarring her painful bones and muscles. She knew if they both got soaked through, the baby would not be able to survive the resulting drop in temperature. Praying now for shelter, she trudged on, barely able to see her way. The track was muddy but still Cora kept going, sure that she could see wheel marks. Just when she was about to sink to her knees, she spotted a discarded tarpaulin by the side of the road. It was the only chance at shelter she had. A darker patch, a dip alongside the track, thankfully not a ditch running with water but more of a trench about four feet deep. Careful with the sleeping child, she lowered herself in, pulling the tarpaulin over, making it straddle the trench to provide basic shelter. It smelt musty but it did the trick and as Cora slumped down with her back against the stony soil of the trench wall, still cradling the baby against her body, she felt relieved to hear the rain gently drumming on the canvas above their heads. With barely enough room to sit with her knees bent, she had no choice but to wait till morning. Then she would follow the tyre tracks that she'd spotted to try and find milk for the baby.

Shivering with cold, jammed against the earthy wall of the trench, she believed there was little chance of catching any sleep, but she must have nodded off. She woke groggy with her arms and legs numb, feeling the baby squirming against her, starting to grizzle. 'There is no more milk, my sweet, not yet' she croaked, fighting for enough breath to speak. Lapsing into a drowsy, unnatural semi-conscious state she wondered if maybe she was dying. Making herself think of home, of walking on the beach with her mother by her side and the sun on her face, she kept herself alert for a while longer. Then she was sure she was at home in her bed in the house by the sea and Evie was singing one of her Scottish ballads as she tucked her in. Cora felt content, knowing she was warm and safe, that she could prop- erly sleep now, without any cares in the world.

Later, annoyed to be woken from her heavenly place, she was angry. She felt her body shifting, she was unable to resist and then the pressure of something on her face, on her lips. Warm breath, air, in her mouth. She wanted to push this thing away, but it was persis- tent, unyielding. She started to cough, twist her face to the side and then she heard a voice, a man's voice, he was speaking in German. A panic went through her, had she been captured? She groaned, wanting to open her eyes but she couldn't force her eyelids apart.

The voice came again, it was calm, soothing, but she couldn't be persuaded by a voice of the enemy. Then a softness, someone was gently wiping her face. It made her feel cared for, loved. She still couldn't move her body and her breath felt stiff, caught in her chest. More pressure on her lips, warm air, like a kiss. Gasping, coughing now, she pushed with her arms, blinking in the light. A smiling face gazed down at her, a young man in uniform, German uniform. 'Did you kiss me?' she croaked in English, rubbing a hand across her lips. 'Get off me!'

The man was laughing, as if it was the biggest joke in the world.

'Kiss of life,' he said, 'You couldn't breathe, I gave you the kiss of life.'

Cora was sitting up now, bright daylight hurting her eyes, she'd been pulled up out of the trench.

'Where is the baby?' she tried to shout, but her voice came out no more than a hoarse whisper.

'Baby is safe,' he grinned, pointing to his uniform jacket on the ground, the infant contentedly sleeping wrapped in a cocoon.

Cora's mind was reeling, 'How... what?' was all she was able to stutter.

'I was passing by this morning, I am lost, looking for my battalion, I heard your baby cry... so I pulled back the canvas and there you were, slumped on your side and the baby was very upset. I knew the little one was doing OK, but you were white and cold, you looked dead.'

Cora felt her heart squeeze with horror.

'So, I dragged you up and out of that ditch and I gave you the kiss of life and now you are alive.'

Tears welled in her eyes, she blinked hard to hold them back, but they spilled down her cheeks.

She knew she should thank him, be grateful to him for the rest of her life, but right at this moment, she couldn't trust him. He'd heard her speak English, maybe he'd been in Paris recently, perhaps he knew they were searching for an American girl.

Studying his face, she saw big eyes, dark hair cropped close to his head. His mouth curved up at the corners even though he wasn't actively smiling. He had the most beautiful face she'd ever seen but she couldn't let herself be fooled. He was a German soldier and she'd seen with what Madeleine had endured, exactly what could happen if one became too friendly with the enemy.

'We need to find shelter for you and your baby, there are houses along the road.'

She was shaking her head, 'No, she isn't my baby, I found her in a bombed-out house, pulled her out of the rubble.'

'Wow,' he said, blowing out a breath. 'This is quite something, is it not? You save the baby, then I save you.'

'Yes,' she said, feeling incredulous herself. He had to be a force for good, she told herself, knowing, despite the wedge of resistance lodged deep inside her, there was no other way she would be able to get herself and the baby to shelter.

As he hauled her up from the ground, she felt dizzy and the world swam before her eyes. 'Whoa... don't worry, I've got you.' His English was American-sounding, friendly. There was no other option, she had to let him support her. Holding on to her with one arm, he stooped down to collect the baby and his uniform jacket with the other. 'Now, let's go,' he said, expertly cradling the child and hooking his other arm under her shoulder, nestling her against his body. 'Can you walk?' he asked with such gentleness, she could have cried.

'Yes,' she said as curtly as she could muster, then stumbling and needing him to help steady her.

'It isn't far,' he soothed, 'I called by there earlier to ask for some milk.'

Who was this man with his kiss of life and his milk?

Even with her first few steps, Cora's heart was pounding and her lungs simply couldn't catch up. He slowed his pace, his voice low, trying to ease her, 'It's not far, you can do it...' and then when she started to sag against his body, 'Let's stop for a minute, hey.'

In that stillness, Cora heard the gentle snufflings of the baby, felt his strong body holding her fast, got back enough strength to take a few more steps.

'You need food and rest,' he murmured, 'you've been on a long march without sustenance.'

Cora swallowed hard to stop herself from crying. She didn't have the extra energy to expend.

'If this takes the rest of my life, I'm going to get you to that cottage,' he said softly, starting to chuckle. 'This is my mission now, finding my comrades... that can wait.'

Even though she held harsh resistance to the young soldier who wore the same uniform as the man who had shot her not so long ago, she had no choice but to let him assist her, she could not have made this journey on her own.

When the baby started to grizzle, the soldier gently rocked his other arm, singing a German lullaby, until the infant stilled.

'Not far now, just ten more steps,' were his next words.

Cora's lungs felt raw, she was counting each painful step, feeling as if her ordeal would never end. She felt him shift his grip, to hold her more firmly against the side of his body.

Afterwards, she remembered seeing the white peeling walls and the low wooden door of a cottage, but the rest was a blank. When she woke on a low couch, she thought for a moment that she was at home in Montauk. But the smell was all wrong, there were wooden beams above her head and the low murmur of voices in the background were a mixture of French and German.

With the piercing cry of a baby, awareness shot through her. Raising herself up on her elbow, she looked towards the other end of the one room, the soldier who had saved her seemed relaxed at the table, he ran a slow hand through his dark hair. Turning his head, as if sensing she was rousing, he got up from his seat with a smile.

'You are awake, how are you feeling?' he said, striding across the space. He was tall, well-muscled and he blocked the light from the window behind him. He crouched at the side of the settee, gazing at her, his face full of concern. Her last bit of resistance simply melted away.

When it came, her voice was weak, croaky, it didn't even sound like her own, but she was able to say thank you and then ask about the baby.

His eyes were hazel, flecked with gold, and the faint lines at the corners turned up when he smiled. 'The baby is fine; she is drinking more milk than Madame Fournier's one cow can provide. Cora glanced past him, to a middle-aged woman with a heart-shaped face and a wild mass of sun-bleached hair held back by a black ribbon. She was completely absorbed by feeding the baby from the glass bottle that Cora had found.

'Have you asked her, does she know who the baby might belong to?'

'No, not yet, but she might when you are able to tell her exactly where you found her.'

Cora made to get up, to walk over there and give the information immediately.

'*Nein, nein*, you don't need to do that right now,' he said, placing a gentle hand on her chest and urging her to lie back down. 'You need to rest up, I have warm milk and honey for you to drink, then you will need solid food and after that you should feel stronger.'

She knew he was right, but she lay down reluctantly. Only she understood how crucial it was to establish whether the baby's family could be found.

As he rose from the settee, she asked him his name.

'I am Max Heller,' he said, with a broad smile... 'and you?'

'Cora,' she said, without thinking, feeling dread clutch her heart when she realised she'd revealed her true name.

'Cora,' he repeated, smiling again, 'that's a nice name... and I can tell by your accent you are an American.'

'Yes,' she gasped, clinging to the notion that unless her country had declared war in the last few days, she was from a neutral country and given the distance she'd travelled from Paris, this one lone soldier, separated from his unit, was unlikely to have heard of a young American woman wanted for spying.

When he came back with her milk, he pulled over a small side table to put the cup on, then crouched down again beside the settee. 'I spent a year in New York, just before the war,' he said.

'Oh,' she remarked, surprised.

'Yes, indeed, my father lives in Brooklyn, he emigrated when I was a young boy. We were meant to go to live there with him, but my mom didn't want to leave her family in Hamburg, so we remained in Germany.'

She saw him take a breath, then he smiled, 'I might have stayed in New York, maybe I should have, but my mom got sick, so I had to go back to make sure she was OK.'

'Is she all right, has she recovered?' Cora asked.

'Yeh, she's stronger now, she had pneumonia and its left her short of breath but she's all right, and now of course, I've ended up in the army as well, so...'

It came back with a jolt to Cora, him being an enemy

soldier. Their conversation had seemed so normal, she'd almost forgotten.

She cleared her throat, tried to adopt a more formal tone. 'Did you like New York?'

'Yes, I did... from the first sighting of the Statue of Liberty, I fell in love.'

'Well, that's good,' she offered, wanting to tell him about her own family, about where she lived, but he was a German soldier, the same as the man who had shot her in Paris. And maybe, who knows, maybe this was a tactic to disarm her, get information. She'd accidentally blurted out her real name, she was right to hold back any further detail, she had to be very careful.

Noticing a fresh bruise around his right eye, she began to wonder what had happened to him, why he was not with his fellow soldiers. 'How long have you been separated from your unit?'

'Two days... we were hit by an air strike. I don't remember much, but when I came to, I'd been thrown from the truck and my friend, the driver, he was dead...'

He lowered his head, swallowed hard. Instinctively, she reached out to place a gentle hand on his arm. 'I'm so sorry to hear that.'

He was silent for a few moments, then he raised his head, his eyes shiny with tears. When he spoke again his voice was tight, 'I left him there, made him decent, covered his body with branches. Then I stumbled away, dazed in the head, trying to find somebody, anybody, who might help. We'd been bringing up the rear, so I knew it would be a while before they came back to look for us. And even if they did, I'd wandered way off track by then. It wasn't until just before I found you and the baby, that I stumbled upon this cottage and Madame Fournier gave me food and drink.'

They both gazed over to their saviour, her head was bowed, she was still feeding the baby.

'Her husband died years ago, she has no children, she lives here alone with one cow and a few hens.'

'Thank goodness for her... and for you,' she said.

He shrugged, offered a small smile, 'I'm so glad I found you both, my sister has a child, a little girl, she looked so much like this one when she was a baby, it was as if it was meant to be, hey.'

Cora felt her breath catch, she didn't want to go into her own circumstances but already in her young life she'd been rescued three times – by Evie, by the Resistance fighters in Paris, and now by a young German soldier. It felt overwhelming, so much so she emitted an audible sigh.

'You need to rest,' he said, his forehead creasing into a worry line.

She nodded, offered a weak smile.

'Drink your milk, and I'll go and find you something to eat.'

Later, when Cora was strong enough to sit propped up with cushions on the settee, Max brought the baby to her and she sat holding the tiny creature, watching her eyes blink open and then her fingers splay in contentment as she drifted off to sleep, her tiny rosebud mouth still working in a lazy suckle. Cora used her free hand to smooth the single tuft of dark fluffy hair, she leaned in to breathe that special newborn smell. It made her feel heady, intoxicated, like one of the new mothers she'd visited with Evie when she'd been helping on the post-natal rounds. Exhausted but strangely content and in awe of the tiny bundle of life that lay in their arms.

Madame Fournier approached tentatively, trying out a few words in English.

As soon as Cora replied in fluent French, the older woman's face lit up with a smile. As Cora told her the story of the baby's finding, Madame listened carefully, nodding here and there, reaching out a hand to gently stroke the infant's head when Cora spoke of the dead woman at the bombed-out house, probably the child's mother.

Madame Fournier frowned thoughtfully, trying to think through who the family of the baby might be. She wasn't sure at first, she sighed, knitted her brow again, but then when Cora mentioned the horse's head carved into the farm gate post, she became animated, speaking forcefully. They were new tenants of that farm, a young couple who had come to church in the village only once but then she'd heard a rumour that the woman had fallen pregnant when her husband had been home on leave from the French army. She didn't know of any other relatives in the area, but she would make enquiries with the local priest.

Cora felt torn – she was delighted there might be a lead but when she gazed down to the baby girl, her eyes began to fill with tears. She'd already formed a deep bond with her foundling ... only now did she begin to realise how it must have been for Evie, the strength of the bond Cora already had with the baby was breathtaking.

Over the next two days Cora ate and drank and grew strong again – as did the baby. Max laughed that Madame Fournier's cow was working overtime and she should be given a medal at the end of the war for saving lives. In the special bubble where they temporarily existed it was easy to imagine that the war couldn't touch them. But then when the drone of allied planes came overhead, they were all jolted back to reality. They knew this had to end, it was only a question of time.

As they waited for news about the baby's family, Cora found it impossible to hold back from the cuddles and kisses she felt driven to give the foundling child. Max was the same and he showed no sign of continuing the search for his unit. The few days they had together ticked by peacefully. Then when news came with a message delivered to the door that the baby's father was thought to be alive, but in a German prison camp, Cora knew that change was coming. Madame Fournier had already said she would keep the child till her family came to claim her, so it should have been easy and of course it was for the best. But Cora felt the news clutch at her heart, even though it would have been impossible for her to take the child on her hazardous journey towards Calais, she felt the ache of separation already.

Only now did she have some idea of how Evie must have fallen in love with her, even in a few short days. It made pieces of the puzzle slip into place... and she understood more fully why Evie had been so devastated when she'd first mentioned the need to actively search for her birth mother. Evie had managed to cover it well, but Cora had still caught glimmers of it – not so much in what was said out loud, but what was left unsaid. It made her want to be home even more urgently, so she could give her mother a hug and tell her how much she loved and appreciated everything she'd done so willingly, so selflessly for all these years.

Hearing the gentle murmur of the baby as she began to stir awake in the basket weave cradle Madame Fournier had been able to secure from a local farmer's wife, Cora felt a painful lurch at what was coming. Thoughts of the baby were inextricably linked to Max now as well; he'd saved both their lives. Snatched memories slid through her mind, appearing and receding – waking from Max's kiss of life to find him leaning over her, the way he supported her while cradling the baby in his other arm. So gently, so carefully. She swallowed the lump in her throat, she walked to the crib to gaze down as the tiny child blinked open her eyes and thrust out an arm from the knitted shawl that had been provided by another neighbour of Madame Fournier's.

Cora reached down to stroke the baby's face, speaking softly, telling her how beautiful she was, how Madame Fournier was going to look after her so well until the war was over. She was sure the child smiled back at her. *Could this be a first smile? How old were babies when it happened?*

'Are you smiling?' she urged, smoothing a hand over the baby's downy head. 'Yes, you are, aren't you,' she beamed, seeing a definite upturning of the baby's mouth. 'Madame Fournier, look,' she called, 'the baby is smiling.'

Madame was there in an instant, 'Aw, yes, you are smiling, aren't you,' she cooed, standing side by side with Cora, both of them basking in the moment. Then, as the baby started to kick her legs and make the grizzly noises she used when she was ready for her bottle, Cora picked her up from the cot, cradled the tiny, warm body against her chest, making the most of what would probably be her last cuddle. As Madame prepared the bottle, she walked up and down, gently rocking the child, singing the '*Mary, Mary, Quite Contrary*' nursery rhyme that had been a favourite of Evie's. Once she handed the hungry infant back to Madame Fournier, she felt a gentle tearing in her chest. Already she was saying goodbye, not with her mind but with her body.

Max had been out foraging for wood for the kitchen stove, she saw her own emotions reflected on his face instantly when he came through the door and heard the news of the baby's first smile. Then when she told him that the child's father was alive but in a German prison camp, the imminent change in their circumstances showed in the set of his mouth, the thoughtful way he stared into space.

In the next moment he was checking with Madame Fournier that she was still willing to take on the care of the baby. 'Of course, of course,' she smiled, nodding her head.

Instantly, he pulled out his wallet, gave Madame Fournier all the money he had. And then Cora went to her gaberdine mac and rooted in the pocket, the gold ring that she'd taken from the child's dead mother was still there, she gave that to

Madame as well. Thanking her over and over for the help she'd given to her, the baby and to Max.

Madame gratefully accepted their gifts but then waved away all mention of her hospitality, 'What was I going to do, turn you all away?'

'Are you going to be all right, alone with the baby?' Cora asked. 'It might be years till her father comes home.'

Madame Fournier smoothed down her apron, 'But that's the thing, I've been here alone ever since my dear Pierre died. Now, I have a baby to take care of so I will be busy, doing good work and never lonely. I always wanted children, but they never came. Maybe this is God's way of giving me that opportunity now,' she smiled. 'And what's more, so long as I have my cow and the help of the priest, I will manage very well.'

Cora admired Madame Fournier's determination and it made her feel confident in leaving the foundling baby with her. But then there was Max. In these few short days, she'd gotten used to having him around, grown to enjoy his easy ways and his beautiful smile. But she had no choice except to move on – Francine's contact in Calais would be wondering what had happened to her. Maybe word had been sent back to Francine that she was missing and she was already frantic with worry. The world was waiting for her and for Max to return to their opposing sides. Seeing Max expertly take the baby from Madame Fournier and settle her in the crook of his arm made her heart ache, she was going to miss him so much.

As he stood rocking the baby, Max looked across the room directly at her. He straightened his back, drew in a breath, and Cora knew what he was going to say, even before he opened his mouth. 'We should leave tomorrow,' the words felt sombre.

'Yes,' Cora said, feeling like a bubble had burst.

That evening, once the baby and Madame Fournier were settled and sleeping, knowing this was their last night together, Cora and Max crept out of the cottage to discuss final plans. 'As soon as it's light, Cora, you need to move, that way,' he pointed firmly in the direction of the nearest town where she would be able to board a train to Calais.

She inhaled deeply, nodded, not knowing what to say to him now, feeling almost as awkward as when she'd come to after he'd rescued her and found him right there, hovering over her. Leaning on the whitewashed stone wall that surrounded the cottage garden, she let the strengthening breeze strip back the hair from her face. Closing her eyes for a moment, she drew in the rhythm of the wind as it rustled the dry autumn leaves in the trees. The rise and fall of it tying her to the sound of the waves on Montauk beach. Aware of Max's presence beside her, Cora could feel the warmth of him. His proximity created a buzz of expectation, electricity flitting between them. She felt it in the pit of her stomach. It had grown day by day as they'd worked together to care for the baby, to chop wood for Madame Fournier and to sit on their opposite sides of the table. Even though she'd tried with every fibre of her being to resist what-ever had been set in motion from the moment he'd found her, she knew now, with every rustle of the wind in the leaves, with every synchronised breath she drew in, that she could no longer resist.

As they stood together, almost touching, Cora saw him with his head back, his eyes closed, feeling the breeze on his face. She knew she would never get another opportunity. She turned to him, stepped boldly right up close and put her arms around him. He responded instantly, drawing her to him. The musky smell of him, the feel of his warm body sent a frisson through her. When the kiss came it was gentle at first, already known. She gasped with pleasure, knowing that she'd never been kissed like this by anyone before. Feeling the powerful thud of his heart through his shirt, they pressed harder together. This was everything she wanted, but completely unbearable all at the same time.

As they clung together, the moment spooled on as the air around them began to shift, move with a stronger breeze. Some of the dried leaves were coming in their direction now as the waves of rustling intensified, tying Cora back to the sound of the ocean, the pulse of life she'd grown up with. It made her body sing.

She kissed him again, then knowing that she would have to walk away from him tomorrow, she disengaged from the embrace and wiped away a tear with the heel of her hand. Drawing back a little further, she started to speak of Long Island and her home in Montauk, the house beside the sea, the breaking of the waves on the beach. She even told him that her father was the local doctor, her mother a midwife who loved to walk the beach and wade into the sea. As the words flowed, she tried to see herself back there, distance herself from how she felt right now, here in the dark with a German soldier, far away from home.

He pulled her close again, nuzzled his face in her hair, breathed her in. 'Maybe when the war is over, I will go to Brooklyn to see my father and we will meet again. What do you think about th...'

He faltered at the sound of engines in the far distance. Cora imagined army trucks bumping over the rough track of road which they'd followed to get to the cottage those few days ago. They both gasped, pulled apart.

As they stood, straining their ears for further sound, the air fell quiet. They sighed together. 'Even if that isn't German army trucks looking for a poor lost soldier... I'm sorry to say, but it's time for us to move on, isn't it?' Max said quietly.

She linked his arm, pulled him close, feeling her voice catch as she replied, 'Yes, I suppose it is.'

He motioned for them to head back towards the house. Hesitating for a few moments on the doorstep, she sensed he was weighing up the best option. 'We should both be safe here for one more night, but you definitely need to get going first thing in the morning. Whatever happens, I will stay with Madame Fournier until I'm sure the army are close, she has been so good to us both, I want to help her as much as I can.'

'Yes, of course, I'm so glad you are going to do that.' Then Cora stiffened, suddenly caught by anxiety for the baby.

'Don't worry, I'll make sure Madame Fournier and the baby are safe and everything is sorted before I leave,' he soothed, 'And when the army come, I won't say a word about you and how I found you.'

Cora felt her chest ache with longing, 'Thank you,' was all that came when at last she could speak. When all she wanted was to shout to the sky and the wind, 'I love you, I love you.'

He pulled her into a tight embrace, crushing her body against him, it was agonising. 'I'll see you in the morning, before dawn,' he murmured at last, stepping back, walking away.

She felt tears sting her eyes, she wanted to go after him, draw him into another embrace, but that wouldn't alter the fact that they would need to go their separate ways tomorrow. She had no other choice, she would have to go inside, pack her bag, snatch a few hours' sleep and be ready to leave at sunrise.

When Cora gasped awake the next morning after a troubled sleep, she dressed quickly. Peering through the half-light she was able to make out the shape of Madame Fournier at the kitchen table feeding the baby from the bottle. She walked through, murmured a good morning to Madame and then reached out to stroke the baby's silken head.

'For now, until her father returns, I have given her my mother's name,' Madame said, looking up with a smile. 'What do you think of Mathilde?'

'I think it is perfect,' Cora smiled, gently reaching out to stroke the baby's head for one last time.

'I have packed food and drink for you...' Madame Fournier murmured. Then with a mischievous smile, 'And yes, he's already been in to tell me what's happening.'

Cora felt a stab of grief. 'He saved my life and the baby's. It will be so strange to leave him behind.'

Madame Fournier reached out a hand to her. 'I know, my child, I know... I have really warmed to Max as well, but we do still need to remember that he is a German soldier, ultimately... he is the enemy.'

Cora felt it like a punch. Her instinct was to jump to his defence, say something along the lines of yes, but first and foremost he is a man. But where would that place her, in the eyes of Madame Fournier? Would she be seen as a collaborator?

It made her feel sick to the stomach, knowing that someone as kindly as Madame Fournier could judge Max simply by the uniform he wore. Yes, she understood the conflict, she'd felt it herself at first, but once she'd seen how genuine he was... he was an enemy soldier, but he'd saved her life and the life of the baby. There had to be a place in the world for the goodness of humans, no matter where their allegiance lay.

As she walked away from the cottage, she heard the door click open, and she turned to see Max's tousled head appear. She raised a hand in farewell as he stood at the door, watching her go, his face reflecting the pain of their parting. Swallowing hard to keep back her sorrow, she paused for a few seconds as he smiled and blew her a kiss, before bowing his head and re-entering the cottage.

She turned back in the direction she was headed, stood motionless, staring for a few moments along the stony track. As she took the first step, she felt something deep inside her chest start to shift and tear. She pressed the heel of her hand to her breastbone, made herself put one foot in front of the other. There was no choice, there was nothing else she could do right now except keep on walking. Even if she stayed on in the cottage, Max would have to go back to his unit anyway and then she'd be worrying about Francine not knowing what had happened to her and her parents still waiting for news. This was the only choice.

The further she walked, with just the crunch of her own footsteps on the stone track, the more she made herself believe in her decision. At least she had food and drink in her canvas bag, her false identity card was securely stashed in an inside pocket, and she knew exactly which direction to take for the railway station. She'd thought of swearing Max to secrecy over her real name, but it would only have raised suspicion. He had already expressed his concern for her safety, aware that a lone American woman walking through the countryside might be picked up by his fellow German soldiers and questioned.

She'd been the one to reassure him that she knew how to keep herself safe and she would be vigilant. He had no idea of what she'd been doing in Paris, it would have been impossible to tell him any of that, but she sensed that he knew there was something askew. He'd never even asked any questions about why, exactly, she was heading for Calais, a city that was fully occupied and fortified by the German army.

She walked briskly, glad of the returning strength in her legs, using the physical activity as an antidote to the residual ache in the pit of her stomach. It would take a while to stop thinking about Max, but she would do it. Maybe, in the end, all that would remain would be an unseen thread, stretching between them. She would probably never find out what happened to him and it made her feel desperately sad. A shudder ran through her body at the idea of never knowing whether he'd survive the war. She made herself march more determinedly, trying to dispel the whisper of that simple, destructive thought.

CHAPTER 19

The port of Calais was almost destroyed – buildings were gutted, rubble and rusting metal shells of cars and trucks littered the streets. As Cora walked the final distance to the Hotel Genevieve, she saw the skeletal remains of a canopy that still clung to the wall of what must have been a street cafe. The shattered buildings with their empty, glassless windows, a scrap of curtain from one blowing back and forth in the breeze. It made her heart squeeze tight with sorrow, she had seen nothing like this in Paris, but Calais had been bombed and shattered first by the Germans as part of their march into France and now that it was occupied, it was being regularly blasted by the British and the allies. All for having strategic importance as a port poised for a crossing of the Channel.

Bertrand had told her stories of Calais during the last war, when his leg had been blasted by a shell in the trenches, he'd been transferred to the hospital here. He'd also known some of the history going back through Napoleon to the Roman Empire. All armies gathered and stood ready to cross the Channel at this point. It sent a shiver down her spine; she was amidst such history yet heavy artillery and air strikes were grinding Calais slowly down to a pile of rubble. What would there be left at the end of this war?

Startled by the sudden appearance of an army motorbike carrying two German soldiers, the one on the back smoking a cigarette, Cora put her head down and picked up her pace. She missed the ease of wearing her slacks and sneakers, but dressing conventionally and in dark, worn clothing gave her much better cover. The motorbike puttered by without so much as a glance in her direction from the soldiers. They seemed deep in some conversation, the one on the back starting to laugh uproariously.

As she approached the dock area, Cora quickly picked out the ancient watchtower, the landmark which Bertrand had spoken of. It now rose from a landscape of rubble, remarkable that it still stood after all the air raids and artillery fire. He'd told her the Hotel Genevieve lay directly across from the watchtower and there it was, the only building standing at the end of a row of other structures shattered and broken. Some of the windows were cracked, others boarded up, but the walls of the hotel stood firm.

Cora walked up two stone steps to knock at a door peppered with bullet holes and to ring the ornate iron doorbell. She could hear it echoing inside what seemed to be an empty building. Then the staccato tap of heels on a hard floor and the door opened a crack.

'What?' a voice called through the nick.

Cora was careful to use the exact words that had been schooled into her by Francine. 'I am Simone Devereux, sent from Paris for work.'

The door creaked open. A tall, very thin woman with sharp cheekbones and wavy chestnut hair, greying at the roots, stood eyeing Cora up and down, a cigarette clamped in the corner of her mouth. Narrowing her eyes against the smoke, she croaked, 'You'd better come in.'

Cora drew in a breath, stepped tentatively across the threshold.

The woman took a drag of the cigarette, then removed it from her mouth.

'You're late, I thought you weren't coming... I had to let Francine know.'

Cora gasped, 'Oh, I hope she wasn't worried.'

'She hasn't got back to me,' the woman declared, her voice matter of fact. 'Don't worry about Francine, she can handle herself. Me and her go way back to when she worked in my mother's cafe here in Calais, long before the last war.'

Cora was about to express her surprise, but she was cut off by the woman: 'The thing is, you've missed your connection now, so you'll have to wait till we can make other arrangements. I'll show you to your room,' she said, impatiently beckoning for her to follow and then walking quickly to the bottom of a set of dark wood stairs. 'I won't be asking for money for board and lodgings, but you'll be helping with cleaning the rooms and waiting on tables for the gentlemen who lodge here until we can get you moved,' she called over her shoulder. 'I'll need you tonight and then for breakfast in the morning, eight a.m. sharp.'

'Yes, all right,' Cora gasped, struggling to keep up as she followed the wiry, chestnut-haired woman up the winding stairs.

'This is your room... the attic,' the woman offered abruptly, pushing open a pitted, white-painted door.

'Thank you,' Cora tried to smile, 'and what is your name?'

The woman narrowed her eyes against the curl of smoke rising from the cigarette in the corner of her mouth. 'Well, the gentlemen who lodge here, they call me Edith Piaf,' she offered, her voice gravelly, 'because I sing every evening in the dining room.'

The spartan attic room was daunting – a narrow, sagging bed with a greasy patchwork counterpane on dusty wooden floorboards. A stained sink in one corner with a cracked, fly-spotted mirror above and a slit of a window high up on the wall. Cora heaved a sigh as she placed her bag down on the bed then shrugged off her coat. All day she'd kept thoughts of Max at bay, but now she ached for his smile, his calming voice. Hopefully it wouldn't be too long before her new escape route was secured.

Suddenly weary, she lowered herself onto the bed, the springs creaking beneath her weight. In that moment she could have sat there and wept, but the strange groaning sound from the bed made her belly start to niggle with a laugh. How on earth had she ended up here from Iris's luxury apartment with a view of the Eiffel Tower. It was so ludicrous, it made her want to chuckle. Thinking of the woman who called herself Edith Piaf and the scathing view she would take, Cora had to work even harder to hold back a snort of laughter.

Standing up from the squeaky bed which complained just as loudly as she relieved the pressure, she quickly unpacked her bag into a small locker. Seeing a greyish white apron folded on top of the cupboard, she donned it over her worn black skirt and plain white blouse. Might as well start work straight away, she thought to herself as she descended the stairs through two floors, each a corridor with numbered discreetly closed doors, not a sound to be heard.

Edith Piaf raised both plucked eyebrows when Cora appeared in the kitchen. Seeing a pile of washing-up in the sink, she walked briskly across the room, 'Do you want me to start with these?'

Edith straightened in her kitchen chair, tapped the ash from her cigarette into an ornate glass ashtray. 'Yes, feel free,' she said, 'then you can help me set the tables for the evening meal... We have eight gentlemen currently boarding; they are German officials working at the Hotel de Ville, the town hall. They have very exacting standards.'

'Is there anything specific I need to know about them?' Cora asked, pushing up her sleeves, starting to run the water.

'They are German officials, beyond that, it's best not to know anything or ask questions. Too much knowledge can cause trouble.'

As she turned from the sink, Cora saw Edith draw a finger across her throat and make a slitting sound.

She focused her attention on vigorously scouring the pots and pans.

When the tables were set and large pans of stew and boiled potatoes stood waiting for the guests, Cora was surprised to see all eight men in dark suits – some paunchy, middle-aged – proceed into the dining room to take their seats. Thankfully, they ate their meal quietly with occasional bursts of murmured conversation and displayed little interest in their new waitress. As Cora served the two tables, she caught snatches of conversation – mostly about bookkeeping, some about vessels in and out of the port. Clearly, the men thought that none of their German conversation would be understood because they seemed to speak freely about their work in the town hall. Already Cora's mind was ticking over the potential for gleaning information, a spark from her time in Paris that hadn't yet died. She was sure that Estelle and Bertrand would be interested in these conversations.

'Hey, waitress,' a pale-faced younger-looking man called, snapping his fingers, 'we need some wine.'

Cora returned to the kitchen. Edith had changed into a flowing robe with a colourful peacock pattern, her hair was up in a loose chignon and she was reading a magazine at the table, another cigarette clamped in the corner of her mouth.

'Where's the wine?' Cora asked.

Edith pointed a long, elegant finger with dark red nail varnish to a small table in the corner of the kitchen where four carafes of red wine stood ready. 'Take them in two at a time, one for each table, then serve the rest later when they are ready.'

Cora did as she was told, none of the men acknowledging her service in any way whatsoever.

After slices of cake and some hard-baked biscuits had been served, the men leaned back in their seats to light their ciga-rettes, ready for a second glass of wine. At this point Edith appeared through the door and walked to the far end of the room. A murmur of approval rippled through the men. Cora stood fascinated, an empty glass carafe in her hand.

Edith cleared her throat, then began to croon a song in French. Her voice was earthy, full of feeling and perfectly in tune. When she started to sing 'Lili Marlene' in German, Cora felt that painful lump she'd tried to subdue as she'd said goodbye to Max fight its way back into her throat. She knew exactly why her hostess had been nicknamed Edith Piaf, her voice made Cora's heart twist as she stood transfixed, the song taking her back to kissing Max as the wind rustled the leaves and then the next morning, the wrench of pain as she was forced to walk away and leave him standing at the cottage door. She drew in a ragged breath, but the feeling of loss released by the song stayed with her. Tightly gripping the wooden tray she held in both hands to stop her body from shaking, she knew she was fighting against all that had happened to her in the months since Paris had been occupied.

As Edith's poignant voice brought the final heart-wrenching notes of *Lilli Marlene* to a close, Cora swallowed hard, readied herself to start clearing the tables. She knew there was a mass of sorrow waiting for her, but it would have to bide its time... she couldn't begin to confront it here in the active midst of war. It would have to wait until she was safely home in Montauk.

The audience gave Edith rousing applause and begged for more. She waved a hand at the men drinking wine at their tables, pretended to say no, but then with a mischievous smile,

she began another number which drew an instant cheer –
Marlene Dietrich's 'The Boys in the Back Room'. The lively
song filled the room with energy, some of the men were
animated, swaying from side to side. Again, it brought back
vivid memories for Cora, she'd seen the film which featured the
song back home with Evie on a trip to New York, shortly before
she'd left for Paris.

After coffee, the gentlemen retired to their rooms and Cora
was again washing up, while Edith sat smoking at the table. 'You
sing so beautifully,' she had to say, even though the shrug she
got in return was dismissive. 'It made me think of when—'

'Nah,' Edith interjected, 'I'm not really interested in what it
made you think of... we are where we are, here, in a war. No
point harking back to past times. Life is grim, sweetie, let's get
on with it.'

Cora swallowed hard; she didn't have an answer to that.
Instead, she scrubbed a large iron pan with extra vigour.

When a knock came to the back door, Edith tutted, then
rose from her seat. 'Who the hell is that at this time of night?'

Hearing her shocked cry after opening the door, Cora threw
down her dishcloth and ran. Edith was holding up an old
woman, bent over, breathless, her grey hair dishevelled. Edith's
voice was soothing, cradling the woman wrapped in an over-
sized black coat, a brimmed hat pulled down low over her face.

'Please sit down,' she crooned, gesturing desperately for
Cora to pull a wooden chair across from the kitchen table.

Only when the woman collapsed onto the seat and straightened her back, did Cora realise who the windswept figure was.
'Francine,' she cried, a sob catching at her voice.

Francine attempted a wobbly smile, she tried to croak out a
greeting, but it set her off coughing. A deep, vicious sound
which racked her body and left her gasping for breath.

'Why did you come here, why did you make this journey?'
Edith called out, exasperated.

'I was worried,' Francine croaked between breaths, then she pointed at Cora. 'I was worried about her; we had no news.'

Cora was in tears now, her throat so tight she couldn't speak. Instead, she put an arm around Francine's shoulders. 'I'm so sorry, my train was derailed by an air attack... I had to go on the run, hide out in the countryside, I've only just got here.'

Francine's eyes lit up then, she was nodding, 'I'm so glad you are safe.'

'You shouldn't have made this long journey, look at you,' Edith's voice had a hard edge which matched the glance she threw in Cora's direction.

Francine was shaking her head, starting to chuckle. 'Oh, I got sick before I started out on the journey and when the doctor came, he wasn't happy with my condition.'

Cora having stopped crying, now felt her throat tighten once more. 'You should have stayed at home, Francine, waited till you were better.'

She felt Francine shrug her shoulders, then she placed a gnarled hand over Cora's. 'I'm sorry to say that I'm not going to get better from this, *ma chérie.*'

'What do you mean you're not going to get better, what is it?' Edith almost shrieked.

Cora felt Francine draw in a laboured breath.

'It's cancer. Lung cancer.'

The words hung in the air, stunning Cora and even Edith to silence.

'How long have you got?' Edith murmured, tears brimming her eyes.

Francine shrugged her shoulders, 'Who knows, hey... but I'm probably not going to see Christmas this year.'

It was all Cora could do to stop herself from sobbing out loud. She pulled Francine close, squeezing her tight.

'Ease off a bit, you're going to throttle the life out of me here and now,' Francine gasped, starting to laugh but then hacking with a cough once more.

Edith took the initiative now, 'We need to get you to bed, you can sleep in the guest room, right next to mine,' she announced, her mouth gripped in a firm line... 'though how the hell we're going to get you up the stairs I don't know.'

'We can carry her, in the chair,' Cora offered.

Edith tipped her head to one side, considering the idea.

'No, no, let me walk,' gasped Francine.

Edith was already shaking her head, 'You are too out of breath. If you want to stay in my house, you need to follow my rules,' she insisted, gesturing for Cora to take the foot of their makeshift stretcher.

Edith was surprisingly strong in the arms for one so wiry, but even so, halfway up the winding stairs they had to stop to rest. At that moment, one of the German guests exited the dining room and came to the bottom of the stairs. 'Let me help,' he said, running up to take over from Cora, who moved up a few steps to work side by side with Edith. The extra muscle did the trick nicely and Francine was soon in through the door of Edith's guest room and deposited on the chair beside a four-poster bed complete with bright red satin counterpane.

'Thank you,' Edith called to the retreating German, who offered a small salute.

Francine was weakening rapidly as she sat. 'Stay with her while I get some nightclothes from my room,' Edith said gently, 'then we'll help her into bed.'

Cora stood supporting Francine in the chair, noting the drooping of her head, the rasp of her breathing. She wanted to speak, say something meaningful, but her mind was blocked, still whirring over the news of Francine's cancer. Beyond the shock she was now thinking about her friend's two sons in America; was there any way they could be told that their mother was unwell? And then the thoughts of Iris and Evie came at her, especially Iris, who had been so close to Francine. *Is* close. Not *had been*.

The war stood as a solid block of iron and steel to all communication across the world. The most she could probably hope for was to send a telegram to Estelle and Bertrand in Paris... she would ask Francine tomorrow, maybe after she'd rested overnight, hopefully by then her hacking cough would have settled and she'd be able to speak more easily without coughing. Cora swallowed hard to keep back the tears, she needed to hold herself together. If she lost control, she wouldn't be able to help her dear friend.

Francine lifted her head, motioned for Cora to help her out of the black wool coat which swamped her emaciated frame. First, Cora removed the brown leather bag which Francine had strung across her body. The contents felt heavy as Cora lowered the bag to the carpeted floor. Eager to get on and help Francine feel more comfortable, she was unbuttoning her coat when Edith returned with the nightdress. As they helped to undress their patient, Cora was surprised by Edith's gentleness, which completely undercut her previous swagger and seeming hardness. Once they were down to Francine's petticoat, Cora was shocked by how thin she was, her shoulder bones sharp, the rise and fall of her chest rapid with an audible rattle. Cora couldn't believe the change that had happened so quickly, but then when she thought back, Francine had been coughing more, she'd been thinner and easily tired. Why had she dismissed it all as due to the war, to rationing, to the stress of their situation?

'Right, let's get you into a nightgown,' Edith announced, businesslike, undeterred by Francine's dismissive wave of a hand. 'I'm giving you the pale blue silk, only the best for you,' she murmured, slipping the garment over Francine's head.

'Thank you, Lulu,' Francine croaked, her voice barely above a whisper.

'Lulu,' Cora blurted out, distracted... 'so that's your real name?'

'Lulu Delacroix, in full, and it's as real as any name ever could be,' she replied.

Cora shrugged, then smiled, with Francine so ill, there was no time to make any more sense of Edith, or Lulu.

Lulu offered a wry smile, her eyes warm, sparkling. It seemed as if Cora's calm acceptance of her elusive response had bonded them somehow. Working together, one at each side, they stood their patient then helped her turn to sit at the side of the bed. Once she'd got her breath back, Lulu lifted Francine's legs and Cora helped shift her upper body into position, propped upright against a wall of soft downy pillows. They both stood by the bed, watching Francine relax, exhausted.

'I'll go and get her a jug of water and a glass, my mom always said that poorly patients need to drink as much clear fluid as possible.'

Francine peeped open her eyes for a few seconds, 'Evie knows best,' she smiled, reaching out a hand to Cora.

Cora took her hand, gave it a gentle squeeze, then exited the room. With every step as she descended the stairs, she emitted a quiet sob. Only when she stood at the sink, running the cold tap, did she manage to rein in the shock of Francine's news, forcing it inwards, transmuting it to a deep ache of sorrow.

The men in the dining room were still singing, a melancholy German song, the tone of which struck a chord with the ache inside of her. Only the thought of being strong for Francine braced her. Who knows, maybe the doctor in Paris had been wrong. Maybe all that Francine needed was to rest up and be nursed back to better health. She'd visited enough very sick cancer patients with her father to know that someone who might seem to be gravely ill and dying could rally round, end up having much more time than expected. As she made her way carefully back up the stairs, carrying the jug and glass, she made herself believe this to be true with every step.

CHAPTER 20

MONTAUK, LONG ISLAND, NOVEMBER 1940

Iris clamped a hand to her hat as she straightened up from the taxi, the sea breeze here as brisk as she remembered from her last visit before the war. 'Thank you, ma'am,' the driver called, as she slipped him a generous tip. So grateful to be back on this side of the Atlantic but missing her beloved Paris even so. Standing for a few moments on the sand-dusted road, she pulled her navy-blue tailored coat straight with one hand, holding onto her hat with the other. Turning gracefully, she picked up her small suitcase containing all the newly acquired belongings which she'd purchased with the money donated by Franz. Lucien's nephew had never communicated with her directly, but he'd instructed a junior officer to treat her with respect and make sure she was well provided for. The case was light: a couple of changes of clothing, some silk underwear and her cosmetics and toiletries. As she stood now, daunted by the prospect of confronting Evie, she was glad she'd used her compact mirror in the back of the taxi to apply her bright red lipstick. She'd need every scrap of courage she could muster to face her friend.

She sensed the house was empty as soon as she approached

the wide porch where she'd spent many happy evenings with
Evie and Cora. It brought tears to her eyes thinking of Cora
now, laughing, chatting as they sat together in the swing seat.
She'd always been asking about coming to Paris, often confiding
in Iris about her birth mother, desperately needing to search for
the woman who'd abandoned her all those years ago. The heavy
feeling Iris now carried in her chest tightened every time she
thought of Cora. She would never be free of it, she knew that,
not until the girl was found or turned up safe and well. Her
instinct had always been that Cora would have gone to
Francine's house. But what about those German officers, the
ones who'd arrested her on the stairs? She'd sensed they were
heading towards her apartment, the best in the building. If they
had occupied it, it's possible they'd been there when Cora
returned. Here she was again, going over and over the same
thoughts, never getting close to any resolution. Having to hold
onto her hazy, illogical understanding that surely she would
know if Cora had been killed. The potential for such a thing
made her heart squeeze painfully tight.

Placing her suitcase squarely down on the boards of the
porch, she straightened up, looked around her; the house was
exactly as she'd left it on her last visit before the war. The
boards neatly swept, two yellow and white checked cushions on
the swing seat. With all that had happened to her, she'd
expected to see change here as well. But thankfully, there was
constancy, and it allowed her to draw in a steady breath of salt
air, steel herself for the imminent encounter with Evie. She
could hear the waves crashing on the beach. Intuitively, she was
drawn there, knowing that's where she'd find her friend.

The closer she got to the beach, the more her heeled leather
shoes dug into the sand. It was almost impossible for her to walk
but there was Evie, standing with her back turned, hands on
hips, gazing out to sea. Iris knew her friend's thoughts would be
at the other side of the ocean, in France. It made her feel even

more daunted, seeing the square set of Evie's shoulders, her hair stripped back from her face by the Atlantic breeze.

Halting for a moment, one hand still holding her new hat in place, she reached down to remove each leather shoe in turn. Her silk stockings would be ruined, but all that mattered now was making the best of this first meeting with Evie. She'd sent a telegram with her approximate time of arrival, maybe her friend even knew right now that she was approaching from behind, the damp sand sticking to her stockinged feet, her heart thudding against her ribs.

When Evie turned, Iris saw the shock on her face and then the full fury of her gaze. Trying not to flinch, she held eye contact as the rage in Evie's eyes began to burn even more strongly. Iris almost turned and fled. Evie was running towards her now, screaming incoherently. Iris stood her ground, she would take what came, it was what she deserved. Stopping short, Evie was growling, shouting words that seemed mixed and jumbled by the wind – why, stupid, mad, my daughter.

Iris felt a sob rising in her chest, she took two steps towards her distraught friend. Evie snarled, looked as if she were going to step back. But something snapped inside Iris and she lurched forward, made a grab for Evie, letting go of her hat and her shoes, the hat whipping away in the breeze, soaring up into the air.

She had Evie in her arms now, but she was spitting and struggling against her, 'Get off me! You! This is all your fault!'

Iris clung to her with all her might, Evie was so strong but Iris was taller and she was determined. If she lost this battle now, she might lose her best friend forever, there would be no going back.

'I am so sorry,' Iris shouted, her voice barely audible above the wind, tears streaming down her cheeks.

Still Evie fought and spat, then she began to sob in Iris's arms, her body starting to relax at last.

'I am so sorry, Evie, I truly am... I did try to tell Cora to leave Paris, she just wouldn't listen.'

Evie drew in a shaky breath, swiped tears from her eyes.

'You should have tried harder,' she shouted, still not ready to let go of the anger that had carried her through the past few months.

'Yes, maybe I should,' Iris conceded, 'but your daughter is very stubborn.'

'I know,' sobbed Evie, 'I know... just like me.'

Iris pulled her properly close now in a real hug. 'I promise you, Evie, I will do all that I can to help you and Adam, I'll pull any strings, do anything, to try and find Cora... Remember when we were together that first night on the hospital ship, how we worked side by side, matching each other's determination. That's the kind of team we will be, Evie.'

Evie snuffled against Iris; she was nodding her head against her shoulder. The two women clinging together with the surf washing their feet now, their hair tousled and entwined by the Atlantic breeze.

CHAPTER 21

CALAIS, FRANCE, NOVEMBER 1940

Although Cora knew that Lulu would be sleeping beside Francine that first evening, she couldn't settle. Somewhere in the early hours of the morning she snuck down from her attic room to the second floor, gently clicking open the heavy door of Lulu's guest room. A lamp glowed on the bedside table, she could see Lulu's chestnut hair spread over the pillow, she was sound asleep. Francine's laboured breathing from the other side of the bed was alarming but by the rhythm of it, Cora deduced that she was also sleeping.

Making her way back to bed, she heard a ripple of laughter from the floor below where most of the men slept, they were probably up playing cards or something. It had been kind of the man to help them upstairs with Francine, but something about the solidarity of the men in suits made Cora feel uncomfortable. Hopefully it wouldn't be long before she was able to move on. But what about Francine? The picture had changed now, it was inevitable that she'd need to spend more time in Calais.

Sighing, she made her way back up the stairs to her attic room. Seeing her bag on the chair, she plunged in her hand and pulled out the tattered romance novel. She hadn't touched it since the train and couldn't remember any of the story, but now it beckoned to her as something that might take her mind away from the harsh reality of the present. Even as she thought it, she saw herself as if from above in this bombsite of a city. Having left behind a German soldier she'd grown to love and would probably never see again, she was fully surrounded by Hitler's army, and now her dear friend was lying very sick in the bed of a woman who she'd only just met and was struggling to trust. She tried reaching back to her past life for any strength she could draw on. Evie's voice came to her loud and clear, as if she were right there: *This is your chance to make a difference. You've visited many poorly patients with me, use what you know.*

'I'll see what I can do,' she murmured in response, 'but first I need to try and get some rest.'

Seeking distraction, her eyes scanned the first page of the novel but the words wouldn't go in. Exasperated, she lay back on the narrow, creaky bed, letting her mind drift. Inevitably, she thought of Max, she could only assume that he was back now with his unit, restored to the army. What a strange world it was where sides had to be taken but then lines became blurred. Wherever Max was now, she hoped that he would always remember what they'd had together. In times of war boundaries needed to be broken down or peace would never come.

Waking with the unread book still in her hand, Cora glanced at her watch: 6 a.m. With all that had happened last night, Lulu hadn't reminded her of her duties, but she assumed she'd still be working on the early breakfasts. She was instantly awake, running on adrenaline. In seconds she was out of bed and at the small sink in the corner of the room. She glanced in the mirror – her hair was growing out now in clumps, more softly curled, dishevelled, it gave her a rakish air. Not much of a disguise really, her red hair was bound to be a giveaway.

Slipping back into her black skirt and white blouse and the

apron from last evening, she exited the attic room, anxious to check on Francine before she descended to the kitchen. As she approached the door it clicked open and Lulu appeared in a cobalt blue silk robe, her hair hastily piled on her head.

'She's not good,' Lulu whispered, her voice breaking ever so slightly. 'I think she might be dying.'

Cora gasped, 'No, surely not.'

Lulu reached for her hand, 'I nursed my mother in her final days, Francine is looking very much the same, I don't think it will be long... I'm going to call for a doctor, see if we can make her more comfortable. You go and sit with her, OK?'

Cora swallowed hard, nodded.

Gently opening the door, she could hear the creak in Francine's breathing. She'd heard that sound before with her father's poorly respiratory cases, the ones who were nearing the end of life.

Squeezing back tears, she walked softly to the bed, reached out to take Francine's hand.

'Is that you, Cora?' Francine spoke quietly, her voice clear.

Cora squeezed her hand, 'Yes,' she replied, 'I'm here.'

Francine opened her eyes, she smiled. 'I need you to find something for me... Look for my leather bag, I had it with me when I arrived, it was strung across my coat.'

Cora knew exactly where she'd put it, it was still there on the floor beside the chair they'd used to carry her up the stairs.

'Find the bag... the gun's in there... and the diamond necklace... I want... I want you to have them...'

The shock of what the bag contained hardly touched her, all her attention was fixed on her friend's laboured breathing. 'Yes, I know where the bag is, there's no need to worry,' Cora soothed, starting to feel light-headed with the grief building in her chest.

'I need you to promise,' Francine said, her voice ragged, breaking into a deep, rattling cough.

'I promise.'

'The gun is loaded... as always,' Francine smiled, drifting off into an exhausted sleep.

'Of course it is,' Cora said, squeezing Francine's hand to stop herself from crying.

Francine opened her eyes, her face scrunched, her chest working like worn-out bellows. Cora stood resolutely, brushing some strands of silver-grey hair from her friend's sweat-stained face. 'Would you like a sip of water?' she asked.

Francine shook her head, 'I need to hold your hand, that's all.'

Cora swallowed hard, her chest tight.

Francine opened her eyes, offered a smile, 'You've always been so good to me, Cora... as young as you are, you feel like a kindred spirit,' she breathed, 'but you are a foundling child and I've often sensed that restlessness in you, always searching for something... maybe one day you'll realise that what you've been looking for is already there.'

Feeling the impact of the words, seeing the effort it took for her friend to communicate, Cora felt her heart wrench and she emitted a sob.

Francine squeezed her hand, her eyes bright now, 'Grief is a natural part of life, *ma chérie*, it goes hand in hand with love, the two are inseparable.'

Cora gulped in some air and nodded, a weight beginning to settle on her chest.

Francine smiled again, 'Don't ever be afraid of living well, Cora, it makes the dying so much easier.'

'I won't be afraid,' Cora croaked, her voice barely audible.

Francine squeezed her hand, but her grip was very weak. When she spoke again, Cora had to lean down close to catch the words. 'Get word to my boys in America, tell them I love them very much... and Iris and Evie, they have always been special...'

'I will, Francine, I promise.'

Francine's breathing was very shallow now, but she was able to whisper, 'I'm going to meet my Sam, we've been apart for way too long...'

Cora felt riven by grief but she held fast, clinging to Francine's hand. 'Is there anything that you want right now?'

'A cigarette would be good,' she whispered.

Cora easily found the pack of cigarettes and the silver dolphin's head lighter in Francine's coat pocket. She lit up for her friend, coughing because she'd never been a smoker. At the snap of the lighter, Francine smiled. 'Sam bought me that lighter...' she breathed, 'all those years ago...'

Cora held the cigarette to Francine's lips, watching as she attempted to take a drag, but she had no strength to inhale. Her eyes were closed again now and when Cora spoke her name she didn't respond. Stubbing out the cigarette in the ashtray on the bedside table, she held onto Francine's hand. When her friend took a deep, ragged breath, Cora thought she might be rallying but the breath was held for a long time before the next came even deeper, rattling her lungs. Another gap, another gasping breath and then nothing, no more air entering Francine's chest.

Cora spoke softly to her, remembering what Evie had told her that at the point of death, people can still hear, so choose your words carefully. She told Francine that she loved her, as did Iris, Evie, and Lulu, and that she was going to a better place far away from the war, where she would be with Sam again. And then, she repeated her promise that she'd get word to Francine's boys as soon as she could, tell them their mother loved them very much.

Gently, she stroked Francine's hair. Her face was smoother now, she looked younger, at peace. Cora hadn't even had a chance to tell Francine about Max, which made her feel even more devastated. Francine would have loved to hear that story... But now it was too late, and as she reached to close

Francine's eyelids, a numbness crept over her. She needed to cry but the tears wouldn't come. It made her feel tense, restless, why couldn't she cry?

Then Francine's voice whispered in her head, *Don't be worrying,* ma chérie, *you've been through so much since the war started. It's best you remember me as we were, laughing together at the table...*

Cora started to cry then, tears streaming down her cheeks. When the door clicked open and Lulu appeared, all she could say was, 'It's too late, she's gone.'

She felt Lulu's arm around her shoulders, drawing her away from the bed, uttering words of comfort that seemed jumbled in Cora's head. Then, 'The doctor is coming, he will certify death,' Lulu was saying, her shoulders stiff, her voice catching on a sob.

'I told her that you loved her,' Cora said, the words echoing in her own head.

'Thank you for doing that,' Lulu said, using the back of her hand to swipe away tears. 'There will never be anyone like Francine, she was everyone's mother.'

Cora felt the deep sorrow in her chest expand, suddenly her breath was constricted. All she knew was that she had to be out of the room, away from the suffocating reality of death. She took a few steps, then seeing the leather bag on the floor she grabbed it, slung it over her shoulder, then walked briskly away, running down the stairs, feeling the weight of the revolver tapping against her body at every step. It linked her to that night at Francine's when she'd run back to the house, rushed in through the door, Francine in her chair pointing the gun straight at her. Francine was fearless, strong, she never lost heart even in the most desperate of circumstances. She could have been arrested or shot herself at any time, but no, she got cancer instead. Thinking about it now, Cora realised that she'd probably had it for a while, she'd seen her out of breath, coughing. But in a war, people don't tend to think of other ways to die.

Hit by rage, she needed to be out of the building, in the open air. Hooking the bag over her shoulder she clicked open the front door, walked boldly out into the shattered war-torn street. With no idea of where she was heading or what she was going to do, she marched down the broken pavement, only knowing that she had to be active, she had to feel the morning air moving in and out of her lungs. She heard Francine's chuckle, felt the energy she always brought despite her advancing age. Life was for living, that's what she would say, war or no war.

Scrambling over rubble, tearing her stockings, numb to the scrape on her leg and the dust which made her cough, Cora had no idea of where she was heading. Glancing behind she could still see the ancient watchtower. Now, in her heightened state it made her feel angry – she imagined all the death and destruction, wailing and sobbing it had borne witness to across the centuries. But still it stood mute, while another war raged, and its walls continued to hold their secrets.

Stopping for a few moments, breathless, gazing around at the broken buildings, the piles of rubble and shattered glass, she felt suddenly desperate for comfort. Why had she thought it was a good idea to come out here? She needed to be back at the hotel with Lulu, helping to lay out Francine's body, make arrangements for the funeral. Gulping in dusty air, she steadied herself and was about to turn around, head back to the hotel, when the sound of an army vehicle making slow, bumpy progress behind her made her freeze. The car was shiny black, filmed with a layer of dust but the distinctive red-and-black swastika flag fluttered bright and clean on the bonnet. If there'd been a doorway to step into, she would have done so instantly. Now it was too late to act, any evasive action would make her look furtive, suspicious.

Instead, she kept her head down, made to walk on as steadily as she could, try to ignore the passing vehicle. The tightness in her chest began to ease a little as the tyres scrunched slowly by. With relief she glanced up and saw the shape of the driver, he seemed to have no interest in a dishevelled woman out in the street. Then, with a clutch of fear, she heard the vehicle stop abruptly a short distance ahead.

With her heart hammering against her ribs she continued to walk steadily by. As she passed the car, there was silence, but she felt as if eyes were boring into her. In the second she thought she was safe, she heard the click of a car door opening behind her and a voice called out. She recognised it instantly – it was Karl Hesse. She bounded forward, all set to run. 'No, Cora, don't be silly,' he shouted, 'I could shoot you in a second.'

Gasping, she turned to confront him, his driver was holding a revolver pointed directly at her. She judged the distance between them and knew he would most certainly hit her if she tried to run. 'Come here, come on,' Karl beckoned, as if she were an errant child.

She had no choice.

With every step the weight of the gun and the diamond necklace in the leather bag over her shoulder tapped against her body. She couldn't even remember why she'd picked the bag up – probably because Francine had stressed the importance of it. A lump of raw grief mingled with terror rose in her throat.

Karl was dressed immaculately as always, clean-shaven, smiling. But his dark grey eyes glinted like pieces of coal.

'Well, my young friend, it looks as if you might have fallen on hard times,' he raised his eyebrows in mock surprise, taking the few extra steps to cover the ground between them. When he stopped, he leaned in, she smelt his sharp cologne as he reached out to push a few strands of hair behind her left ear. 'We meet again... And you've changed the style of your hair. Why cut it so short? Did you need to disguise yourself for some reason, Cora? Was that it?'

The loathing she had for the man ran through her like electricity, kept her together. Whatever happened to her now, she would not let this man feel that he'd beaten her.

'You are very quiet today, Cora... maybe you're tired? It can't be easy for a woman like you, on the run from Paris, probably no friends in Calais. Do you have anyone here?'

'I've just arrived,' she replied, making her voice steady.

He tipped his head to the side, 'No luggage?'

'I travel light.'

'So I see,' he smirked. 'I don't like you wandering the streets alone, Cora. You need to come with me, I can find you somewhere comfortable to rest. Maybe we could read through some passages of that journal of yours... it is so sweet, so lovely.'

She held her body rigid, every muscle yearning to punch him in the face. But his driver still held the gun.

'Come on,' he said, adopting the tone of a kindly uncle. 'Let's get you in the car. We can't be standing out here in the street all day.'

As Cora walked to the car, she calculated with every step how easy it would be, once she was in the back of the vehicle, to slip her bag off, reach down for the gun. But then Karl muttered something about her being far too dusty to sit next to him and gestured for her to get into the front seat, next to the driver. As the car bumped over the pot-holed remains of the road, she tried to form a plan, but her mind was still in shock from Francine's death and her thoughts struggled to connect. Working on instinct alone, with hardly any movement of her upper body, she stealthily reached into the leather bag and pulled out the silk drawstring pouch containing the diamond necklace, tucking it down the side of her body, waiting for the moment the driver was distracted enough for her to be able to secrete it. She knew the gun would be discovered as soon as she was searched, but the diamond necklace could be hidden, maybe used as a bribe. She heard Francine's voice in her head, telling her to be patient, bide her time. Once they were past the watchtower, then the

Hotel Genevieve, she felt the invisible thread which linked her to all that she had left stretch thin, so thin she didn't know whether it would be able to support her. But when big drops of rain began to fall against the car windscreen, clearing the dust, the driver had to lean forward and give every scrap of his attention to the road ahead, Cora gripped the blue silk drawstring bag and pushed it inside her coat, down the front of her blouse. This small victory made her feel elated, buzzing with renewed energy and with every heavy swoosh of the wiper blades. She knew that one day, this would all be over and, living or dead, she would have found some way to make her mark.

CHAPTER 22

Cora gasped awake after her first night of captivity, sure with the light flooding in through a high window that she was in Iris's Paris apartment. She shot up in bed, her heart pounding, her brain sluggish, feeling drugged. She was in a high-necked night-gown, the bed sheets were immaculate, white, covered by an embroidered counterpane. But the room was all wrong, white walls, stripped wood floor with a built-in wardrobe on one wall and no other furniture apart from this narrow bed, a small locker and a commode in the corner of the room.

Horrified, she saw her silver necklace with the spiral-patterned pendant on the bedside locker. She never took it off, someone else must have removed it.

A shudder went through her body as she remembered where she was, and who must have been here with her. With a rush, the detail of the previous day came back to her. The ride in the car, the search of her bag and removal of the gun. Then a wait in a locked room and later, after she'd been given bread and cheese and a glass of water, she'd been escorted up some stairs and into a small furnished apartment – Karl's quarters. She'd felt grubby, aware of her dank hair clinging to her head, the dust on her shoes, grittiness of her face. And the weight of the silk bag resting between her breasts, close to her heart. He'd said a few words she couldn't remember and then dismissed her to the care of an older German-speaking woman with a blank expression, dressed all in black. She'd been shown to a bathroom where nightclothes were laid out, the bath full of warm water with scented soap and clean towels. She'd been left alone, there was even a lock on the door, so she'd been able to hide the diamond necklace behind the pedestal of the sink. Then, despite her misgivings, she'd slipped into the bath and used the soap and shampoo to scrub herself clean. The relief of cleaning her body, the ease it gave her. Stepping out of the grey bath water that left a line of scum around the enamelled bath, she'd enjoyed the feel of the clean towels against her skin. The white nightdress was demure, but she'd still needed to wear her brassiere underneath, so she could use it to secrete the necklace.

The woman had been waiting for her when she emerged, ready to show her into the bedroom. A milky drink had been waiting, and she had stood over Cora while she consumed all of it. She'd thought at the time it might contain a sleeping draught, but she had no choice but to comply. As soon as the woman had retreated from the room, after Cora had heard the turn of a key in the lock, she'd slipped out of bed, searched frantically for a hiding place for the diamond necklace and as sleep began to hit her, thankfully she'd found a loose floorboard in the fitted wardrobe.

The last memory she had was slipping gratefully into bed and falling into a dead sleep. The silver chain had been around her neck then, she never took it off.

She knew it must have been Karl who had come into the bedroom. She imagined him sitting on the edge of the bed, brushing her hair back from her face and then slipping both hands around her neck to remove her precious family heirloom. It sent a cold shiver through her, she knew he'd only done it so she would know that he'd been in here as she slept, while she'd been vulnerable.

Her body began to shake uncontrollably, a sob threatened but she bit it back. She forced herself to think of the house by the sea in Montauk, imagined herself sitting at the kitchen table, then out on the porch in the swing seat. She conjured up the sound of the waves crashing on the shore, her mother's face as she turned with a smile before she waded into the ocean.

Evie shot up in bed, her heart pounding. What was this? She was sure she hadn't been having one of her nightmares from the past, they were so familiar, she always recalled them on waking. But she felt haunted, her chest tight with dread. Adam was snoring gently beside her, his face pale and unlined in the moonlight seeping in through a gap in the gauzy white curtains. She lay her head back down, but her pillow felt crumpled, uncomfortable, and she was so wide awake her eyelids felt pinned back.

She had no choice but to get up, go downstairs, make her customary cup of tea.

As she placed her bare feet on the floorboards, she knew as if a voice had whispered in her ear. It's Cora, something's happened to Cora. She made herself remain still for a few seconds, trying to shrug it off. After all, she carried visceral anxiety about her daughter every single day. But this was sharp, inexplicable.

Blowing out a lungful of air, her body felt tight, wound up with the stress of it all.

She felt the weight of it increase as she descended each step of the stairs where Cora had laughed and run and snuck down on Christmas morning full of mischief and excitement. Evie's throat contracted and tears welled in her eyes, she yearned for that past life, prayed that one day she would be reunited with her child. *Her child.* Yes, Cora would always be hers, part of her own body, even though she hadn't carried her in the womb, the girl was there with every beat of her heart, with every breath.

Flicking on the kitchen light, she almost screamed out loud, thinking she'd seen a ghost. 'Iris,' she called out at the same moment as her friend shouted, 'Evie.'

'What the blazes are you doing here?' Evie called across the room, still clutching a hand to her chest.

'Same as you, I couldn't sleep,' Iris smiled, taking a deep drag from her cigarette before stubbing it out. Patting the chair next to her she then said, 'Come on, sit down, you look absolutely dreadful, I'll make you a cup of tea.'

Evie nodded, she wasn't going to argue, she always knew when she wasn't functioning properly.

As Iris busied herself, filling the kettle and putting it on the stove, then taking care with the measuring of the tea leaves into the pot, Evie told her about how she'd woken, what she'd felt.

Iris gave a grim smile, 'My awakening wasn't as dramatic, but I felt the same, I can't even explain it.'

As soon as her friend had poured the tea, Evie reached across the table to take her hand. 'Iris, tell me I'm right. I would know, wouldn't I, if Cora had died?'

Iris's voice was quiet when it came, 'Yes, I think you would.' She seemed no way near as certain as Evie would have liked.

'I know it sounds far-fetched, but it's all I've got to keep me going,' Evie said, her voice strained, overly eager. 'Adam doesn't believe in intuition so his rational mind can't even allow him that small comfort. He walks around with that haunted look in his eyes, he can't even talk about it.'

'You both have your own ways of coping, it's so hard...'

'And I've seen your face sometimes, Iris. I know you feel it too.'

'Yes, I do,' she replied, her voice throaty.

They sat quietly for a few moments, listening to the rise and fall of the waves out there in the dark, breaking on the beach.

At last Iris spoke, 'This is excruciating, this waiting, isn't it? But we have to believe that one day Cora will come in through that door, she'll be bright and smiling and she'll walk with you down to the beach.'

It eased Evie a little, she only wanted to hear positive things.

'I hope you're right,' she breathed, 'because this is tearing me apart.'

'Oh, Evie,' Iris groaned, 'I'm so sorry that you're having to go through all of this. If only I'd been much firmer with Cora, told her she had to go home.'

Evie sighed, 'Let's not start that again... like we've said already, Cora is a grown woman, she is stubborn, headstrong. She will only come back when she's ready.'

Iris was shaking her head, 'I know, I know... just like her mother,' she said with a fleeting smile.

'It wouldn't be so bad if there was some way of us knowing how she was doing,' Evie groaned. 'She's an American citizen in Paris... all she needs to do is keep her head down and she should be safe, but you know Cora, she's not likely to do that, is she? It really gets to me, the not knowing... Then again, if she *was* in danger, well maybe it's for the best if I'm in the dark. I don't know anymore; it all gets jumbled in my head and keeps going round and round...'

Iris squeezed her hand, 'Would it help if I travelled back across the Atlantic, if I was closer to France? I wasn't going to tell you this till later because it isn't confirmed yet. But I was thinking of going back to Southampton, to Netley hospital.'

'Oh,' Evie said, her mind already whirring. 'You mean to work as a nurse.'

'Yes,' Iris said, both eyebrows raised as if she'd surprised herself by saying it. Then, when Evie didn't reply, she continued with, 'I've written to the matron there, I'm waiting for a reply.'

'Southampton is very close to France, isn't it, just across the Channel?'

'Yes, it is,' Iris replied, scrunching her brow. 'But now, seeing you in this state, I don't want to leave you here like this, Evie.'

'No, you haven't clicked what I'm thinking, Iris.' Evie was impatient now, her voice rising. 'You wouldn't *have* to leave me here – I would go with you to Netley hospital.' The moment Iris opened her mouth to protest, Evie reached out to take her hand. 'No, don't waste your breath, you know me better than anyone: once I've made up my mind, there's no stopping me. I'm coming with you, Iris. When you get your reply, write back, tell them we're both qualified nurses, we'll both be there.'

'But what about Adam?' Iris frowned. 'Will he be all right on his own?'

'He'll be fine, you've seen how self-contained he is. He might even be better if he's not fretting about me all the time. My way of coping can be quite dramatic, as you know.'

'True,' Iris said. 'I always used to imagine you like some romantic heroine, running along a clifftop with your hair flying in the breeze.'

'Ha, yes, that's about right,' Evie smiled. 'Poor Adam, we got married so fast he didn't know what he was letting himself in for.'

'I don't think it would have made a jot of difference,' Iris replied. 'You two were destined to be together... I didn't see it as definite when we were on the hospital ship, but when we got back to Netley hospital, his face that day when he first saw you in the corridor. I knew exactly what would happen, right there and then.'

'You never said a word, Iris, not one word.'

'As if you would have listened even if I had! You'd have denied it; you might even have set out to do the opposite for devilment.'

'You knew me so well, even back then.'

'It wasn't that difficult, Evie. You do tend to wear your heart on your sleeve.'

'Sorry about that,' Evie laughed. 'I even exasperate myself at times. But if I come with you, Iris, I will be the best nurse on your ward, I promise. I will work so hard.'

'I know you will,' Iris smiled. 'And, as always, you've completely talked me round without me even being able to think through any objections.'

'So, that's settled then,' Evie said, offering a firm nod, then reaching out to shake Iris's hand but knocking the salt pot over, spilling it on the table. Instantly both women grabbed a pinch of salt and threw it over their left shoulder.

'Look what you've got me doing now, Evie Munro – I'm as superstitious as you are.'

Evie laughed, getting up from the table, suddenly distracted by a shift in the weather, a strong wind buffeting the sides of the house making the waves crash louder on the shore.

'The breeze over the ocean is telling us something,' Evie cried, walking to the door, bracing herself to open it. She gasped as the wind came straight at her, feeling the force of it whip back her hair, mould her nightdress to her body. It caught her off guard, made her shriek with laughter. Clinging to the door, she turned back to Iris, still laughing. 'It's Cora, she's calling to us from the other side of the Atlantic, she knows we're coming.'

Even when a chair blew over and clattered to the kitchen floor, still Evie held her ground in the doorway. Iris beside her now, both of them laughing and shouting, 'We're coming, Cora, we're coming.'

Evie, delighted to see her friend joining in, put an arm around her, pulled her in close. 'Here we are together, Iris, running along that cliff, you're up there with me this time.'

'Yes,' Iris gasped, the wind catching her breath. 'Yes, it's you and me together against the world.'

CHAPTER 23

CALAIS, FRANCE, NOVEMBER 1940

Still groggy from sleep, Cora grabbed the silver necklace off the bedside table and refastened it around her neck. It felt like an act of defiance. If she ended up being incarcerated here in this stark room for a second night, she would remove and hide it so Karl Hesse couldn't play mind games with her whilst she slept. The thought of being locked away, completely at his mercy, sent a shiver through her body. She gritted her teeth and made herself sit up straight. She would not be beaten, not by this man who had haunted her since that first day of the occupation when she'd found him in Iris's apartment.

Her rally was short-lived because in the next second her heart twisted at the thought of Francine dying right before her eyes. Was that only yesterday? It felt like weeks ago. The deep sadness hit her afresh. She bit back a sob – she couldn't let herself grieve here, in this threatening space. She was stuck, she knew that for sure, the sound of the key turning in the lock last night had stayed with her and now it made her feel sick to the stomach. It took all her willpower to force herself to draw in deep breaths, to reinvigorate her senses, but slowly she began to settle.

Feeling less panicked, she lay back against the pillows, her thoughts returning to Francine. Cora knew it was unlikely she'd get back to the hotel in time for the funeral. And what would Lulu be thinking now that she'd disappeared with a bag containing a gun and a diamond necklace? Maybe she hadn't even known what was in Francine's bag. She hoped at least Lulu would realise she had been forcibly taken and hadn't decided to abscond. It felt important for Lulu to know that Francine was a true friend, that Cora would never abandon her.

An abrupt shout, a man's voice on the other side of the locked door, made her current situation snap back to the forefront of her mind. She felt the shock of it through her body, bringing her back to the present with a jolt. She was trapped here, a prisoner, and she had no idea what was going to happen next.

Making a conscious effort, she tried to weigh her predicament rationally, the way her father had taught her. *When you're dealing with a problem, stay calm. There's always a plan if you think it through.* Sitting up in bed, almost as if she'd heard his voice, she felt the connection, it gave her a sense of having some degree of control over her situation. So, she was being held captive by a German officer, for a reason she daren't even contemplate. What could she do to improve her chances of escape? She had no way of knowing what Karl Hesse was up to, but she'd sensed that first time she'd met him in Iris's apartment that he was physically attracted to her, and then what he'd said to her in Paris when she'd been out with her camera was an even stronger hint. Something about the way he looked at her reminded her of the gauche teenage boys at high school dances, like Danny had been when they'd first got together. Again, she thought of the journal, but now, with the distance of time it didn't send a rush of shame through her body, it seemed almost irrelevant. She knew, however, that it wasn't irrelevant to Karl, he made a great deal of it, probably revelling in the discomfort it caused her. Right now, his belief that the journal was still a potent force was all she had. Not power exactly, but if she could tap into his need to have that control over her, if she could keep up the act, make him believe she was still that naive young woman newly arrived in Paris, precious about her private scribblings, it would give her some hold over him. She would be playing for time, she knew that, and she would have to be clever, but it was all that she had for now.

With a turn of a key in the lock, the door clicked open and the woman in black appeared with a breakfast tray – coffee, croissants, butter and strawberry jam, presented on a willow-patterned plate with silver cutlery and a white, starched napkin.

'Thank you,' Cora smiled.

The woman offered a single nod and then withdrew, she still hadn't spoken a word.

First things first, Cora thought, her mind already working on how to make some connection with the silent woman – keep smiling, say kind things, show appreciation. And then, who knows, maybe a woman like that who had probably been conscripted into her housekeeping role would risk all she had for a diamond necklace.

The smell of the freshly baked croissants made Cora's mouth begin to water. Tucking into the food with gusto, she ate every morsel. It was important to eat and drink to keep her body strong and her mind sharp, then she would be ready to face whatever came through the door.

Later, after she'd had her lunch and the light was still bright outside, the woman returned with some books, toiletries, cosmetics and a selection of brand-new shoes and clothes to hang in the wardrobe. The items were high quality, expensive. The woman hung the dresses in the wardrobe with care, running a loving hand down the fabric to straighten each one.

The colours were bright greens and blues and one damson shade of silk evening gown.

'You will wear this one tonight, for dinner with Captain Hesse,' the woman said.

The sound of her spoken voice took Cora by surprise. Instantly however, she mustered a smile, thanked her, said she was looking forward to the occasion.

The woman narrowed her eyes, clearly suspicious of her response. Cora made a mental note to tone down her reaction, make it more credible.

'What is your name?' she asked the woman as she prepared to leave the room.

She saw her press her lips in a firm line. 'I am not allowed to say, mademoiselle, 'I am here only for your maintenance... I will return in due course with some jewellery for you, Captain Hesse has expressed a wish to see you wearing diamonds.'

Cora choked back a laugh at the absurdity of her situation... could it be that he knew about the hidden necklace and was teasing her? No, it was impossible, no one had seen her hide it. 'Yes, I would be very happy to cooperate with Captain Hesse's request. He seems like a very charming man.'

The fleeting look in the woman's eyes told Cora all she needed to know – she lived in fear. She no more thought Karl Hesse was an honourable man than Cora did.

'I'll see you later,' Cora called after the woman as the door clicked to.

Once she was alone again, she went straight to the wardrobe to inspect the evening gown, relieved to find that although it had a V-shaped back, the cut and the sleeves would easily cover the tell-tale bullet wound on her shoulder. Then, dragging the bedside locker beneath the high window, she clambered up on it. Standing on tiptoe she was able to snatch a moment's view of the outside world. She'd been so tense in the car yesterday, she'd struggled to gauge how much distance they'd travelled, time had seemed to stretch on interminably. Seeing intact rooftops, she surmised she must be on the outskirts of the city. It didn't help her case; she would have preferred to have less ground to cover to get back to the Hotel Genevieve if she were able to escape.

Restless now, clambering down from the locker, she began to pace the floor, increasingly agitated at the reality of being confined and not knowing her status. Was she a prisoner? If so, would she be held here indefinitely, would she be interrogated? She had no answers to these questions and the uncertainty was gnawing at her. She yearned to be out in the streets again, making her way back to the Hotel Genevieve, able to properly grieve for Francine and help Lulu with all that needed to be done.

Seeing the stack of books brought by the woman, she glanced through them. They were all very dry, obviously there was a very tight list of suitable reading material for a young woman confined to a small room. None of it appealed, but she did find a notebook with a pencil tucked neatly into the spine... Karl must be hoping for a new chapter in the journal, she thought, taking the book back to the bed and propping herself up against the pillows. Channelling the much younger woman she'd been when she'd first arrived in Paris last year, she began to write. Reflecting on missing home and family and, of course, Danny, she poured out the thoughts and feelings of a pure young woman who only wanted to be loved by the right man – someone noble, strong, a man who could truly look after her. Crossing out part of one section which when she read it back appeared to be a little overdone, she settled on her final version, making sure to leave the journal accessible to anyone who wished to read it.

The day straggled on. She paced up and down some more, picked up the books in turn, put them down again, watched the fading light at the narrow window. When the sound of the key in the lock came, she was eager to see the woman, relieved that at last she would be able to leave the close confinement of her room, even if it was to have dinner with Karl Hesse.

The woman placed a small square jewellery box on the bedside locker, then she went straight to the wardrobe to remove the damson silk evening gown. Cora had never in her life worn anything like it; she was hoping it would sag around her, make her look frumpy. But as the woman helped her to dress and the silky fabric slipped over her body, she glanced down and saw that the garment fitted perfectly. It clung to her lithe body and made her look elegant. Darn, she thought, I wasn't expecting that. Denying the frisson of nerves it gave her, she felt the weight of the silk against her skin and knew with a sinking heart that the dress would fuel Karl's interest in her. If only she were getting ready to see Max, this would be the most perfect moment in the world.

'You have a scar on your shoulder, are you all right, mademoiselle?' the woman's deadpan voice broke through.

'Yes, I had a tumble from my bicycle, it's all fine now.'

Cora realised she'd clenched her jaw tight.

'You seem very tense, are you sure you're all right, mademoiselle?' Was that a hint of concern in her voice?

'Yes, thank you,' she breathed, exhaling heavily.

'If you sit on the bed, I will do your hair.'

Cora nodded, lowering herself clumsily in the long evening gown.

The woman placed a soft white towel around her shoulders and clipped it into place. Then she not only brushed and combed Cora's short hair, but she also used a pair of sharp silver scissors to snip and shape. 'The last time it was cut, I didn't have a good hairdresser,' Cora offered by way of explanation.

The woman remained silent, just the snip, snip of the scissors until the towel from her shoulders was removed.

Cora was beginning to feel impatient; how long did it take to get ready for dinner? Usually, she slipped into her best blouse and slacks and ran a comb through her hair. With that thought came the knowledge that it had been months since she'd sat down to any kind of formal meal. The last time was with Iris in the apartment when they'd marked the anniversary of Cora's arrival in Paris. It had been a warm spring evening and they'd sat by an open window. Chatting easily, enjoying a few glasses of wine, afterwards they'd walked out to the balcony, gazed at the silhouette of the Eiffel Tower. It had been one of the most perfect evenings of Cora's young life. Now, it felt like decades ago, a filmy memory of someone else's story. She sighed audibly, feeling her shoulders slump.

The woman made a sympathetic murmur, placed a gentle hand on Cora's shoulder. 'Now, we need to apply a little make-up and the diamond earrings, and you are ready to go.'

Cora nodded, offering a small smile. But whatever had peeked out from behind the woman's facade had been fully withdrawn. Her mouth was set in a polite line, and her hands were deft as she applied face powder, a trace of eyeliner and some red lipstick. The most Cora ever did was apply one quick layer of lipstick, so her face felt heavy with the powder, as if she were wearing a mask. It didn't feel natural, but then Cora would be playing a part, so maybe this could be the equivalent of stage make-up.

When the woman grasped the clip of her spiral-patterned necklace, Cora reacted instantly. 'No, I have to keep it on.' The woman murmured an apology but then she insisted, 'It is Captain Hesse's orders, no other jewellery, only the diamond earrings.'

Cora felt her throat tighten. Knowing she had no choice, she undid the clip herself, kissed the enamelled pendant before placing it on the bedside table.

She swallowed hard, sat perfectly still as the woman fastened the diamond earrings in place. With a glance to her necklace, she felt a pang of loss, but she had no choice except to trust that her most precious thing in the world would be waiting for her when she returned to the room. The cool weight of the diamond earrings pulling on her ear lobes felt like a betrayal, a travesty, but Cora straightened her back, lifted her chin.

'You look beautiful,' the woman said, her voice flat, but when Cora made eye contact, she saw a sheen of unshed tears. It was a chink in the woman's armour, and it reassured her that there was a thinking, feeling human being within the seemingly empty shell.

The slip-on evening slippers which matched the damson silk felt odd on her feet. With the first few steps she teetered, feeling as if she were about to fall. At least if she got the chance to escape, she would easily be able to kick them off, she could run fast in bare feet.

Retracing her steps from yesterday, she followed the woman down a stone staircase, the clip-clip of her new shoes echoing in the cold, empty space. Goosebumps prickled on her arms; she tried not to be distracted by them as she memorised every detail of the route they were taking. Standing outside a heavy carved wooden door, she waited as the woman knocked. A muffled call from inside and then the woman pushed open the door and gestured for Cora to enter. The light was low, and as Cora stepped over the threshold, she needed to allow her eyes to adjust. An oblong table, shiny wood, was set for two with white starched serviettes and polished silver cutlery that glinted in the light cast by an elegant candelabra. A carafe of red wine stood ready, cut-glass wine goblets waiting expectantly.

The door clicked shut behind her and Karl rose from a leather armchair in the shadowy corner of the room. Cora felt a stir of unease in her stomach. Snatching a quick breath to steady herself, not wanting to show any sign of discomfiture, she held her ground as he walked towards her, his boots making a heavy sound on the boarded floor. As he emerged into the light, she saw he was without his uniform jacket, his shirt open at the neck, loosely tucked into his trousers. Even though he looked less formal, he held his shoulders square, the way he moved was stiff. There was something odd, incongruous about him. The semblance of a smile he offered took her straight back to the first time she'd seen him in Iris's apartment. Again, she was aware of something tightly coiled, waiting.

She watched as he crossed the distance between them, his eyes looking her up and down, starting to burn with intensity. He liked what he saw. 'You have become a woman at last, Cora,' he said. As he leaned in to scrutinise her, she saw the clean lines of his face, his chiselled jaw, and smelt his citrus cologne. He was a handsome man, there was no doubt about that, but there was something dead behind his grey eyes, and it made her stomach twist.

He reached for her hand and when he raised it to his moist lips, she had to stop herself from wrenching it away. He walked with her to one end of the dining table and gestured for her to be seated, pulling the chair out for her. His fingers brushing her bare arm felt like the crawl of an insect; she swallowed hard to repress it and then offered a polite smile from behind her mask of face powder and lipstick, reminding herself that she was playing a part. As he walked to take his seat at the opposite end of the table, she unfolded the white starched serviette and slipped it onto her knee.

As he sat down, she discreetly took deep breaths in and out, steadying herself. What could she possibly have to say to this man who had cold heartedly abducted her from the street and now held her captive? 'I trust your quarters are comfortable,' he stated, sounding like a gentleman from a novel set centuries ago.

'It would be much better if the door wasn't locked,' Cora countered, slipping back to their previous sparky banter.

He laughed. 'But then you might disappear into the night and where would that leave me, without your lively company?

And then of course, there is the other matter of the issues we need to clear up.'

'Oh,' she said, forcing nonchalance, 'what issues?'

'This, for a start,' he replied, lifting a large revolver up from the table.

She held back a gasp, not wanting to give him the satisfaction. It was Francine's gun and now he was pointing it straight at her chest.

'Well?' he said, his eyes alive with a dark light.

'It's a family heirloom,' she said. Francine had been like family, so it wasn't fully untrue.

'So why would you bring it with you, all the way to Calais?'

'It's very precious, it belonged to my father, he fought in the last war.'

Karl was smirking now, shaking his head. He laid the revolver back down on the dining table, by the side of his plate.

'Who were you staying with, in Calais?'

Her reply was interrupted by a knock on the door and then a soldier in uniform appeared carrying a large white ceramic jug with an ornate handle. He came to her first, didn't ask but poured soup into her bowl. The warm mushroomy smell was homely, it helped her relax a little.

Once Karl had been served and the soldier had retreated, Cora took up her spoon, hoping Karl would now be distracted.

'Well?' he said, waiting for a reply.

'I told you; I'd only just arrived when you found me on the street, I was lost, looking for somewhere to stay.'

He picked up his spoon then, the clink of it against the bowl seemed to fill the room.

'There is something else...' he paused, dabbing at his mouth with his serviette. 'The matter of what you were up to in Paris, before you came to Calais, who you were working with, that kind of thing.'

She swallowed a mouthful of soup, it was too hot, it burned

the roof of her mouth. 'I have no idea what you are talking about.'

He looked up from his soup bowl. 'Oh, I think you know full well... and if I were to examine your body, I'm sure I'd find a fresh scar from a healing bullet wound.'

Cora could barely swallow her next mouthful. Her mind was reeling, she had no idea what to say. Maybe the woman had already reported back to him, and he was only tormenting her, dragging it out.

She made herself cough, as if choking on a piece of mushroom. Delicately placing the starched serviette to her mouth, she gently croaked, 'Please, can I have some wine?'

He rose from his seat immediately, taking up the cut-glass carafe, coming to stand at her shoulder, leaning in to pour the blood-red wine.

'Thank you,' she said, still pretending to clear her throat.

As he stood, he ran the fingers of his free hand down her neck. 'If you weren't so beautiful, I would not tolerate your inability to tell the truth. I'd be questioning you much more aggressively,' he said, his voice husky.

Cora fought against the revulsion creeping through her body. At least now she had absolutely no delusion as to his intentions, she had no choice but to play his game, hopefully stave off further progression of this clumsy charade.

As he walked back to take his seat, her mind was scrabbling for calm, trying to work out a plan. But there was no plan. Seeing the way his bright eyes bored into her from the opposite end of the table, she knew she had him in her thrall, but it would only take a tiny gesture out of place, a snap of a twig, to send him in the opposite direction. She was walking a tightrope with no safety net.

Drawing in a slow breath, she tried to change tack as they waited for the main course to be served. 'Tell me about yourself, Captain Hesse, where did you grow up?'

He started to smile, rested back in his chair, 'Oh, I'm a Berliner, I love the city life, it is the best place in the world to—'

The slamming of a door, a woman's voice screaming, 'Where is she? Where is my waitress?'

Karl leapt up from his seat. 'What is this outrage?' he shouted. 'I cannot tolerate this!'

Cora sat frozen; she had recognised the voice instantly, it was Lulu. Lulu had come to rescue her.

CHAPTER 24

Karl stormed from the room, shouting. The sound of running, boots on the stairs. Tentatively, Cora rose from her seat, the door wasn't locked, she opened it a crack. She could hear a loud commotion downstairs, Lulu was ranting, unstoppable. It made Cora feel emboldened, ready to take a chance. She kicked off her silk slippers, then seeing the gun on the table she ran back, grabbed it, started to make her way to the top of the stairs. Holding her breath, every step sending a clutch of anxiety through her body, slowly she made her way down, keeping close to the wall, feeling each step with her bare feet.

Lulu's voice was ever closer, full of energy, demanding to have Cora released right now. 'I brought her from Paris, especially, to assist in my hotel... we have eight German guests to cater for, important men who work at the town hall.' Then when she wasn't getting anywhere with Karl, she heard her mention a high-ranking officer. Cora couldn't catch the name, but it was someone who would be very displeased if Lulu were disrespected like this.

She heard Karl state bluntly, the edge to his voice chilling, that he had reason to believe that Lulu's young waitress was involved in espionage. Lulu laughed out loud, telling him not to be ridiculous. She could tell by Karl's tone that he was barely holding his own, his voice was impatient now, on the edge of shouting again. 'I will speak to those in authority tomorrow morning and send word to your hotel,' he said. 'There is no more I can do for you this evening, Madame Delacroix.'

Cora was almost at the bottom step, she could feel the blood rushing in her ears as she sent up a prayer that Lulu could keep him engaged for a minute longer.

But silence had fallen, she heard a door closing then a young soldier with blond hair rounded the bend at the bottom of the stairs. She caught him off guard and he had no time to reach for the rifle slung across his shoulder. When she pointed the revolver directly at his chest and pressed a finger to her lips for him to be quiet, he raised both hands in surrender. Whispering in German, she ordered him to be silent or she'd shoot him and gestured for him to retreat, back down the stairs. His face was stricken, she almost felt sorry for him, but she narrowed her eyes, made herself look fierce.

A heavy tread on the stairs and Karl appeared behind the young soldier, his eyes registering the situation, then he was smirking. He pushed past, marched up the stairs towards her. 'Stop or I'll shoot,' she shouted, but still he came.

Her heart was about to burst, her hand was shaking, she had seconds to decide. She gritted her teeth and pulled the trigger. Nothing happened, the trigger clicked, clicked again when she tried another shot.

Karl was laughing at her, loud, aggressive. 'Stupid girl, do you think I would leave a loaded revolver lying around for you to use?'

She fell in on herself, the gun heavy in her hand, her arm drooping. She'd assumed that it had been loaded because it always was, that's how Francine had kept it.

He pushed roughly against her, pulling the revolver from

her hand, throwing it at the young soldier who stood with his mouth still dropped open in disbelief. He shouted angrily at the soldier, some German words Cora couldn't understand, and the young soldier disappeared rapidly down the stairs, leaving her alone with Karl.

He grabbed her arm, dragging her back up the stairs, her bare toes catching on the rough stone. The physical strength of him was terrifying, but not as terrifying as the look in his eyes. She knew it was in him to kill her there and then, snap her like a twig. She had never been close to anyone in this state before, she had no idea how to manage the situation. Boldness was the only thing that came naturally to her in that moment. Once he'd dragged her back into his room, to the abandoned meal on the table, she straightened up, tried to struggle free.

'No you don't,' he growled, increasing his grip on her upper arm, his fingers digging painfully into her flesh.

'Let go of me,' she yelled, kicking out with a bare foot.

His reaction was so fast she didn't even see it coming: he swiped her hard with the back of his hand, full across the face. The pain was excruciating, she was sure her nose was broken. With her head swimming, she half-collapsed, thinking that he might now finish her off.

Instead, he grabbed her again, pulled her up close, face to face. 'You think you're something, don't you, Cora, but look at you,' he spat. He took his thumb then and ran it hard against the scar on her top lip. 'You are nothing, worthless. You weren't even born right, look at this ugly mark.'

Cora growled with rage, pushed his chest hard, desperately trying to struggle free. He was laughing now, gleeful. Suddenly powerful, she freed her arm and then punched him as hard as she could in the face. He gasped with pain then he had her arms pinned again, his eyes blazing, 'Get away from me, you ugly whore,' he shouted, pushing her so forcefully she toppled and fell heavily onto the wooden floor. As she tried to scramble up, he kicked her hard in the stomach. She had never felt pain like it, she couldn't breathe, she felt broken. He left her lying there, discarded, with blood flowing freely from her nose and mouth, not even able to reach up a hand to stem the flow. A front tooth felt wobbly, her jaw was stiff, it felt as if he'd split open her belly, so painful was the kick. She might even have blacked out for a moment because when she came to, he was crouched beside her. 'There is more where that came from, if you don't behave properly,' he hissed, pulling her up, making her stand.

It took all her strength to stay erect, but she would not lose her dignity. Swaying ever so slightly she held eye contact with him and repeated the same words she'd used when she'd seen him outside the Ritz when she'd been on her first mission with the camera. 'You are not a gentleman,' she rasped.

His eyes narrowed. 'And you are not a lady,' he spat, 'you are a spy. And I will prove it.'

Cora took a ragged breath, desperately trying to steady her shaking body, she made herself laugh in his face, 'My friend Lulu came for me, and I heard what she said, she told you that questions would be asked about your behaviour from higher ranking officers.'

He grabbed her again, started to shake her roughly, then he had his arms around her, grappling her into a stifling embrace. Despite the blood on her face, he tried to kiss her hard on the mouth. She pushed against him, twisted her head away, but he held her in a vice-like grip, ripping at the bodice of her dress, the damson silk peeling apart. The animal noise he made as he pushed his hand down, cupping her left breast, squeezing it hard till she gasped in pain. 'You are worthless, I will do whatever I like with you,' he groaned, 'and no one will stop me.'

As he was about to kiss her again, there was a knock at the door.

'Yes,' he shouted.

Cora heard the door click open and then the woman's voice,

telling him there was a very urgent telephone call from headquarters.

'All right, all right,' he shouted, stepping back, walking to
the door. 'Take her away, clean her up,' he ordered as he left the
room.

Cora was shaking uncontrollably, clutching at the tattered
remains of her silk gown, tears streaming down her cheeks now
at the gentle voice of the woman. 'No, no,' she was saying, 'this
is not right.'

Carefully, she put an arm around Cora, supporting her,
leading her away, back to the room. Once the door was closed
and locked from the inside, the woman spread a clean white
towel on the bed and helped Cora remove the torn gown. 'Lie
down, my dear,' she soothed, 'I will wash away the blood, I will
make you better.'

Cora's body was trembling uncontrollably, her mouth felt
caked with sticky blood, but slowly, agonisingly, she lowered
herself onto the bed. The pain in her face had spread now, her
head was pounding. Tentatively she reached up a hand, the
flesh around her nose and eyes was swollen, but she could still
see, at least she could see. For this to be deliberately inflicted
by another human being made her want to howl with pain.
She knew in that moment that if she didn't manage to get
away from here in the next few days, Karl would probably
kill her.

She must have blacked out for a few moments again
because she startled with fear when the door clicked open. 'It's
me, it's only me,' the woman soothed, appearing with a bowl of
warm water and a soft flannel. Gently, so gently, she sponged
the blood from Cora's face, applying antiseptic to the areas of
broken skin. Cora gritted her teeth at the sting of the cream, as
the woman tended her wounds and then helped her change into
a clean nightdress.

Cora knew she had one chance at this, it was now or never.

'Thank you,' she murmured, taking the woman's hand, 'you have helped me so much.'

The woman's face was blank, she seemed to have retreated into herself again.

Wincing with pain, Cora raised herself up on one elbow. 'If I don't get away from here soon, it will not go well for me.'

The woman didn't reply, she simply stood by the bed, expressionless, listening.

'I might be wrong, but I sense that you are not altogether happy with your work here.' Still the woman stood mute.

'I want to show you something,' Cora said, crying out in agony as she struggled up from the bed, dragging herself unsteadily to the wardrobe where she'd stashed the blue silk drawstring bag containing the diamond necklace.

When she came back, she pulled out the necklace, held it up to the light, made the diamonds glint and gleam enticingly. 'This can be yours,' Cora whispered. 'We can both disappear from here tonight.'

The woman drew back, shaking her head, her eyes wide, terrified. 'He will hunt me down, kill me.'

'Not if you come with me, I have friends. Lulu Delacroix – the person who came tonight – she will help you, I promise.'

The woman bowed her head, hiding her face from view.

Cora held herself rigid, fighting against the throbbing pain in her body. If she'd misjudged this, there was no going back and she'd played her only card, she'd played it straight away.

Silent seconds ticked by with the diamond necklace now resting idly in Cora's hand. The woman sighed, then reached out and took the necklace, let it run through her fingers. 'I can tell it is the real thing,' she said at last, her eyes wide, the corners of her mouth turning up ever so slightly with the ghost of a smile.

Cora repeated a silent prayer, her heart bumping in her chest.

'I need to know where you got it from,' the woman said at last.

'It's a family heirloom, it belonged to my aunt,' she said, her throat tight with tears when she thought of Iris, and how Francine had shown her the necklace that night in Paris before any of this.

The woman nodded, holding it up to the light again.

Hearing a heavy tread on the stairs, they both froze. The woman grabbed the blue silk bag out of Cora's hand and pushed it with the necklace straight into her apron pocket. She almost dragged Cora to the bed. 'Pretend to be asleep,' she whispered urgently, helping her lie down.

Cora wanted to scream out loud with the pain in her body but she held it all tight, closing her eyes as the door creaked open.

She sensed Karl standing in the doorway, she felt his eyes on her, it took all her concentration to give the appearance of sleep.

'She is exhausted,' she heard the woman say, 'and I've given her the sleeping draught again, to make sure she will be rested for tomorrow.'

Karl didn't reply, he merely grunted, 'Make sure you clean her up properly,' then with a rush of relief, she heard the heavy tread of his boots on the stairs.

As soon as the woman had closed the door and locked it from the inside, she helped Cora to sit at the side of the bed. The woman spoke rapidly, her eyes gleaming: 'If he can't sleep, he might come back during the early hours of the morning – we need to act quickly.'

Cora reached to the bedside locker, retrieved her spiral-patterned necklace, squeezing it tight in her hand for a second, feeling the power of her lucky talisman.

'Let me,' the woman said gently, taking it from her. With her hands shaking ever so slightly, she fastened the necklace around Cora's neck. Then she removed the diamond drop earrings, placed them in the square box and slipped it into her apron pocket as well. 'These are for you,' she said, matter of fact. 'It's a disgrace what that brute of a man did to you.'

Cora felt her throat tighten, the sheer violence of that blow, that kick, came back to her, but she had to force it away. If she didn't focus right now on getting herself and the woman safely away from this place, she would die. 'Take these pills, for the pain,' the woman said, handing her two round tablets with a glass of water. In that moment, Cora had to make an important decision – to trust or not to trust. For all she knew, these could be a sedative, something to knock her out so the woman could leave her behind, taking the necklace with her. Cora hated being so vulnerable, but she knew the pain would slow her up, hold them both back.

'Look at me,' the woman said. 'You can trust me, I have as much reason as you to hate Captain Hesse.'

Cora held eye contact for a few seconds then she nodded, took the tablets, washed them down with the water. The woman was already retrieving Cora's bag, packing her meagre belongings. Then she helped her strip off the tattered remains of the damson silk evening gown and don her worn black skirt and serviceable blouse.

'I always take the kitchen scraps out to the back yard around this time of night. I will come for you then and we will leave the house together. Where do we need to go?'

'The Hotel Genevieve,' Cora said, 'then from there my friend will be able to arrange for us to leave the city.'

The woman nodded, 'I have family in the free zone, in Marseille, I can make my way down there now, with this,' she patted her apron pocket. 'I can pay my way and have a little left over on the side.'

Cora smiled, placed a gentle hand on her arm. 'What is your name?'

A fleeting look of uncertainty crossed the woman's face, but then she spoke, 'I am Anna Muller. I was born in France, but I married a German man, a communist, he is in a prison camp. I don't know where. They took me to work for them because I was already a housekeeper at an officer's home in Berlin. They said it was only right that I served Hitler's regime, given my husband was a traitor. They give me board and keep, but no pay. I too am doing penance.'

'Not anymore, Anna, you are getting out of here with me, tonight.'

Later, as Cora crept down the stairs, following Anna, she felt an icy shiver of fear run down her back and all the while her heart hammering so hard it made her feel even more light-headed. Even though Anna had reassured her that none of the men used these stairs at this time of night, she expected to hear Karl's heavy tread at any second. The sound of a man's raised voice in a room further down the corridor made Anna freeze and sent what felt like an electric shock through Cora's body.

As they entered the kitchen, Anna beckoned for her to follow. The room was spotlessly clean, all plates stacked neatly, crumbs swept, not a teaspoon out of place. Anna cast her eyes around one more time then pulled her coat from the hook behind the door, slipping a hand into her deep apron pocket to check that the precious jewels were safe.

Once the back door was closed behind them and Anna was almost dragging Cora down an alley, she whispered, 'Just checking where we need to go: is it the hotel close to the watchtower?'

'Yes, are you sure you know the way?'

'I do,' Anna said firmly, putting an arm around Cora now, helping her walk, leading her out of the alley onto a broader street. 'Keep your head down,' she murmured. 'If anyone stops us, I'll do all the talking.'

As they proceeded through the blasted landscape of the

city, with only moonlight to guide their way, their pace was slow due to the beating Cora had taken. She was so relieved that she'd taken Anna's tablets, she would hardly have been able to walk without them. After one terrifying moment when a patrol vehicle passed by slowly and the two women pressed their backs against the rough wall of a bombed-out building, Cora felt as if they might never reach the hotel. Then she saw the imposing silhouette of the watchtower in the near distance. 'There it is,' she whispered to Anna, 'not far now.'

Cora felt tears prick her eyes as they approached the street from where she'd been snatched after Francine had died. Seeing the tower had brought the sorrow back to her.

'Don't be scared, we're nearly there,' Anna whispered.

It wasn't worth risking an explanation. Cora squeezed Anna's hand and they continued the final leg of their journey.

'There's a door around the back,' she murmured when the Hotel Genevieve emerged from the gloom.

Cora led the way now, praying the door had been left unlocked.

Yes, they were in luck. Gratefully she led Anna through into the cluttered space, lit only by the stub of a single candle on the kitchen table.

'I knew you'd find a way,' a voice came at them out of the darkness.

Anna let out a scream as Cora gasped, 'Lulu!'

Lulu struck a match to light up a cigarette, her form materialising as Cora's eyes adjusted to the light.

'This is Anna,' Cora said, 'she's a housekeeper at the place where I was held, she helped me escape.'

Lulu rose from her seat, the cigarette clamped in the corner of her mouth. She walked around the table, came up close to Anna. 'Can we trust you?' she whispered fiercely.

'Yes,' Anna replied, lifting her chin.

Lulu's eyes narrowed, she took a drag of her cigarette and

then gave a single nod. She let out a gasp when she switched her gaze to Cora. 'My God, what have they done to you? Was it him, that Captain Hesse?'

Cora gulped in some air, 'Yes.'

'I'll find some way to make him pay for this,' Lulu growled, placing a gentle hand against Cora's cheek. 'I've seen him around the city, he's a beast of a man.'

'How did you know where I was?' Cora asked.

'I have my contacts, I can't tell you more than that,' she said distractedly, still looking Cora up and down, already leading her to a chair.

Cora lowered herself carefully down and then let out a long-held breath, suddenly exhausted.

Lulu was busy at the stove now, 'First things first: coffee and something to eat... then I will arrange for you both to move on as soon as possible. He will be here as soon as he discovers you missing, I'm sure of it.'

'Let me do the food and drink,' Anna said, 'then you can get on.'

'Good plan,' Lulu agreed, pushing a tea towel in Anna's direction, before heading out of the room. 'I need to make a telephone call,' she offered over her shoulder. Closing her eyes, Cora managed to drift into a sleeping-waking state, only rousing when Anna touched her arm gently and instructed her to eat and drink. Lulu must have come back into the room at some stage because she could hear Anna's voice telling her story. Then Lulu's response, 'I can get you out of the city. There are no guarantees of full safety, but with the asset you have, the high price you can pay, you will stand a good chance of making it in one piece to Marseille.'

Relief that Anna would be safe eased Cora and allowed her to drift into a deeper sleep for a while.

'Wake up,' Lulu said firmly, 'You need to eat more food, drink some water – you will be on the move soon.'

Cora reached out a hand to her, 'What happened to Francine, it seems so long ago. Tell me how everything went, did you manage to arrange the funeral?'

'Yes, she was buried this morning, I gave her as good a send-off as I could, a plain coffin is all they have in the city right now, what with the demand, but it was decent. She's buried in the same graveyard as my mother, close to the harbour, and I've marked the grave with red silk flowers. I said a special prayer on your behalf... told her not to worry, that I'd found out where you were, and I'd do all that I could to rescue you.'

Cora smiled, reached out a hand. 'Thank you for that, Francine was such a special person... I wish I could go to see her grave before I leave but...'

'You can't, there's no question about that, and Francine would understand. I've already told her, one day, when all this is over, you'll come back to lay some flowers, pay your respects, maybe stay for a while and chat. Francine always loved to listen, and she was so kind and so wise, as you know...'

Cora swallowed hard to stop herself from crying; she would let herself grieve properly when the time came.

'Thank you,' she said, reaching out a hand to Lulu, 'I will miss her so much.'

'Oh, I almost forgot, there is one more thing,' Lulu cried, 'I found it on the table by Francine's bed...' Cora heard the scrape of a kitchen drawer then Lulu was back by her side, 'This,' she announced, placing the silver dolphin's head lighter right in front of her.

Cora grasped it in her hand, choked out a sob, there was no stopping the tears now and it made her ribs hurt terribly. She clung to the lighter, feeling the hard silver dig into her palm, she was back in Francine's kitchen with the smell of the coffee, the crackle of the stove and all the love and the warmth Francine offered to those she chose to sit at her table.

Drawing in a shuddering breath, Cora swiped the tears from her eyes.

'I know, this is so hard, I was choked up when I found it, the lighter was her special thing,' Lulu soothed, 'and she would have wanted you to have it.'

Cora started to shake her head. 'No, Lulu, you must keep it. I don't smoke, and it needs to be used – Francine wouldn't have wanted it to be sat in a drawer.'

With one more stroke of the smooth silver, Cora slid the lighter towards Lulu. 'Please, you must have it...'

Lulu shrugged, offered a smile, then slipped a cigarette out of her pack, using the dolphin's head lighter immediately. She glanced up to the ceiling. 'Thank you, Francine... you know I'll make good use of it.'

As Cora breathed through the stabbing pain in her sore ribs, she began to feel calmer than she'd been for weeks. It was as if she could feel Francine's soothing presence and it made her so sad that they would never sit at the table together again, sharing their stories. She released a heavy sigh.

She felt the gentle pressure of Lulu's arm around her shoulders, then heard her voice as it almost broke on a sob, 'I feel it too, Cora. I will miss her so much, but her spirit is strong and it will stay with us forever. There will never be anyone like Francine King... she was a mother and a friend to us all.'

CHAPTER 25

Within the hour, a single knock came to the door and a gruff-voiced man with a double-breasted jacket and a cap worn low over his face stepped into the kitchen. Lulu stood up from her chair, pulled her peacock pattern blue silk robe close around her body. 'Please, Anna, show him the necklace,' she said. Anna produced the necklace from her apron pocket, and he held it to the candlelight for a few seconds, then he tested one of the stones with his teeth.

'It's good,' he grunted, 'and you said half.'

'Yes,' Lulu replied.

He took a pair of pliers from his pocket and with two firm snips the necklace was divided. Half given to Anna; the rest slipped inside his jacket pocket.

Anna went for her coat.

'Good luck,' Lulu said, pulling her into an embrace, 'Don't worry, you can trust Gustave... he knows I'll remove his balls, snip snip, if he double-crosses anyone I place in his hands.'

'Ha!' Gustave laughed, 'she's not wrong there! No man in Calais would dare cross Lulu Delacroix.'

Cora got up shakily from her seat at the table, she reached

out to Anna. 'Thank you. If it hadn't been for you, I don't even want to think about what would have happened to me.'

Anna pressed her lips together, then she placed the palm of her hand gently against Cora's bruised face. 'Don't forget you saved me as well, so you are very welcome, *ma chérie.*'

The way she spoke, in that moment, brought Francine back instantly. Cora felt it like a punch in her chest, but then it softened, left her with a warm glow and Francine's voice in her head, *Grief is the price we pay for love... that's the deal, with the pleasure comes the pain...* Cora nodded her head, 'That's true,' she whispered to herself, then, raising a hand to Anna, she called goodbye as the woman turned at the door to wave a final farewell.

Lulu lit another cigarette, took a drag, then shifted her attention to Cora. 'I know you are in pain, but you will have to be on the move very soon. Here,' she said, pushing a bottle of pills across the table. 'Anna left these for you, they're painkillers. She said they will help you.'

Cora reached for the bottle and slipped it into her pocket.

'I've told your guide that you are injured, you will have to take it slowly and you might need to rest up from time to time. Our aim is to get you out and along the coast to Brittany. It's a long journey and it will be hard, but I've seen your mettle, you can do this, I'm sure of it.'

Cora forced a smile, made herself step up to Lulu's expectations.

'Your destination is a small coastal village, far enough along the coast so that you are less likely to run into any German patrols. From there, you will travel by fishing boat across the Channel to Plymouth. Put your trust in those along the way, they are there to help you. If they ask you for a code word, it is Piaf.' Lulu grinned.

'Of course it is,' Cora laughed, instantly caught with a sharp pain in her ribs.

At the sound of a knock on the door, she heaved herself up from the table, picked up her bag and made ready to leave. A shadowy figure stepped into the kitchen and stood quietly waiting.

'I won't kiss you on the cheek or hug you too hard, for obvious reasons,' Lulu said, placing a gentle arm around Cora's shoulders. 'But you stay safe, hey. Francine thought the world of you, and she mentioned your mother, Evie, and another friend Iris. Sounds like you have a good team.'

'I do,' Cora croaked, her voice thick with emotion. She pulled Lulu into a gentle hug. 'Stay safe... the work you do here, it's—'

'I do what I do,' Lulu cut in, 'now go, just go... and one day, when all this is over, come back to the Hotel Genevieve, there will always be a warm welcome for you here.'

The shadowy figure waiting for Cora stepped into the light, it was a young woman with a tuft of black hair peeping out from a dark green knitted hat. 'Come with me,' she said, reaching for Cora's bag. 'We will be on foot for this first leg of the journey.'

Even as they were walking away from the back of the hotel, Cora heard with a jolt of panic the scrunch of tyres in the street and the loud hammering of a fist on the front door of the Hotel Genevieve. She knew it was Karl and the thought of him hurting Lulu made her chest tighten.

'Don't worry,' the young woman whispered over her shoulder. 'Vehicles can't get round the back to this narrow alley and Lulu, she can stick up for herself. She also has German friends in high places. She will be safe, even from Captain Hesse.'

Cora steeled herself, all she had was trust, and the knowledge that she was heading to Brittany, that almost mythical place where her birth mother had originated from. How strange that her escape route was via Brittany... it had to be a good omen, didn't it?

As darkness receded, Cora struggled on, every step of the

way sending a jolt of dull pain through her body. They were leaving the broken city of Calais behind, reaching a place where the houses thinned and blended into more open countryside. Her guide had slowed her pace, stopped for momentary rests as required and made sure Cora had a chance to take her painkillers. But all the while it was as if they had the devil on their shoulder, needing to push on, feeling at any moment they could be stopped.

It was a relief to see the first light of dawn breaking through, Cora took it as a sign that she was almost there, that all would be well. Even though she could barely walk, and her face ached in the cold morning air, she would not give in. She kept going, determined not to let what Karl had done to her prevent her from achieving her goal. Thinking of the fishing boat waiting for her in Brittany, imagining the kindly smile of the captain, helped her to keep moving.

'You will rest soon,' the young woman turned with a concerned glance. 'You are doing very well.'

Cora had no concept of time, all she knew was that it was now almost fully light, and she could hear the sea breaking on the shore, even smell the salt air. It soothed her soul, the familiar rhythm of it helping her put one foot in front of the other.

When they came to an abandoned building, what looked like a disused barn or a storehouse, the young woman stopped as if getting her bearings. 'This is it, the place you will rest,' she said. 'There will be food and drink waiting in a paper bag, you can sleep here till the evening, when darkness falls someone else will pick you up from here.'

Cora nodded. 'Thank you,' she breathed.

'You are welcome,' the young woman smiled, handing over the bag which she'd carried for Cora all the way through the city. 'I hope you get home safely.'

As her guide walked away, Cora took a few seconds to breathe in the salt air. Hearing a vehicle in the distance, she roused herself and hobbled towards the door of the rough stone building. With a firm shove the white-painted door creaked open. It smelt musty inside but with relief she saw a bed of straw covered by a blanket. *You can rest here, the food is in the bag*, the young woman had said, and there it all was, ready and waiting.

Cora collapsed down, groaning in pain as she settled herself on the makeshift bed. I'll close my eyes for a few moments she thought, sinking instantly into a dead sleep. Gasping awake hours later to the scrunch of tyres on the gravelly track outside, she shot up on her bed of straw, holding back a groan of pain from her stiff body. She sat waiting, holding her breath. In her head it was Karl, he'd tracked her down, he was outside in his car, waiting to drag her back to that locked room. She'd be his plaything, and then when he tired of her... Suppressing a sob, the bones of her face pulsing with pain, she sat completely still, like a statue. With no strength left to run, she was at his mercy now.

She could hear voices, the sound of boots on gravel. In a matter of moments the white-painted door would burst open...

Her heart skipped a beat at the slamming of a car, or could it be a truck door? The sound was heavy. Then an engine revved and the scrunch of tyres again... the vehicle was leaving. She sat erect, straining her ears, but there was nothing. It must have been passing traffic. A surge of relief ran through her body, making her light-headed, almost giddy.

She wanted to laugh out loud, but her body was too sore and she needed to bottle it up, in case someone else was passing by. Instead, she collapsed back onto her bed of straw and stared up to the roof of the barn. A missing terracotta tile allowed a shaft of sunlight to stream in, casting a square of light on the hard-baked earth floor. It was the most beautiful thing that Cora had ever seen, a bright ray of hope. If she'd had the strength, she'd have got up, raised her face to the sun, let it warm her soul.

Instead, she lay back, content to gaze at it, a smile starting to tweak at the corners of her mouth.

She must have drifted back to sleep because when she woke again the shaft of sunlight had gone and her belly was growling with hunger. Remembering the food in the paper bag, she pulled it towards her. Drinking greedily from a glass bottle of water until she'd slaked her thirst, she then devoured bread and cheese and a red, juicy apple. She'd never tasted flavours so pure; her mouth ran with saliva at the deliciousness of the meal. She revelled in the tastes, smacking her lips, searching the corners of the paper bag for any crumbs that she'd missed.

Gradually the light faded, and she began to feel chilly, so she wrapped the blanket around her shoulders over the top of her gaberdine mac. She knew that someone would come for her soon. Still, when she heard the rumble of a heavy vehicle followed by the sound of the barn door scraping across the earthen floor, she sat rigid, both fists balled. Then she heard a man's voice calling from the door, asking for the code word.

'Piaf,' she whispered into the gloom.

Only when she stood up from the bed, shedding the blanket and letting it fall to the straw, did she recognise the shape of a revolver in the man's right hand. Thankfully, he had lowered it now. He was smiling, walking towards her with an outstretched hand, which she took. His handshake was reassuringly firm and the gentle smile that played around his mouth helped to ease her anxiety.

'Are you ready?' he asked, walking to her straw bed, removing the blanket and then dispersing the straw with his feet across the floor of the barn. 'Don't want to leave any clues,' he twinkled, casting his eyes around, snatching up the paper bag, then gesturing with his head for her to follow. He raised a hand to hold her back inside for a few moments while he made sure their way was clear. Then he moved and she followed, keeping pace with his long stride. He lifted the canvas flap at the back of a covered truck, 'Get down amongst that pile of blankets,' he urged. 'Snuggle up. I'm taking you along the coast and I'm not stopping till we need to fill up with petrol.'

His sense of urgency chimed with her own, she was eager to be on the move again, even though as soon as they set off the rattle and bounce of the truck over the rugged road shook through her sore body. Wedging herself into a corner, she managed to find some relative comfort but with the movement of the truck and the seep of exhaust fumes, she knew this was going to be a challenging trip. It was daunting, but she made herself think of that beach in Brittany, where she would sit listening to the sound of the sea as she waited for her fishing boat.

Despite her discomfort, she must have fallen asleep because she woke with a start as the truck bounced through what must have been a deep pothole. She'd been dreaming that she was back at the cottage, Max was there, he was gently stroking her face as she lay helpless on the settee with the sound of the baby and the low murmur of Madame Fournier's voice in the background. Then it wasn't Max, it was Karl and he was dragging her off her bed, almost pulling her arm out of its socket. His voice rough, growling as he let her fall. She fell endlessly, rigid with fear till she banged down hard onto the floor. Her hip hurt so much she was sure the bone was broken.

She woke, shocked and in agony, almost sobbing, her heart racing with fear. It took a few moments for her to realise her hip was hurting because in her sleep she'd slipped off the blankets and now lay on her side against the hard boards. She groaned, shifting her position, able to ease her physical pain but her heart was still pounding from her dream. Karl was haunting her, maybe he would for the rest of her life. Inevitable, she supposed, given the brutality, the sheer inhumanity of the attack. She'd never been subjected to any physical violence in her whole life. Maybe Evie might have smacked her when she was a child, she could be naughty at times, but no one had ever hurt her so badly and so deliberately before. Then she remembered the gunshot, how could she forget that? But it was different, it seemed clinical in comparison. Karl had been right up close, she'd felt his breath on her face, seen his vicious gaze. He'd known exactly what he was doing. He'd punched her deliberately. A shudder cut through her body as she lay on the bed of the truck. Even a scraped knee had been lovingly kissed better by Evie or Adam. She was so homesick now. Instead of yearning for her birth mother, all she wanted was to be at home, safe in Montauk, with Evie and Adam, doing ordinary, everyday things in their house by the sea. 'You'll be back soon,' she told herself out loud, but there were so many stages of this journey yet to come, she daren't even think about what could go wrong.

At some point the truck stopped, she could hear the driver clambering down from the cab and slamming the door. He was whistling a mixed-up tune, then he shouted out, asking for fuel. She held her breath, sensing the presence of someone near the truck, then the inevitable sound of a fuel cap being unscrewed. The fumes were strong and they caught the back of her throat. She held a hand across her mouth, fearful of a cough giving her away. Desperately swallowing her own spit, she struggled to hold it back. But as the man was screwing the cap back on, out it came, a single cough. Instantly, her driver was coughing, making a real scene of it. She could hear the man with the fuel laughing, telling him he needed to cut back on the smokes.

Cora swallowed more spit, just to be sure, and she folded a piece of blanket and held it across her mouth till the truck started up and they trundled on their way once again. Miles and more miles went by, she dozed and slept and dreamed some more. Then as the light of a new day began to peep through the gaps in the canvas, she sensed that her driver had lost the urgency of their mission, their pace was slower, she knew they would be stopping soon.

When the truck ground to a halt, she waited, listening, not sure if they'd been stopped by someone or they had reached their destination. 'Come on, then,' the man called, sticking his head through the flap of canvas at the back of the truck. 'We're here, at your next stop.'

'Thank you,' Cora breathed as she struggled up, then took his hand to help her down.

He shrugged and smiled, didn't say anything except, 'You're over halfway there... you'll rest up again now, then you'll catch a train for the rest of the way. This far west, you should be safe on public transport – all locals here, not many Nazis.'

Cora didn't feel reassured, she'd rather have lain in the back of another truck, but she had to trust that these people knew what was best. She supposed that if she was found hiding in a vehicle, then that would immediately raise suspicion and there would be consequences for the driver.

She followed the man around the back of a single-storey whitewashed cottage with a red tiled roof on the outskirts of what looked like a village. He tapped three times on the door. It was opened by an elderly woman with white hair, her thin face lined with wrinkles, her dark eyes alive with mischief. 'Ah, monsieur, you are ahead of time,' she said, Cora barely able to decipher her thickly accented French dialect.

He tipped his cap and offered a smile to the elderly woman then turned to Cora, 'Madame will look after you now,' then he disappeared around the corner of the cottage before she could even say thank you.

Madame gestured for her to come in, then she closed the door firmly, locked it and applied a bolt top and bottom. 'Can't be too careful, not when there's another war on,' she chuckled, leading the way for Cora to follow. From the tiny kitchen which smelt of fresh baked bread they went through a sitting area and then Madame opened the door to a small bedroom with a neat single bed complete with a lace bedspread. 'You will stay in this room,' the woman said, 'I will bring you food, and then you can sleep for as long as you need.'

'Thank you, madame.' Cora tried to smile but her mouth felt lopsided and then she realised the woman had already gone from the room.

In her exhausted state, Cora began to wonder if she were caught up in a dream or a fairy tale, maybe the woman was a mirage. Then she heard the clatter of pots in the kitchen, and she knew that this was indeed real. Placing her bag by the side of the bed, shrugging off her coat, she sat on the bed, her black beret still on her head.

When the woman appeared with a tray of soup, homemade bread, fragrant cheese and some tiny, iced buns, Cora felt her stomach growl with hunger. Without saying a word, Madame placed the tray on Cora's knee, before pulling the beret from her head and placing it down on top of her bag. 'Enjoy your food,' she smiled, 'I bet you don't get bread and cakes like this in America.'

'How did you know I was from America...?' But the fairy-tale woman had disappeared yet again.

CHAPTER 26

After a magical unbroken sleep, for the first time free of nightmares, Cora woke to find herself refreshed. She yawned and stretched, feeling so comfortable she could have turned over and gone back to sleep. As if sensing the exact moment of her awakening, Madame tapped at the door and bustled in with coffee and pastries. 'No, no,' the woman said, as Cora made to sit at the side of the bed. 'Prop yourself up against the pillows, you must rest as much as you can.'

Madame placed the tray across Cora's knee. It reminded her of when she'd been ill at home and Evie had brought in her supper, made a fuss. She breathed in the memory, blinked back the tears, and then lost herself in the delicious food and the aromatic fresh-brewed coffee. When she was done, the tray was removed and, against orders, Cora sat at the side of the bed, pleased by how free her body felt, how much the pain had improved.

Standing up, she straightened her skirt and checked her bag: her fake identity card was still there – Simone Devereux. She hadn't needed to field any questions about her personal details yet, so it had been redundant so far. The other meagre items included the tattered paperback she'd started to read on that first train journey out of Paris, and down at the bottom of the bag she found a small leather-bound box that she hadn't seen till now. She recognised it immediately. 'The earrings,' she murmured to herself, clicking open the lid to reveal the diamond drops neatly slotted in, side by side. Anna must have put them there. Cora remembered now what she'd said when she'd pushed them in her apron pocket with the necklace, she'd told Cora, 'These are for you.' It seemed that she'd kept her promise, but seeing them took her back to Karl's brutality, it clutched at her, triggered hollow dread. She snapped the lid shut and threw them back to the bottom of the bag. She wouldn't be beaten by what that man had done to her.

A young, blonde-haired woman wearing a blue coat, teamed with a bright red scarf and matching felt hat set at a jaunty angle, was her escort for the next leg of the journey. 'Stay close,' she ordered, her tone businesslike. 'You can call me Lizette, you're a friend of mine from Paris, if anyone asks.'

Cora nodded, feeling not relaxed exactly but aware now that after all the distance she'd covered, this was probably the easy part of the journey. 'What happened to your face?' Lizette asked.

'I got the wrong side of a German officer,' Cora replied.

The young woman gasped, muttered some swear words under her breath.

'We are going for a day out at the seaside, I will buy the tickets,' she said, 'when the train comes sit quiet, do you have a book to read?'

Cora nodded.

The small local train arrived in a cloud of smoke and steam, it was narrow and rickety with only two carriages. 'You sit by the window,' Lizette ordered, 'keep your head down.'

As soon as they were settled in a seat, Cora took the tattered paperback out of her bag and started to read. The words swam before her eyes, she read the same paragraph over and over for some time before turning the page. Glancing out of the window she saw open countryside, clumps of trees with some copper and gold autumn leaves still clinging on. The sky was clear today, the landscape of whitewashed farmhouses with red terracotta roofs pleasing. She found herself starting to relax, rocking with the motion of the train as the steam swirled around them and they moved towards the sea, closer to her escape.

'Not far now, just one more stop,' Lizette said, her voice clipped, sounding a little tense.

Cora was about to say some soothing words, try to encourage her to relax as the train stood at the tiny station. But two young men boarded and instantly their eyes were drawn to Lizette.

'Hey, blondie,' one shouted, 'can we come and sit next to you?'

Lizette tutted, kept her head down, but the young men came anyway, sat on the seat in front. One of them, the bolder one, immediately turned round to stare.

'What you reading?' he said, grabbing Cora's paperback and tipping it up so he could see the title. 'Ooh, a love story, hey, what do you think about that, blondie?'

Cora's companion was steadfastly staring at her hands.

'She doesn't think much,' Cora piped up, the hairs at the back of her neck prickling, irritated now with the young man – his bearing, his entitlement. He was a younger, much milder version of Karl Hesse and he had the same grey eyes, a whippersnapper in comparison but, given the right circumstances, she knew that he had the potential to be just as brutal.

'You've got a funny accent. Not from round here, are you?' the young man said, narrowing his eyes, scrutinising Cora's face.

'No, she isn't, she's my friend and she's visiting.'

'Your friend is she, blondie? Well, pardon me for saying this, but I think you are talking bullshit.'

Cora had had enough now. Her head snapped up. 'I am her friend,' she spat, 'mind your own business.'

The young man was smirking, leaning closer over the seat.

'Leave it, Marcel,' his quiet mousy-haired friend said, pulling on his arm.

'I don't think I can,' the young man growled. 'I suspect there's some funny business going on here... have you not heard of the smuggling that's going on? People needing to get out of Europe, escape from the Germans... What better place to come, hey.'

Cora heard the young woman's breathing quicken, she was sitting stiffly, erect in her seat with her head bowed.

'Now, if that is what we have here, I think we could come to some arrangement, hey, mademoiselle?' he leered, reaching out to grip Lizette's chin, roughly yanking it up so she would look at him.

Something snapped inside of Cora, she couldn't bear it. She leapt up from her seat shouting, 'Leave her alone.'

The young man jumped to his feet, face to face with her, 'Got you,' he cried, his spittle hitting her cheek.

'What's going on here?' the train conductor shouted as he came into the carriage.

'I think we have an illegal travelling on this train,' the young man said, 'someone who should be reported to the gendarmerie as of interest to our occupying forces.'

Lizette looked petrified. She glanced to Cora, her face stricken. If she was found and reported, Cora knew that her guide would be arrested too. This was all too much to bear; she was prepared to deal with her own situation but in no way was she going to be responsible for the fate of a young woman who had taken a risk to guide her to safety.

Cora felt anger flare and fought hard to keep it at bay. 'I think we can sort this out,' she said to the conductor. 'I need to speak to you in private.'

The conductor looked dubious; he glanced her up and down, very unsure.

'Please,' Cora said, her heart pounding with fear for Lizette, she'd been through so much herself that her own worries felt of little consequence now. 'These men have been harassing my friend. Imagine if she were your daughter – you would be outraged at their behaviour.'

'Is this true?' the conductor asked, raising his voice, scowling at the young men.

When they didn't reply, Lizette started to sniff, dabbing at her eyes with a handkerchief. 'Yes, it is true. This one' – she pointed at the perpetrator – 'he's been saying bad things, trying to kiss me.'

The conductor growled, 'I'd put you two boys off the train,' he said, 'if we weren't almost at the last stop. And if either of you say another word to this young lady, I will report *you* to the gendarmerie.'

For the rest of the journey the young men sat rigid in their seats, staring straight ahead, while Cora held onto Lizette's hand.

It was such a relief to pull into the station, the young men were up right away, waiting at the door, ready to descend to the platform. Cora and Lizette followed demurely, not showing any sign of hurry, but all the time Cora's heart was hammering in her chest. As the train door opened and the fresh sea air met her, she knew that she was almost home, she sucked it into her lungs, enjoying the salty smell, the promise it gave.

Stepping down onto the platform first, she waited for a second to make sure that her travelling companion was safe. The moment she turned back, she saw with horror the young man, Marcel, marching down the platform towards her with the stationmaster in tow.

'Run,' urged Lizette, but Cora knew if she did, they would know that she had something to hide. Yes, she might escape, but if she didn't, she'd have real difficulty explaining her actions and as Marcel had already pointed out, her French accent sounded strange in this part of the country.

'Best to stand my ground,' she muttered to Lizette, 'But you must go, just go.'

A moment of indecision in the young woman's eyes, then she walked away.

'Where's your friend going then?' Marcel called. 'Deserting you, is she?'

Cora didn't answer, instead she turned to the stationmaster with her eyebrows raised, 'Is there something I can help you with, sir?'

The stationmaster was middle-aged, paunchy, and he looked like he was on the verge of a yawn, as if he'd been woken from a nap. 'This young man, he thinks I should ask you some questions – who you are, where you're going, that kind of thing,' he said sleepily.

'That's perfectly fine,' Cora said, 'but I'd rather do that in private if you don't mind. This young man has been harassing my friend on the train, I don't trust him.'

The stationmaster ran a hand around his face. 'All right, follow me,' he grunted.

Irritatingly, Marcel followed along behind, he wasn't going to let this drop easily. Cora clocked Lizette in the distance, waiting by the station gate. She discreetly raised a hand, then stepped out of view.

Once they were inside a small dusty office, stacked with papers on almost every surface, the stationmaster gestured for her to take a seat and he slipped behind the small desk, leaning back in his chair for a moment, removing his peaked cap, brushing back his few straggles of greying hair, then replacing it further forward on his head.

'I need to see your identity card,' he yawned, holding out a hand.

Cora unfastened her bag, confidently pulled out her fake papers.

He studied it closely. 'So, you are Simone Devereux,' he said. 'Where have you travelled from?'

'From Calais,' Cora replied, her heart starting to beat a staccato rhythm, feeling as if she couldn't breathe cooped up in the tiny room.

'Calais?' he frowned. 'What the heck were you doing there, the place is no more than a bomb site, or so I've been told.'

'I was working as a waitress at a boarding house,' she said.

'What's the name, what's the address?'

Cora knew instantly that she couldn't disclose Lulu's address, it would be too compromising, especially if it were linked to false papers, if that's where this conversation was leading.

'I'm so sorry, I can't remember.' She tried to form an innocent smile, but it must have fallen wide of the mark.

He narrowed his eyes, suddenly wide awake. 'I'm beginning to think the young man has grounds for his suspicions,' he growled.

Cora knew that what she said next was crucial, it would make or break her chance of escape.

She cleared her throat. 'I truly can't remember, I am so sorry. And the young man in question, he was very rude to my friend, he was trying to force her to kiss him.'

The man waved a hand as if all of that was unimportant.

'I have sufficient grounds here,' he said, making his voice pompous, 'to make a call to my senior officer, who may, in due course, check with the town hall in Calais for any discrepancies relating to a Simone Devereux.'

Cora felt her heart clench, the palms of her hands were clammy.

'I have recently lost a dear relative, a wealthy woman,' she said, fishing in her bag. 'I need to be with her family. I don't want to be delayed in my journey, so I'm wondering... if I offered you an incentive, would you be able to overlook your checks, this once, so I can be on my way?'

He leaned back in his chair, weighing up his options.

'What's the incentive?'

Cora pulled out the box containing the diamond earrings. As soon as she clicked it open, she saw his eyes spark with greed. He grasped one of the earrings, pulled it from the case and held it up to the light. 'I've only ever seen real diamonds once,' he murmured, 'a necklace around the neck of a wealthy first-class passenger. I always said to myself, "one day, I'll buy some of those for my wife", but on a stationmaster's pay...'

Cora sat praying he would take the bait. All she had between being arrested or going on her way were these two diamond drop earrings.

'They're the real thing all right,' he said, pulling out the second earring, holding it up next to the other one.

Time stretched on interminably, agonisingly.

She made herself breathe, wiped the palms of her hands on her coat.

'I'll take them,' he said abruptly, pushing them back into the box and shoving it into his coat pocket.

Cora stood from her chair, wanting to run from the room, but instead she made herself smile, 'Thank you for your consideration,' she said. 'My grieving relatives will be most grateful.'

He tipped his hat to her and she exited the room with him following along a few steps behind.

Marcel leered at her as she emerged, standing up from where he was leaning, a cigarette in his hand.

'There is nothing to investigate here,' the stationmaster shouted in Marcel's direction, 'and if you don't shift yourself, you'll be the one arrested.'

Cora saw the young man's eyes widen; he almost tripped over his own feet as he ran.

She walked steadily, kept going away from the stationmaster's office towards where she'd spotted Lizette by the gate, adrenaline still pulsing through her body, making her heart dance in her chest. It thrilled her and scared her all at the same time, thinking about what might have happened if she hadn't had those earrings in her bag. 'Thank you, Anna,' she whispered, 'thank you for saving my skin yet again.'

As she exited the station, she saw Lizette pacing, one hand balled into a fist. Cora called to her softly and she bounded forward to greet her. 'I am so relieved to see you, I thought I'd lost you for a moment there... how did—'

Gasping, Lizette froze in horror as two tall, broad-shouldered SS officers strode towards them. Both men unsmiling, keeping pace with each other.

'Shall we go down to the beach?' Cora spoke loudly enough for the officers to hear, linking Lizette's arm, turning her face away so there was no chance of being recognised.

Catching on straight away, Lizette replied, 'Yes, let's do that.'

Cora almost groaned with relief as the officers turned into the gate of the station. 'Let's get moving right now,' she urged, 'in case they've been summoned by the stationmaster.'

'This way,' Lizette gasped, grabbing Cora's hand and pulling her into a run. Cora's legs felt wobbly but as soon as the exhilaration of the near escape hit her, pure joy shot through her body. She wasn't home and free yet, but it was so tantalisingly close she could taste it as surely as the salt in the sea air.

'This way,' Lizette called, completely out of breath now, she had to pause for a moment bent over at the waist.

Only then, as she waited by Lizette's side did Cora feel the ache in her shoulder, the residual pain in her ribs. 'How much further?'

'It's up there,' Lizette pointed to a weathered house on the cliff overlooking the beach.

Lizette struggled a little to open the warped wooden door with a large iron key she produced from her pocket... 'I'll show you up to the room which has been prepared for your arrival.'

Coughing on dust, Cora stepped through into what would be her final resting place before the Channel crossing. After the exertion of running, her body felt alive, buzzing with excitement. Following Lizette up the creaky, worm-eaten stairs, she forced herself to hold back any thought of this being a done deal. 'Don't tempt fate,' was a phrase that Iris often used. Thinking of her aunt now, it was all she could do to steady herself.

'In here,' Lizette motioned, pushing open a flaking, white-painted door. The room was cluttered with rope and rusting iron tools, but a space had been cleared in one corner for a tattered armchair and a small table. Dust motes danced in the light streaming through the window. 'Stay in the corner so you're out of view,' Lizette instructed. 'You'll find food and drink in a bag beside the chair. When night falls, someone will come. It won't be me.'

Cora nodded, sensed some regret in the young woman's voice.

'I've learned a lot from this mission,' Lizette smiled, reaching out a hand, 'You be careful now. I sense you have a taste for excitement and sometimes you take a bit too much of a risk?' Then she leaned in closer, 'There was a woman from the next village with the identical hair colour as you, and the same fiery spirit. She met a British soldier during the last war and followed him to England.'

Cora felt the words like a punch, it took her breath away.

'Was she pregnant, did she go to Southampton?' she gasped.

Lizette scrunched her brow. 'I don't know, why are you asking?'

Cora's heart was thumping in her chest, she could barely speak, 'This is unbelievable but... that woman might...' Her throat was tight with shock, she was unable to continue till she'd taken a deep breath to steady herself. 'I was abandoned as a baby during the last war by a French woman with dark red hair, exactly like mine. I was found in the grounds of a British military hospital across the Channel in Southampton.'

Lizette's mouth dropped open, she reached out a hand. 'How strange... do you think it could be her, the fiery woman?'

'It's a strong possibility.'

Lizette was frowning now. 'This is unbelievable.'

'What was her name, do you know her name?'

'Erm, it was, oh, what was it... such a long time ago for me, but my aunt and uncle who live there, they used to tease me: "You'd better be a good girl or you'll end up like..." Ugh, what was her name?'

Cora's stomach twisted with frustration, she felt like shaking Lizette.

'Thérèse, it was Thérèse! Yes, that was it: "You'd better be a good girl or you'll end up like Thérèse." I never knew her surname.'

Cora groaned, a warm ache of longing in the pit of her stomach. 'Can you remember anything else?'

Lizette started to shake her head. 'I'm not sure you really want to know...'

Cora felt a stir of unease, Lizette's brows were knitted tightly together.

'I do want to know,' she blurted, 'I've waited so long to hear about her, I want to hear everything, even if it's bad.'

Lizette reached for Cora's hand. 'The thing is, if this Thérèse is your real mother, she's not the best person in the world.'

Cora's stomach swooped and fell, she made urgent noises, encouraged her to go on, even though she'd begun to feel daunted by what might be coming.

Lizette cleared her throat, looked Cora in the eye. 'It's just that... well, when she left the village to follow the soldier to England, she already had two children.'

Cora snatched some relief, sighed, 'Well, that means I have a half-brother or—'

'No, I'm not making this clear, I'm so sorry. The story goes that Thérèse left secretly at night, leaving her five-year-old son and her three-year-old daughter behind. They woke alone in their cottage the next morning to find her gone. The poor little mites were heartbroken.'

Cora felt a deep painful lurch in her chest. 'Maybe she was desperate, maybe she had to leave in a hurry,' she gasped, but even as she heard herself saying it, she knew she was inventing excuses for her birth mother. She'd done the same to Cora, after all, hadn't she?

Lizette squeezed her hand, 'The thing is... she'd had the time to pack all her clothes, to make sure she had her essentials. The whole village was outraged, why leave the children alone? She could have asked any one of them to look after the kids if something urgent had come up. In the end the village school-teacher, an unmarried middle-aged woman, took them in... Thérèse never came back.'

Cora's whole body heaved – all this time she'd held onto an image of her mother as a woman who might have been desperate and bereaved, but who was also a beautiful, caring person. Someone to seek comfort in during her darker moments. If what Lizette had told her was true, it smashed apart the whole invented image of her birth mother which had been built, layer upon layer, since she'd been old enough to understand the story of her finding.

She felt a jagged pain in her chest.

Lizette's face was full of concern, 'I'm so sorry to have told you this – and how strange that it's me, the person sent to accompany you on your journey to safety.'

Cora swallowed hard. 'It was meant to be.'

Tears stung her eyes but she wouldn't cry, she was determined not to.

'Thank you,' she croaked. 'It's not what I wanted to hear, but at least I know now what the woman was capable of.'

Lizette bowed her head, almost in tears herself, 'You might be right, though, maybe Thérèse did mean to come back but something prevented her.'

Cora forced a bitter smile. 'What, for the whole of that time... twenty-three years?'

'I'm worried about saying this out loud,' Lizette said. 'But maybe she died.'

'Maybe she did,' Cora murmured, shot through with a second's hope that it was the case, rather than the stark reality she'd been presented with. No, Thérèse was alive, Cora felt it in her gut, and now a bubbling fury was starting to build inside of her.

'Keep an open mind, if you can,' Lizette offered, as she pulled her knitted hat down more firmly and made ready to leave.

'I'll try,' Cora said, her mind still reeling, stricken, as she sensed deep anger now at the edges of her shock.

Lizette reached for her hand, leaned in and gave Cora a quick peck on the cheek. 'I wish I'd kept it all to myself now.'

Cora cleared her throat, made her voice steady. 'No, you did the right thing, it's best that I know.'

Lizette didn't look so sure, but she offered a smile, 'This is quite something we've been through together, isn't it... and not only our narrow escape from the stationmaster.'

Cora pressed her lips together, nodded, then managed to utter, 'You take care out there, Lizette, stay safe.'

'I will,' she offered, lifting a hand in farewell as she walked briskly towards the door, impatient now to be away.

Even after the sound of her footsteps had receded and Cora had heard the heavy clunk of the front door being closed, she stood like a statue, her mind struggling to absorb the new version of her birth mother which had come at her with force. How incredible to at last have the woman's name but how devastating to be told that this Thérèse had cruelly left behind two very young children, who would probably be scarred for life. They were her half-siblings; it broke her heart to know how they'd been treated. Her breath felt stuck, she cleared her throat to try and relieve it.

The chair was in the corner of the room, she slumped down into it, raising a cloud of dust which made her cough. At least it brought her back to the present and the realisation that she had no choice but to absorb the shock, lock it deep down, because right now she needed to stay calm so she could get out of this place. She felt like screaming out loud to relieve the reaction that had hit her like a punch. But she daren't risk making any noise.

Her birth mother had suddenly become a heavy, haunting presence she needed to leave behind so she could return to her real mother, Evie, and her kind, patient father with an open, unclouded heart. Feeling the weight of the spiral-patterned necklace against her breastbone, a wave of revulsion flooded through her. She grasped it, wanting to rip it off and throw it into the sea. But even as the edges of the pendant dug uncomfortably into her hand, something held her back. Evie had kept the necklace safe for her, given it to her on her sixteenth birthday. It had become a talisman and she had wholeheartedly believed in its power to keep her safe. It felt way too drastic, as she hovered on the brink of escape across the Channel, to jettison her good luck charm now. With an angry growl she squeezed it hard for a few seconds then let go, feeling it settle back to where it had always been.

CHAPTER 27

Later, after the sun had set over the sea and Cora had emerged from her final hiding place in the house on the cliff, she sat with her back against a rocky outcrop, listening to the waves breaking gently on the shore. The rhythmic sound, the smell of salt air helped her settle the haunting thoughts of Thérèse. In a way it was good to have time alone on the beach, to compose herself as she waited for the signal to move.

She hadn't had much rest in the house, with what Lizette had told her scurrying through her mind. Eventually, knowing she needed to calm herself, she'd been drawn to the ebb and flow of the waves on the beach below and she'd lapsed into an almost hypnotic state. Drifting between sleeping and waking, time suspended as she hardly dared to breathe between one wave and the next, in case she missed the three knocks on the thick wooden door. When the signal to move finally came, she gasped as if waking from a dream. Her heart painfully tight.

Now, she was waiting again, so close to escape, too close to comfort. If something went wrong at this stage, maybe she would never get home. Lizette had told her she would be smuggled onto a fishing boat, the route across the English Channel had been used before, it should be safe. *Should*. The boat would land her at Plymouth in Cornwall. Cora couldn't imagine beyond that, she had to rein back all expectation of what she would do then, safe on British soil. Coherent thoughts of what she'd experienced since that day in June when the swastika had been raised on the Eiffel Tower were too much for her right now. Instead came flashes of memory – Francine with her gun, the joy of running gleefully through the streets of Paris after escaping from Iris's apartment, the excitement of her missions with the camera. Later, finding the baby and loving her so fiercely for a short while. Lulu singing 'Lili Marlene', her cigarette clamped in the corner of her mouth. And Max, always Max, those moments they'd shared and that kiss on their final night, outside the cottage with the rustle of leaves in the breeze. The memory of him would be with her always, she was sure of that.

The flashes she tried to block were those which she already knew would come back to haunt her later – the brutality of Karl's assault, Madeleine punched and beaten by her own countryman, the searing pain of her gunshot wound, the baby's mother, crushed beneath the debris of the farmhouse. Then, Francine sick and dying in Lulu's bed.

She gulped in some sea air. If she hadn't been instructed to stay in the shadow of the rocky cliff, she'd have kicked off her shoes, walked over the smooth sand, waded into the sea to find some solace. She imagined lying down, letting the waves wash over her, renew her body and mind. The pain of the revelation about her birth mother would need to be salved somehow but she was still too shocked to work it out. Now that she knew Thérèse had lived by the sea, that they'd had that shared experience, it drew her and repelled her all at the same time. The ebb and flow of the tides, the cry of the gulls overhead, it tied them together from Brittany to Long Island and back again. It infuriated her that the new version of Thérèse shared this link... but it also energised her, made her more ready to sort out the intense feelings she now had for her birth mother. Not make her peace, but make sure that she worked through it so she could keep all of the joy and the solace that she'd always drawn from the sea. She was determined not to let Thérèse spoil that as well.

Another wave of distress hit her as she recalled her own sense of loss, after only a few short days, at leaving the baby with Madame Fournier. And little Mathilde wasn't even her own flesh and blood. How could Thérèse have left *all* her children behind? Was she some kind of monster? Cora shuddered, forced herself back to listening to the breaking of the waves... this was *her* sea, it would steady her, keep her safe.

A sound in the water startled her, someone wading through, a murmur of voices then a short, stocky figure approached. She got up from the sand, supporting herself with one hand against the rocky outcrop, feeling the gritty solidity of it as she strained her eyes to make out the detail of the approaching man.

As he came closer, he hissed, 'What is the code word?'

'Piaf,' she replied.

He nodded, gestured for her to follow him to a small rowing boat pulled up on the beach. Her heart was dancing in her chest, breath coming quick. She thought of Evie and Adam at home in Montauk, waiting for her, she prayed for the power of her parents to keep her safe. The fisherman helped her into the boat, 'Hurry,' his single word. She gripped the sides as he pushed the boat out then he jumped in, the small vessel swaying violently with his weight. 'It's all right, you are safe,' he murmured, those were the sweetest words that Cora had ever heard.

Once they'd boarded the darkened fishing vessel, she began to feel more at ease. But until they were well out into the Channel, in sight of the Cornish coast, she would not let herself believe that she might be saved. As they moved further away from the French coast, she felt glad to be leaving behind the heavy weight of the German occupation. The occupying force was strong. She'd seen first-hand the brutality of the German army in Karl, but then she'd also seen the other side with Max, a conscripted soldier, someone so kind and gentle, she couldn't even imagine him firing a gun, never mind trying to kill a fellow human being. As always, thoughts of Max eased her, she saw his smile, it made her feel safe and warm.

Propped against the side of the boat, she must have fallen asleep because a gentle hand was shaking her shoulder. 'Almost there now,' a lighter voice than the captain of the ship was saying. Groggy, Cora opened her eyes, and in the early morning light she made out the smiling face of a young man with dark red hair, like her own. With a gasp, she wondered if he might be her half-brother.

'Is your mother called Thérèse? Does she have red hair?' she croaked, sitting up lopsided, peering at him.

He started to laugh, 'Come on, wake up properly, you're dreaming.'

'No, no, I was just wondering...'

'My mother is called Celestine and she has black hair, like the rest of my family... I'm the odd one out,' he said, leaning in to inspect Cora's hair, 'Like you, hey.'

'Yes, I'm definitely the odd one out.'

'Here, I have sweet coffee for you... time to wake up, you are free now, free.'

She swallowed hard, pulled herself up at the side of the boat as it pitched in the swell of the waves; she had to hold on tight. The young man had reinforced her realisation – she had a half-brother and a half-sister, they might still live along this stretch of coast... if she came back one day and found them, she might be able to get to know them. The thought gave her a warm glow – this was where the search for her birth mother had led her... to the siblings she'd never had. And if a return visit didn't offer any clues, there was always the promise of obtaining

more information from that letter, the one Iris had sent to the
address in St Malo. Maybe by now a reply had come and it was
waiting in the apartment on Avenue Rapp. Not that she wanted
any more news of her birth mother, but if she couldn't trace her
siblings any other way, a letter might provide useful information. She wondered if her French half-brother had joined up,
maybe he was in a German prison camp right now or... she
couldn't even go there, she would not countenance the loss of
his life before she'd even been able to begin her search for him.

Thinking of a time in the future when the war would be
over felt impossible as she breathed the night air aboard a boat
smuggling her to safety. But it had to come one day, didn't it?
Her mind was too exhausted to think about how the war might
unfold, it would probably mean many more years of struggle.
The thought was overwhelming.

A whispering voice came to her – her mother, Evie. *Listen
to the sea, feel the boat beneath your feet... you are safe now and
soon you will be able to rest and heal. You will be home soon...*
Cora began to smile, it was madness she knew, but she could
already sense the presence of her mother and it made her feel
reassured. As she sipped the sweet coffee, she began to expand
her thoughts to her father, Adam, at home in Montauk in the
house by the sea that she hadn't realised she'd missed so much
until right now.

As the dramatic sweep of the Cornish coast became clearly
visible, silent tears flowed down her cheeks. She revelled in the
view, feeling the rise and fall of the solid fishing boat beneath
her. She would never forget this moment of return; it was pure
bliss.

As soon as she was ashore and safely installed in a quaint
boarding house close to Plymouth harbour, she asked to use the
telephone. 'Don't be talking for too long,' the grumpy proprietor
of the establishment said, reminding Cora so much of Estelle
she had to hold back laughter as the woman led her to a small

room where the black telephone stood in the middle of an oak table. With shaking hands Cora dialled for the operator, asking to be put through to their house by the sea in Montauk. She waited and waited, feeling the beat of her heart as time stretched on and then there was a click and the operator's voice, fuzzy now, 'Just putting you through.'

With another click her father's voice spoke, 'Hello, can I help you?'

Hearing his voice felt like catching the thread of a dream's edge, she wasn't sure if it was real. She tried to speak but her voice wouldn't come, she was holding her breath, anxious not to break the spell.

'Hello?' he said again, as she clung to the edge of the wooden table, her heart racing in her chest, so fast it made her light-headed.

She cleared her throat and then she croaked, 'Dad...'

'Cora, is that you, Cora?

'Yes, Dad, it's me,' her voice breaking.

He was crying at the other end of the telephone; she'd never heard him cry before but he was sobbing and sobbing. Once he was able to speak, he sounded frantic, asking all the questions at once: 'Where are you? Are you safe? Are you injured?'

When she'd given enough information to soothe him, he cleared his throat, began to use his doctor's voice to give direction.

'So, you are in Plymouth, Cornwall right now... so that's good because I think there's a direct train you can take. It might surprise you to hear that your mother and Aunt Iris are now also in England, along the south coast in Southampton.'

'Iris,' Cora gasped. 'Iris is safe!'

'Yes, she is safe, she came to us in Montauk months ago... she was arrested by some German soldiers who came into the apartment that day you went missing.'

Cora's heart jolted, it felt as if Karl Hesse would haunt her forever. She knew he and his sidekick had been involved, he'd almost told her as much.

'Was she hurt, is she OK?'

'She was thin, troubled, when she arrived in Montauk, but your mother soon had her eating and drinking, looking more relaxed. She was held for a while in a prison cell... she never really talks about it.'

Cora felt her chest constrict; she knew first-hand how that kind of trauma played out.

'Cora, are you all right? You've gone quiet.'

Hearing the alarm in her father's tone, she cleared her throat, 'Yes, yes, I'm fine... just so relieved to know that Iris is safe.'

She heard her father sniffing, he gave a rough cough then wrestled back his doctor's voice. 'So, what happened was, your mother had already been talking about going to France to search for you herself or getting stuck in and helping with the war effort. So, after Iris had recovered, that's when they decided to sign back on as war nurses, working at the Netley Military Hospital in Southampton.'

It all clicked into place now, of course they would do that, she knew how spirited the two of them were, especially working together.

'Obviously, another big part of doing that was that they would be right across the English Channel, ready and waiting for you if you managed to get to England.'

Cora felt a bubble of relief rise through her chest – Evie and Iris were already there. It made her feel choked up to know that they'd been so determined to be as close as possible to France. She swallowed hard but she couldn't stop the ache in her chest.

Her father's voice was thick with emotion again. 'Cora, are you sure you're all right?'

She started to laugh to stop herself from crying, 'Yes, yes, I'm absolutely fine, I promise.'

She heard him breathe deeply, she could sense him pulling himself together, 'I'll give you the number for the hospital, call your mother and Iris, let them know you're safe, that you are coming to Southampton. Have you got a piece of paper and a pencil?'

His practicality, the tone of his voice, made her smile. 'Yes,' she called down the line, grabbing the stub of pencil and a scrap of paper already written on, no doubt by some other stray. After he'd recited the number, he told her: 'I'll wire you some money, so you can pay for your travel and board and lodgings.' Then with a catch in his voice which made Cora's heart twist, 'You have no idea how wonderful it is to know you are safe, my daughter, my beautiful daughter.'

Her throat tightened, she had to take a moment before she could reply, 'I'll see you soon Dad.'

Iris and Evie were busy on a ward still packed with casualties recovering from the evacuation at Dunkirk. Their morning shift was full of dressing changes, penicillin injections and the detail of care of the mainly bed-bound patients. They'd both been surprised at how easily they'd clicked back into the routines of work at Netley hospital. On their first day, Evie had joked that hopefully they wouldn't be haunted by the ghost of Sister Pritchard – the strict, uncompromising but utterly professional ward sister who had overseen all their work previously. They'd heard that she'd died years ago. 'She's probably ruling the roost on one of those wards up in the sky,' Evie had joked. But the strange thing was, the sister on their current ward was almost a reincarnation. An uncompromising, straight-backed woman with an eagle eye, knowing and seeing everything, Sister Jones was strict but fair. It had made them laugh and reminisce even more strongly about the last war.

For Evie, being here was hard. It was where she'd found

Cora that summer evening towards the end of the war. This is
where it had all begun and where she was now waiting,
desperate for news of her adopted daughter. On the first
evening of their return visit, she'd walked to the small pier
which jutted into Southampton Water, where she'd stood when
she'd heard Cora's first cry. The trees in the hospital grounds
were stripped of their leaves and an icy wind blew but she'd
wrapped her red-lined nurse's cloak around her and clutched
the rail, gazing up to a sliver of moon in the dark grey sky, letting
her mind reach back to the time of Cora's 'finding'. She'd found
contentment standing there and it had brought her closer to
Cora, made her even more sure her daughter was still alive.
Shivering with cold, even in her wool cloak, as she'd walked
back down the pier, she'd seen again the red-haired woman
deposit a blanket bundle in the grass, she'd heard the strident
cry of an abandoned baby. She'd felt reconnected with her
daughter.

'Cora,' she'd whispered to the night, but all that had come in
reply was the haunting cry of a herring gull.

As the days ticked by with the all-consuming work on the
wards, Evie grew stronger, less preoccupied. She found again
the reward of working with the injured soldiers and as she
observed their slow recovery, it gave her hope, made her feel
part of the war effort, helped her manage her own demons. And
the relationship she had with Iris had been restored so well it
felt new-found – she had a friend who shared her anxiety over
Cora, fully understood how she had to live with the loss day
after day, and how hard it was to wait for news that never came.

This morning, Evie was working with a probationer nurse
while Iris, slipping back into her more senior role, was checking
through the notes with Sister Jones. When a voice called down
the ward, 'Nurse Mayhew, telephone call for you,' Evie didn't
think much of it. Adam sometimes called and because he was a
doctor, Sister Jones didn't mind her speaking to him, providing

their conversation was short, and mostly related to the patients she'd left behind in Montauk.

Evie raised a hand to Iris, who was sitting at a desk at the other side of sister's office, mouthing, 'It's Adam...'

She picked up the heavy telephone receiver, 'Hello,' she said. When no reply came, 'Adam? Is that you?'

She could hear a snuffling sound, 'Adam, are you OK?'

Then a tiny voice from far away said, 'Mom, it's me, it's Cora.'

Evie gasped out loud and clutched the desk, now she was the one who couldn't speak.

Iris jumped up from her desk, she was already by her side, her voice urgent, pleading, 'Evie, what is it?'

'It's Cora,' Evie croaked.

Iris took the receiver, 'Cora, is that you?'

'Yes,' came the tiny voice, 'I'm in Plymouth, I'm safe.'

Iris was choking on tears now, clinging to Evie, 'She's safe, she's safe.'

Evie retrieved the heavy receiver, gasping, 'I can't believe it's you, I've been so worried... are you sure you're all right, are you injured?'

As she talked on and on, Iris stayed right by her side, leaning in, her arm supporting Evie, tears still streaming down her cheeks.

On the day Cora arrived in Southampton, Evie and Iris were both waiting for her on the station platform. Evie had already given her notice, so she'd be ready to escort her daughter back to America, but Iris had chosen to stay on at the hospital, carry on with her war work. Evie was either jigging up and down or pacing back and forth, she couldn't keep still. Iris felt like her mother – soothing, cajoling, trying to occupy her.

With the sound of the train approaching, the gusts of steam

and swirling smoke, both women began to spiral out of control. They clung together, taut with excitement. Passengers were pouring off the train, frantically their eyes searched up and down the platform.

'Oh God, what if she missed the train, what if she's lost,' Evie was saying, her voice on the edge of panic. When Iris glanced up, she saw a young woman who looked like Cora, but she was too thin, and her red hair was cropped short. Only when the young woman stopped in her tracks did Iris realise it really was Cora.

'She's there!'

As the two words landed, Evie turned to look in the direction Iris was pointing. She screamed out loud, running headlong towards Cora, who seemed rooted to the spot. Iris followed along behind, content to stand back and witness the reunion of mother and daughter.

'Mom,' Cora was sobbing as Evie crushed her in an embrace, stepping back only to reach up to her daughter's face. 'Your face is bruised, what happened?'

'Oh, it's nothing, I was hitching a lift on the back of a truck coming out of Calais and I had a fall, that's all. It's fine, honestly,' Cora wasn't sure if it was right to lie to her mom, but she couldn't stand here at first meeting and tell her what had happened to her that night with Karl.

Evie kissed her hand and placed it against Cora's cheek, like she'd done when she was a little girl. Then they were hugging again, crying some more.

'Aunt Iris,' Cora said at last through tears, reaching out a hand to her. 'I was so worried about you... I stayed on in Paris to look for you, but we never had any information.'

'Did you stay in the apartment all by yourself?' Iris asked.

Cora felt her chest tighten. 'The apartment was taken by the Germans on that first day, I never got back there.'

Iris sighed. 'I thought as much, I knew those two soldiers I met on the stairs were up to no good.'

Cora couldn't speak of Karl Hesse, not yet, maybe she never would, so she didn't elaborate. 'I didn't manage to rescue much from there, but I got your rubies and the blue silk evening gown you were so fond of... and your tortoiseshell brush. I had to leave them at Francine's though, I wasn't able to—'

Iris was thanking her, 'I hope you didn't take any risks, getting those items. And I know Francine will take good care of them.'

'No,' Cora gasped, 'I somehow thought you might know.'

'Know what?' Iris and Evie asked, their voices rising together with alarm.

Cora opened and closed her mouth but no words would come, her chest so tight she could hardly breathe.

'Cora, please, what is it?' Evie pleaded.

She pressed a hand to her breastbone, spat it out, 'I'm so sorry, but Francine... she died.'

'No,' Evie shouted, while Iris stood silent, frozen.

Cora felt the shock of their loss, absorbed it.

'Did she die in the war, was she shot or something?' Iris asked at last.

'No, she had cancer. You know how tough she was, she must have known she was ill for a while, but she never said anything. Then when I was getting out of France, staying in Calais with a friend of hers, she turned up at the door looking very sick. She told us then that she was dying.'

'How long did it take? Was she in any pain?' Iris asked, her eyes wide, breath coming quick.

'It was an easy death, and I was with her, holding her hand... she died with a smile, thinking about Sam.'

Iris put a hand to her chest. 'She always said he was still with her, and that thing about getting used to living with our ghosts... I've thought of that so many times...'

'She was a very intuitive person, so special,' Evie sniffed. 'I'm so glad you were there with her, Cora... and were you able to ensure she had a decent burial?'

Cora swallowed, 'Yes, she was buried in a cemetery near the harbour, the grave is marked with red silk flowers.'

Iris started to cry. 'She'd be glad of being near the sea, hearing the sound of the waves.'

Evie grabbed hold of Iris, trying to comfort her with tears running down her own cheeks.

Cora put an arm around one and then the other, pulling them close. 'I'm so sorry,' she soothed, 'but there was no way I could let you know. Her sons in New York probably don't know either.'

Iris had her handkerchief out now, dabbing at her eyes. 'It's good at least that you were with her, and she died peacefully.'

Evie used the back of her hand to wipe her eyes and then her nose, she nodded, then pulled Cora close again. 'You must have been through so much over there. Cora, when you're ready, you need to talk about it, tell us everything.'

Already, Cora knew that she wouldn't be able to be completely open, there were some things that she never wanted to revisit, but she would speak about the better times, when she was living with Francine.

Feeling Evie link her arm and give it a squeeze, like she used to when they were both ready to go down to the beach, Cora felt a painful lump in her throat, the disconnect from where she was now to her uncomplicated life in Montauk felt too great. Now that she was so close to being home, she felt the weight of what she'd brought back from France drag at her even more. The thoughts that came at her were like the smuts of smoke in the air, barely visible to the naked eye but clinging to her all the same. To stop her body from trembling, Cora squeezed Evie's arm, snuggled closer. Overjoyed to have her mother by her side, she felt grateful for the lilt of her voice, her vitality, the love that she'd always given. One day soon she would share with her the news about Thérèse, but not today. She would keep it to herself until she was sure her mother fully understood how much she loved her. And that no one could ever take her place.

'First things first: we all need to eat,' Evie announced, starting to pull Cora along, out of the station. 'Iris has booked a table for us at a hotel nearby. Let's have a few glasses of something to celebrate your arrival.'

'Yes, yes,' Cora nodded, her mind drifting back to Paris, the clink of the wine glasses at Francine's table, the love and the laughter she'd found there.

As they walked together through the steam and the smoke and out of the station, Cora began to feel lighter, more able to connect with the emotion of the day. She'd only dared let herself think of this reunion once she was safe on British soil. Even on the journey to Southampton, as she'd dozed and woken at each stop, her mind had lurched between anxiety and excitement and back again. Seeing Evie and Iris was so good, so big a part of coming home; it frustrated her that she couldn't yet feel it as cleanly as she should. But when Evie started to hum a tune as they walked, then broke into one of the ballads from her days of working as a fisher girl, it connected Cora straight back to her childhood, when they'd sung and danced and run along the beach together.

EPILOGUE

MONTAUK, LONG ISLAND, FEBRUARY 1941

'Hope' is the thing with feathers
That perches in the soul,
And sings the tune without the words,
And never stops – at all

Emily Dickinson

Alone in the swing seat on the porch, wrapped in a woollen blanket against the frosty air, Cora listened to the blissful rhythm of the waves breaking on the shore. The relief, the joy of being home still actively buzzed through her but this morning she'd gasped awake from a nightmare, slaked with sweat, the wound in her shoulder throbbing. Strangely, the flashbacks of being trapped, beaten, running for her life had become even more persistent now she was safely home.

Instinctively she reached for the spiral-patterned necklace and grasped the pendant. She'd planned to remove it as soon as she was home, but even as she'd thought it, a hollow feeling had opened up in her chest. Despite what she'd found out about Thérèse, the necklace was her talisman and she still believed in its power to keep her safe. She'd wanted so much to banish it to the bottom of a drawer, but even as she'd unfastened it, she'd felt the loss. Squeezing the pendant in her hand now, she knew she had no choice but to keep wearing it. As she slipped it back inside her thick sweater, the icy coldness against her skin sent a shiver through her. It heightened her senses, rekindled a spark she'd had last night, as she was drifting off to sleep... What if she wore the necklace now, not for Thérèse, but for her half-brother and sister? She let the thought rest for a moment, then she snuggled it close, pulling the warm woollen blanket more tightly around her body.

The whistle of the mailman as he approached the house made her look up. His breath was misting in the cold air. Seeing her, he shouted a good morning and came to the porch, handed her a letter. 'Thank you,' she called to his retreating back, immediately gasping in disbelief when she saw the pencilled address on the tattered envelope. It was her letter to Evie, the one she'd written all those months ago at Francine's kitchen table, showing the arduousness of its journey through war-torn France. She turned it over, planning to tear it open, but the worn, discoloured paper and a distinct thumbprint across the seal stopped her. The pristine white envelope she remembered from Paris had been passed from hand to hand by people like Bertrand and Estelle, and through all of that, it had remained intact. She couldn't bring herself to disrupt it now, not after all it had been through. The miles it had travelled from the occupied zone to the free zone and then across the ocean to America... It felt wrong to rip it open, particularly since she could remember almost word for word what she'd written, and all that and more had already been told to her mother.

Turning it over to see her own handwriting once more, she felt her heart surge. Instantly she was back at Francine's table with the soft scratch of a new pencil on notepaper, the spit of the kitchen fire and the smell of freshly brewed coffee. Those innocent first few weeks of the German occupation, before Madeleine had been attacked, before she'd even been out on her first mission with the camera, when she'd naively assumed she'd be perfectly safe to stay on in Paris. She closed her eyes, sensing Francine's presence so strongly before her soothing voice came, as it often did, telling her not to be afraid to live life, that all would be well. A ripple of pleasure spread through her body, the comfort of knowing Francine was still with her, still looking after her. What she'd said about the ghosts who live with us, it was absolutely true. She would ask Evie about the letter, see what she thought, but she was sure her mother would agree... leave it as a permanent memento. This was no secret correspondence – it was a simple, reassuring message from a daughter to her mother, speaking of love and homecomings.

Almost immediately, before they'd left Southampton, she'd told Evie and Iris about Thérèse and her half-sister and -brother. Iris had cried but Evie, although visibly shocked, had said straight away, 'Those poor children, we must try to find them when this war is over.' It had made Cora love her even more. What *had* hit her mother hard was the scar on her shoulder. Evie's face had been the picture of pure horror when she'd first seen the bullet wound. She'd gasped out loud, broken down. Then, once Cora had explained the circumstances of the shooting, thinking it would reassure her, Evie had gone quiet, looked even more worried. 'So, were you involved with a spy network?'

Cora had done her best to explain the nature of her work with Francine, Estelle and Bertrand, but Evie hadn't looked so sure, and it had compounded how bad Cora already felt about the terrible worry she'd caused her parents. Even now, there were moments when she caught Evie off guard, sitting at the table, lost in her thoughts or throwing an anxious glance in her direction. The rawness of her own experience still came to her in flashes and it permeated through to her parents.

Although she knew it was a lost cause, she still thought of Max every morning on waking. It tied her back to the moment he saved her with his kiss of life. The story of Max had been on the tip of her tongue to tell her mother, but it had never come out. She'd told it to her old friend Martha and she'd gasped out loud, pressed a hand to her chest and said it was the most beautiful story she'd ever heard... Martha had made Cora cry with her enthusiasm for it, not tears of joy but tears of loss, because it was inconceivable that she would ever see Max again.

Week by week, as time ticked by in the house by the sea, Cora began to feel more settled. She was still struggling with the persistent flashbacks, but walking the beach helped her. She spent hours breathing the salt air, listening to the withdrawing roar of the sea. She was sometimes able to get things straight in her head when she was out there and the harder the waves broke, the better she felt. The more time went by, however, the more she felt at a loose end, as if she didn't fit any more with the life she'd had before. Going out with friends, catching up with Danny, engaging in superficial chit-chat about this and that with people who had no concept of what it was like to be caught up in a war. It was wearing. She was sick of pasting the same smile on her face and telling everybody that she was fine, just fine. And if they tried to ask for specific detail of the war, her stock response was, 'Oh, I didn't see much of that, I was in Paris, it was safe for Americans there.'

She felt as if she were involved in a dance, a performance, trying to show everyone she was all right, that nothing had changed. But it had changed, *she* had changed. After all the distress the scar from her bullet wound had caused her mom, she'd been even more wary of how much she told Evie. Her dad seemed to have some understanding. He'd spoken of the unseen wounds that people brought back from war. She hadn't gone into much detail with him, but she'd been grateful for his recognition. She'd told him, because she knew it to be true, that it was the unseen wounds which were the most difficult to heal. A gunshot was clinical in comparison to what Karl Hesse had done to her.

She'd been thinking of chasing up the application she'd made in her previous life, for medical training at the Bellevue hospital in New York. When she'd mentioned it to Evie and Adam last week, after supper, she'd seen the frozen look on their faces and then her father had said immediately how it might be better for her to wait a while longer, the work she was doing for him and Evie in the practice was indispensable. It was nice going around to the patients, delivering medication, staying for a chat, or helping her mom with the pregnant women and the new babies. But that was her old life, she didn't fit with it anymore.

Don't be afraid to live life, Francine had said. Hearing it again now spurred her to walk out onto the porch, feel the gentle sea breeze ruffle her growing strands of red her. She drew in a deep breath and looked up to the blue sky and scudding white clouds. It was spring, the sea air felt warm, and Iris was arriving today from Southampton to spend a few weeks with them before she went back to her war work at Netley hospital. It made her feel joyous to know that Evie and Iris would be reunited, and she could be a part of the laughter and the love they shared, sitting at the kitchen table, reminiscing about old times or telling new stories.

She said a quick prayer for Francine, for Lulu, for Madame Fournier and the baby, and for Max. And then, feeling the weight of the spiral-patterned pendant against her breastbone, she grasped it and lifted it to her lips, gently murmuring, 'I know you're out there somewhere, my brother and sister. Stay safe, one day I will come and find you.'

Seeing a herring gull soaring on the breeze, she felt a moment of pure happiness. Gazing across to the horizon, it was almost impossible to believe that war was still raging in Europe.

Inevitably, it would come to America, she was sure of that, but right now the sun was warm on her face and the beach was calling for her.

She slipped on her sneakers and ran to the shore, feeling a ripple of excitement in her belly at the sound of the ocean. Running full pelt towards the sea, she splashed through the water, glad of the waves breaking against her legs, making her feel even more alive. After she'd splashed and waded, she continued to walk the beach with sand clinging to her damp feet. There was nothing she needed to do right now, she was having time off, going to see *Gone with the Wind* with Martha and Justine later. It had made her feel sad when Justine had suggested it, tying her back to her promise to Francine that when the war was over, they'd go together to the best cinema in Paris. But quickly she'd realised that Francine would want her to honour their agreement, and in some way she'd be there with them.

As she slipped her sandals back on her gritty feet, the April sun peeped out from behind scudding white clouds. She closed her eyes and turned her face to the sky. As she stood, enjoying the warmth, a faraway voice began to call, 'Cora! Cora!'

She tutted, her mind had been so jumbled with flashbacks, this had happened to her before. She stood firm, kept her eyes closed, breathed deeply, in and out, in and out. She knew exactly how to beat it back.

'Cora,' again, a man's voice, accented.

She knew that voice.

She opened her eyes. A tall, lithe young man was running towards her, one arm of his white shirt flapping loose. What? Who?

He was only a few strides away and with a lurch in her chest she recognised exactly who it was. 'Max!' she shouted, bounding towards him.

He stopped for a second, grinning at her, his dark hair

grown longer, slightly wavy, ruffling in the breeze. Still split between thinking he might be a flashback and knowing he was real, she gazed at him, stunned. Then he laughed, took a step towards her, and the spell was broken.

'Max,' she cried out loud, pulling him to her, wrapping her arms around him, feeling the scratch of his stubble against her cheek. His body was warm, he smelled of sea air and when his lips met hers, that moment of realisation she'd experienced on their last night together in France connected with the swell of the ocean, the cry of the gulls overhead and the heat of the spring sun. As they kissed, she felt the blossoming of a rekindled ache in her chest. The moment they'd shared on their last night in France blending seamlessly into the press of his lips and the feel of his body right now. It made her mind sing with expectation.

'I thought you were a mirage,' she gasped.

'I'm real, Cora. I've come to find you,' his face lit up with a smile.

'How have you got here?' she breathed.

'I remembered all the detail of where you said you lived, so I got myself down to Lisbon in Portugal and onto a refugee ship that was heading to New York.'

'But how did you get out of the army?'

'Ah,' he said, pulling his mouth down at the corners. He stepped back and pointed with his right hand to the half empty left sleeve of his shirt.

'You lost an arm!'

'Well not really lost, it got blown off. I had an accident clearing some munitions, got on the wrong side of a faulty grenade.'

Cora could hardly breathe, she was so shocked, feeling the pain for him.

'Honestly, I'm fine, it's just the hand, I've still got the elbow,' he said, showing her how he could flex the arm.

'It must have been awful,' she gasped.

He lowered his head, breathed in. 'Yes, it was... but there are so many others who are worse off or even dead...' He held up his injured arm, 'I'm lucky to get away with this, that's how I think about it.'

Cora pulled him close, fought to hold back tears.

They stood for a moment, breathing as one, then he roused himself. 'At least it got me out of Hitler's army and the first thing I thought of was coming to America. All the time I lay in hospital, I thought about you and me in the cottage with Madame Fournier and the baby. I remembered how safe, how happy I'd felt there for that few days and then, on that last night...'

His arms tightened around her, 'I can't believe I'm here and I saw you straight away, walking along the beach, exactly how you described it to me.'

'Is this real?' Cora murmured, reaching up a hand to stroke his face, then kissing him again with the sound of the waves breaking on the shore and the warm spring sun on her back.

'It's real,' he laughed, 'and we're going to make the most of it.'

As they walked together along the beach, if felt like a scene from a film... his arm around her, pulling her close, she still wasn't sure if she were imagining the whole thing. Yet she felt the relief, the warmth of his smile as it settled over her.

'When did you get here? Where are you staying?' she asked, trying to make it more real.

'I arrived two days ago and I'm staying with my father in Brooklyn.'

'Of course, your father... you told me he lives in New York.'

'Yes, Otto was very shocked to see me... especially with this.' He held up his left arm, it felt so stark, it made Cora's stomach clench.

'But is it all right in New York, you being German, does it cause any problems?'

He shrugged, 'If people ask, I always tell them, but there are so many people and so many accents from all over the world in the city, so it all seems to blend in. There are lots of Germans in the area where my father lives and it's all OK, I think. They know that if America does join the war, things might change. But most of my father's friends were born in New York or they've lived there forever. It has to be fine.'

Cora wasn't so sure, but she was so happy right now, she didn't let the thought settle.

'And how are you?' he asked, slipping an arm around her waist.

'I was going to say fine,' she laughed, turning with him, so they could walk back together towards her house, 'but that's what I tell everybody else. It's hard, isn't it, coming back from a war. It's impossible to leave it all behind.'

'Yes, it is,' he said, pulling her closer against the side of his body, stopping then at the water's edge to kiss her again, so tenderly it made her heart almost break.

Cora felt the hard lump inside her chest that she'd carried since France start to crumble a little around the edges. It would take her a while, but she knew now, if Max stayed around, she was going to be better in time.

'I'm going to see *Gone with the Wind* tonight,' she said, 'Do you want to come?'

'Why, yes, ma'am, I surely do,' he replied, using a mock American accent to imitate Clark Gable. Cora giggled. When he followed up with, 'Frankly my dear, I don't give a damn,' they both cracked up laughing together.

As they walked side by side, Cora imagined the sound of their chat and their laughter drifting out to sea, echoing across the Atlantic. She knew it was only a matter of time before America was drawn into the war, but until it came, she would enjoy this opportunity she'd been gifted to spend time with Max. She wasn't sure how her parents were going to react, but she had enough confidence in them to know that they would only want what was best for her. Maybe a lanky ex-German soldier with a missing left hand wouldn't be quite what they bargained for, but once they got to know Max, she knew they would be persuaded.

'You'll have to teach me some more German,' she said.

'Only if you'll instruct me how to be American and buy me hot dogs,' he quipped, pulling her close, pressing his cheek to her hair, breathing her in.

'I keep thinking about Madame Fournier and the baby,' he said. 'One day, when all this is over, we'll have to go back there to see them.'

'Yes,' she breathed, 'we will. But for now, it's all about me and you and Montauk and the ocean.'

Taking his hand she pulled him into a run, they raced together along the beach, laughing and shouting in the space between the sea and land. Their joyous voices drifting in the clear spring air, up to the big blue sky above.

A LETTER FROM KATE

Thank you so much for reading *The Last Letter from Paris*. I hope you enjoyed reading it as much as I enjoyed writing it. To keep up to date with the latest news on my new releases, just click on the link below to sign up to my newsletter – I promise never to share your email with anyone else:

www.bookouture.com/kate-eastham

It's always difficult to leave characters behind, particularly when they're so well loved as Iris and Evie from *The Sea Nurses*. So it was an absolute treat to keep them close in this story, see how their lives were unfolding, acknowledge them as older women alongside their good friend Francine – now elderly but still a lively, potent force. Even more satisfying was to take our foundling baby, Cora, and show her progress from a confused teenager yearning for knowledge of her birth mother to the resilient, adventurous young woman she would become as part of the early Resistance movement in Paris.

The proximity of the two world wars, one ending in 1918, the other beginning in 1939, and how that must have felt for those forced to endure both experiences, provided a desperately sad but also rich backdrop for the book. I've lived long enough to have met – as part of my previous life as a registered nurse – a few war veterans who had been called to serve in both wars. One man, still having flashbacks and suffering daily trauma from being caught on the wire while serving in the trenches in the final months of World War One, described the shock of being called up again in 1939. Like many old soldiers, he never talked much about his experience, but the screaming nightmares he experienced, often needing to be helped back to bed by the night staff when they found him crouched beside his bed, told that story for him.

I've always been intrigued by the German occupation of Paris, how it would have felt to experience a seemingly innocuous enemy roll into the city and take it over. I deliberately set the novel during the first year of the occupation, at the beginning of the Resistance, wanting to create an impression of how it might have felt not to have been bombed or overtly threatened, but to have had an ominous, unseen tension hanging over the city alongside the all-pervading obstruction to normal life. And then, Cora, a strong, courageous young woman right there among it all – safe but not safe. I felt so much for her parents, Evie and Adam, not knowing what was happening to their daughter, having to hold fast and believe that all would be well. In our modern world, we rely on smartphones and emails to offer ongoing reassurance that our loved ones are safe. Even thinking about a time where instant communication was impossible gave me goosebumps. Yet the ties of love still held fast, stretching as far as they needed until the joy of reunion or the agony of a telegram bearing the worst news came.

In writing this story, I tried to present the history as truthfully as possible – after all, it's there that we find the strength and durability of the human spirit, especially during wartime. And as we know, there are lessons to be learned and hope to be derived from the hardships faced by our predecessors. *The Last Letter from Paris* has been an immersive experience. Even as I write this letter, I'm still alongside Cora, dodging through the alleyways of Paris, with Francine hiding a gun beneath her blanket – and, of course, with Iris and Evie as they wait and endure, still forging ahead with their work as nurses, holding back their fears and embracing what comes from yet another world war.

 twitter.com/eastham_kate

ACKNOWLEDGEMENTS

Sincere thanks to my new editor, Lucy Frederick, and the amazing team at Bookouture for all their work, enthusiasm and ideas to enhance the story. As always, without you, this book would not be out there in the world.

I'd also like to thank my agent, Judith Murdoch, for her unwavering support and sound advice.

And, as ever, I am so grateful to my wonderful family for their love, encouragement and for always believing in me.

Printed in Great Britain
by Amazon

34683869R00162